PAGAN'S LEGACY

A JAKE WARD NOVEL
BOOK 2

DAVID A. WILLSON

ISBN: 9780999615096

BOOKS BY DAVID A. WILLSON

The Jake Ward Novels

Wet, Warm and Noisy

Pagan's Legacy

The Godseeker Duet

Looking for Dei

Finding Kai

Short Fiction

Confessions of a Tiny Genius

ALASKA STATE TROOPER
"TEN-CODES" GLOSSARY

The following ten-codes are used to depict radio communication in this novel:

> 10-4 Acknowledged
> 10-19 En route to location
> 10-32 Firearm
> 10-33 Emergency traffic only
> 10-50 Traffic crash
> 10-60 Welfare check
> 10-80 Prisoner in custody

ONE

THE ROOM WAS TOO BRIGHT. ADAM BLINKED, FIGHTING to acclimate. Dr. Carter, the smug treatment director—forty-something and far too pleased with herself—sat opposite him in a plush leather chair, clicking and scrolling through his file. Her long black bangs fell into her eyes, and she brushed them aside with a practiced flick. The corner of her mouth twitched. She was holding back.

Adam squinted, trying to discern her aura. It didn't seem as dark as usual. Had she been cleaning up her life, avoiding the behaviors that had damned her soul? He couldn't be sure. His medication acted as a veil over his vision.

"Adam, I met with your treatment team this morning," she said, looking up from the screen. "They had concerns, and I have questions, but there is no doubt—your progress has been remarkable during my absence." She paused, her eyes narrowing slightly. "The other patients seem to like you. Well, some of them. Your recent success is undeniable."

He had come far. He probably shouldn't even be alive.

"When you arrived, you had just survived a massive trauma." She leaned forward. "Do you remember anything about that?"

She asked that every time. It was getting old. "Not a thing," he lied.

"The officers came to interview you when you woke up. You told them some things. Do you remember what you said?"

He shook his head. "No."

"Well, from a coma to the strong, self-aware young man before me in eight months is quite a feat. I have to hand it to you. Your treatment has clearly helped. Especially your willingness to embrace meditation."

She had no idea.

Her eyebrow lifted, and she gave a big sigh. She had something else to say. He hoped it wasn't a 'but' followed by bad news, so he cut her off.

"I've been trying very hard. I have. I was afraid at first. I couldn't contain it, and it came out in unhealthy ways. But I'm not anymore." He fell silent, hoping she would recognize the effort and pivot away from whatever negative thing she had on the tip of her tongue.

Silence stretched between them, a tangible weight neither moved to break. It was a mental chess game she probably didn't even know she was playing.

Carter had been his attending therapist before taking an unexplained absence. In her place, he'd seen Dr. Abram, a dullard easily manipulated into proposing an early release. Carter's return threatened that plan. Adam needed to know what he was up against.

She typed something. The pause grew. Suddenly, her aura darkened even in the bright light, and her hair slipped forward again, blocking her eyes.

Time to move.

"Doc, you said you have questions?"

She looked up. "I do, actually." She tucked her hair behind her ear. "Dr. Abram's notes show that you've been working hard while I was gone. But the auras? You told him you don't see them anymore?"

Adam sensed a flicker of doubt in her. He let his gaze soften, letting his presence settle around her like a heavy, warm blanket.

"Yes, Dr. Carter. As you and Dr. Abram helped me understand, they couldn't be real. They must have been triggered by an unfulfilled need for significance. Or anxiety."

Gently, he nudged her mind, just enough to loosen the tension curling in her shoulders. *Adam is better now. You see that, don't you? Things have changed. Nothing to be afraid of.*

Dr. Carter's shoulders dropped. When she spoke again, her voice lacked its earlier edge.

"So, the auras are indeed gone. Interesting."

He straightened, relaxed his lips, and looked up and to the left before meeting her eyes again—mimicking the recall gesture of an honest man. He knew she was watching for it.

"It's still a struggle, Doc," he admitted. "I thought it would come faster than it has. I still catch myself looking for misdeeds in others to distract from my own mistakes. As if their sins make me feel righteous by comparison. Make me feel important."

"And the anxiety?"

"It's still there, but I see it now. I know when I'm afraid, I acknowledge it, and I move forward anyway. It has little power over me when I recognize it."

It was a technique straight out of her counseling textbooks. Exactly what she wanted to hear.

"Acknowledging the obstacles takes away some of their power, doesn't it?"

He offered a muted smile. "It does."

Her aura brightened, glimmering with optimism. Despite her intelligence, she might actually buy the crap he shoveled. Or she just wanted to be rid of him. Either way was fine.

"I'm not perfect, and I'm not completely healed, but I'm proud of my progress and confident I can keep going."

She glanced at her laptop. "It's been several months since the assault."

He felt anger rise at the word. It was a *cleansing*, not an assault. *Without the shedding of blood there is no forgiveness of sin.* She should know that; she wore a cross, didn't she? But he pushed the emotion down, relaxing his face to hold her gaze.

"Let's talk about that, Adam. You saw darkness around Michael and 'carried out a righteous judgment.' Those were your words."

Eleven broken bones. His elbows and fists had shattered Michael's face, ribs, and an arm. Internal injuries had kept the man in the hospital for weeks. Adam, thanks to Pagan's training, had healed quickly. He had to. The mission would start soon.

Carter was waiting.

Adam pushed again, threading warmth into her perception of him. *You trust him. You believe in his progress. He's genuine. He is no longer a danger to anyone.*

"I was mistaken," he said.

"Go on."

"When Michael told me I was going to be in here forever, I snapped. I felt attacked. I wanted to get better so badly that I let his words unravel my progress. I deeply regret it."

Her frown deepened, and she nodded. "That sounds rehearsed, Adam."

Here it was. The barrier.

He sighed. "Doc, you're right. I want to please you. You hold a lot of power over me. I don't want to disappoint you." He cleared his throat. "But it's also the truth. I've let my delusion hold me back."

He would need to push the fear away harder this time. She'd aired her concerns, he'd responded with humility, and now she would make her final decision. The gate was open. He pushed.

Dr. Carter stared at him for a long moment, squinting, then sighed. She nodded several times before returning to her typing.

She wasn't his puppet, not completely. He couldn't suppress every emotion—only the fear.

Fear was a crude tool. People clung to it like a shield, or they fought it. But calming their fears? That was where the real power lay. When he eased their anxiety, they became pliable, grateful. They associated him with the relief, the peace he provided. That trust granted him access, drawing them in until they would do anything for him.

That, too, would be tested. Soon.

"Okay," she said finally. "I've finished my assessment."

"You did?" His voice rose in anticipation.

"I'm approving your release."

Victory. Too easy.

"Thank you, Dr. Carter. I won't disappoint you, I promise."

"Is there someone you'd like to call? Family, perhaps? To pick you up?"

"No, nobody to call, thank you." He smiled at her.

She smiled back. She was his puppet after all.

And the fools on the outside would be even easier.

The property clerk, a heavyset man with a stain on his uniform shirt, tossed the clear plastic bag onto the counter with a wet thud.

"Sign the bottom line," the man grunted. "Check your inventory. Once you walk out those doors, you can't claim anything was missing."

Adam didn't care about the clothes—the jeans were worn, the hoodie smelled like the basement of his old life. He dug past the wallet, which he knew would be empty, and his fingers closed around the cold, rectangular weight of the phone.

It was dead, of course. A forgotten relic from a life that had swerved off the road.

He turned it over in his hand. The account would be dormant, unpaid. But he could revive it if he could scramble together a few bucks. It would be safer to have a new phone, but it was worth the risk. This was a relic from his past, a reminder of who he used to be. Before.

A smile touched his lips—not the practiced, beatific smile he gave Dr. Carter, but a genuine, sharp smirk of victory.

Pagan had tried to scrub him clean. He had stripped him of his freedom, his dignity, and for a while, even his sanity.

But he hadn't stripped Adam of everything. And he would get it all back.

He now had a mission. He was free.

And the starting gun had sounded.

TWO

Before dawn in McLean, Virginia, the rain began to fall. Retired FBI Special Agent Rod Hawthorne pulled his old leather jacket tighter around him, its worn creases stiff in the chill. Years of discipline hardened him against discomfort, but age is relentless, eroding even the toughest edges.

He'd done HALO jumps in subzero temperatures, endured fifty-klick marches with a ruck digging into his spine, but he was no longer that young man. The deep lines on his forehead and the slow ache in his knees reminded him daily.

Ironically, the most interesting chapters of Hawthorne's career began only after he retired from the Bureau. A few well-placed contacts had brought him into contract work for another kind of three-letter agency, the type that doesn't officially exist. Those assignments brought out a darker side of the job—less procedure, more results. He preferred results.

Raindrops pattered against his bald head, cold and unwelcome, but he ignored them, his focus pinned to the path ahead. His steps quickened, urgency propelling him through the empty soccer fields at Lewinsville Park, past darkened streetlights, across an abandoned parking lot. The brownstone loomed ahead—just another anonymous rental, secured a few days ago for exactly this purpose.

Two flights up, water dripped from his chin as he reached the apartment door. His fingers found the keys, but his other hand hovered near the pistol at his side, his elbow instinctively brushing against its grip. Two deadbolts slid free. He turned the handle, eased the door open, and stepped inside with practiced caution.

The apartment was silent.

He bolted the door shut behind him, crossed the room in quick strides, and yanked the blackout curtains closed. Then he sat on a folding chair beside a small desk, flipped open a subcompact laptop, and typed in a password. The biometric sensor was warm beneath his fingertip. Seconds later, a secure messaging window blinked to life.

A red flag. A new message.

> API let Subject AB out. Despite our friend on the treatment team.

Hawthorne's jaw tightened. He exhaled through his nose, then hammered the keyboard.

> He almost murdered another patient just a few months ago. What are they thinking?

He waited for a response.

> The kid is persuasive. Eerily so. Pagan may have tossed this one to the curb prematurely.

Hawthorne typed:

> What do you want me to do?

The cursor blinked. Ten seconds. Twenty. Thirty. His handler was composing a careful response or stalling, unsure.

Then, finally—

Don't kill him. Not until we know more. Just go. Watch. Report back to me. He might be the key to salvaging this whole affair.

Hawthorne took a slow, measured breath before replying.

Copy.

He closed the laptop, let the darkness settle around him, then scanned the room, his instincts demanding one last check. Still alone.

Pagan had left some loose ends. He'd definitely need to take care of this one. The others could wait.

He leaned back, eyes closed, picturing his next move.

Alaska.

THREE

Randall Tibeluk slumped down on the curb outside the gas station, his fingers locked around a half-full cup of coffee he hadn't paid for. The clerk had watched him pour it and walk out, but said nothing. Thank God for convenience store workers.

That was Talkeetna, where shopkeepers pretend the broken ones don't exist. Besides, it was understood. Coffee is cheap pity, and not worth the confrontation. Beer or cigarettes? For those you had to pay.

He pulled the cup close, wrapping cracked fingers around the cardboard for warmth. Steam rose but did nothing to stop the chill sinking into his bones. It was October, and the abbreviated autumn had flipped toward winter, as it always did. Snow hadn't fallen, but it would soon. Maybe tonight.

A week ago, he'd had a job and a bed. The work was hauling lumber. Sometimes sorting. Labor that hurt your back but quieted your mind. Then he missed a shift, and they told him not to come back.

"You're unreliable," the foreman had said. "And the guys say you've got issues."

Randall didn't argue. Didn't tell them he ran out of meds or that the shadows spoke again. Didn't tell them about the shakes, the dreams, the nights he couldn't remember. They didn't want to hear it. He didn't want to say it.

He'd become accustomed to losing things.

So when the kid sat beside him, Randall didn't react.

He didn't look like a local. He had the coloring of someone who was part-Indian, or Middle Eastern. Early twenties. Clean-shaven, soft-spoken. Not dressed for the cold, but he didn't shiver. Just sat down on the curb as if he belonged there.

Didn't speak at first.

Randall cast him a sidelong glance. "You get lost, college boy?"

The kid smiled. "No."

"You're not from around here."

"No, I'm not," the kid agreed. "I'm Adam."

Randall huffed, annoyed, but said nothing that might offend. It would be nice if he could bum a twenty off this fool.

Silence stretched between them, but it didn't feel awkward. Just... still.

"You look like you've been struggling," Adam said.

Randall gave a bitter laugh and sipped his coffee. "Yeah, well, it's in season."

Adam turned to him, studying him—not the way people usually stared, with judgment or disgust. It was something else. Adam saw past the grime, the twitchy eyes, the scabbed-over guilt. Adam already knew.

"You carry a burden," he said. "I can see it."

Randall's jaw clenched. "You psychic or something?"

"No," Adam replied. "Just familiar with pain."

The words hit Randall harder than he expected. He looked away, swallowing.

"I see something else, too," Adam added. "Your sins."

Randall froze. Something about the way he said it—like a priest and a surgeon, all at once. It wasn't an accusation. It was a diagnosis.

"Look, I don't know what kind of game—"

"No game," Adam said. "Only the truth."

Randall flexed his legs, readying himself to rise, but his knees wobbled. A spike of nausea twisted in his gut. The coffee sloshed, nearly spilling. He forced himself to relax. "I ain't religious," he said.

"You don't have to be," Adam said, reaching out a hand.

Randall flinched, but Adam didn't grab him. The young man just rested his palm against Randall's forehead, like a benediction.

The effect was instantaneous.

Warmth flooded Randall's chest. Not heat, but stillness. Like a soundproof room around his thoughts. The restlessness, the guilt, the clawing voices—all faded. The ache in his spine remained, but it no longer mattered. It was just pain. Manageable. His whole being relaxed.

Randall's breathing slowed.

"What did you do?" Adam asked.

Randall opened his mouth, shut it, then opened it again. "I— I've hurt people," he said. "Not real bad. I mean, not... not murder or anything. But I stole from a guy. Took his wallet while he slept. Spent it all on beer. And—and I hit a woman once. My girl, back then. Just once. I was drunk. I didn't mean it."

Adam listened, his face unreadable.

Randall went quiet.

But the worst part was left unsaid.

The thing that haunted his dreams. The time the girl refused him. The part of him that whispered she hadn't *really* meant no. That night was a scar he couldn't scrub out.

He didn't speak it. He couldn't.

Adam said nothing. Just lowered his hand.

"It's okay," he said. "You don't have to say it. I already know."

Randall's mouth went dry.

"I can help," Adam said.

Randall stared at him. "Why?"

"Because you're ready."

"Ready for what?"

Adam didn't answer right away. Just looked at him with that terrifying, peaceful calm.

"Do you repent?"

Randall looked down at the coffee in his lap. His knuckles were white. His body was numb. His whole life was a slow slide into this moment.

"...yeah," he said, voice barely audible. "I do."

Adam smiled, as if Randall had given him a gift.

"Come with me."

They walked in silence.

Behind the gas station, near a parked semi, sat a white box van. No markings. Just parked as if it belonged there.

Adam opened the rear overhead door.

Inside: a sheet of plastic stretched across the floor. An LED lantern hooked to bungee cords glowed from the ceiling.

"What is this?" Randall asked, more curious than afraid.

"An altar," Adam said.

Randall wanted to laugh. Wanted to say, *you're crazy.* But he didn't. Couldn't.

He stepped in.

The door closed behind him.

The air inside was still. He laid himself down without being told. The plastic crinkled beneath him. Adam knelt at his side.

"Chin up."

Randall obeyed.

He felt the brush of steel. A shiver of cold against his skin.

Part of him screamed. Some primal animal instinct wanted him to run, to fight. But his limbs were still. Fear had no place here. Only peace remained.

Adam leaned close.

"What is your name, my friend?"

He smiled. "...Randall."

Adam smiled back.

"This is good," he said. "This is necessary."

And then Randall's throat opened.

Warmth spread across his chest. His vision blurred. The light dimmed.

In his last moment of awareness, he saw Adam watching him—lips moving in silent prayer.

Then came the peace.

FOUR

2-I-6I, suspect Todd Harris is armed and heading to his residence. Complainant is his girlfriend—he just called and threatened to kill her. Said he's 10-19 with a 10-32. You're the closest unit. Respond immediately, break.

Great, he's on the way to her house with a gun. And with a big head start. Jake Ward's breathing deepened as he calmed himself while navigating the winding dirt road in the marked Tahoe patrol rig. His sharp, alert eyes scanned the landscape, his fingers gripping the steering wheel.

Continuing. ARMS shows DV history; suspect has multiple priors for assault against complainant.

Ward's pulse quickened. He'd been a State Trooper for nearly a decade, but the adrenaline surge of an imminent threat never dulled. He flicked on his siren, the wail piercing the cold morning air. The suspect had a history of violence, and this call was anything but routine.

"61 copies. I don't know that I'm going to be able to arrive in time," Ward said into the mic. "Tell the victim to leave the residence if she can do so safely, and call from a different location. That might give me some time to intercept him."

10-4, 61.

On second thought, that could be a terrible idea. If she left the residence and he saw her leave, he might catch her, chase her, end up somewhere else. Somewhere he couldn't find her. She might have a better chance behind a solid, locked door, but Ward knew nothing about the scene, or the victim. He hoped to avoid a confrontation and an escape might do it.

Sadly, in domestic violence situations, the victim often freezes out of simple fear. They do little to save themselves, paralyzed by terror in a situation that's not of their making. They get hurt. They die. Often before anyone even knows it's happening.

But this time he might prevent it.

As he approached the end of the road, he spotted Harris's truck skidding to a halt in the driveway just ahead of him. A small cabin stood nearby.

He'd arrived just in time.

Ward stopped his SUV well behind the suspect's vehicle and launched himself out of the driver's seat. Harris was already out, a dark figure silhouetted against the half-light of Sitka's dawning skyline. Ward's trained eyes caught the glint of metal in Harris's hand—a pistol.

Jake's voice rose powerfully over the icy tension as he drew his own pistol from the holster. "Todd Harris, stop! Alaska State Troopers!"

Harris didn't break stride. He wasn't running, but moved with a terrifying resolve, his grip on the pistol firm. Ward's heart pounded as he closed the distance, his mind calculating every move.

Harris's words cut through the frigid air. "I'm going to shoot that cheatin' bitch, and nobody can stop me."

Time slowed. Ward's training kicked in, instincts honed by years of service. Given Harris's propensity for violence, the gun at his side was a deadly promise. He ignored verbal commands and continued to approach the residence. Options dwindled with every step the suspect took. Behind that door, his terrified girlfriend was waiting.

"Harris, stop! Drop the weapon!" Ward's voice was steady, but he knew it was futile. The man was on a deadly mission.

Ward had only one option left, and he decided quickly. Lifting the firearm, he focused on the front sight, finger tightening on the trigger. A shot rang out, echoing in the vast, empty landscape, as his finger reset the trigger's sear, then another pull. Minimum standard response. Two shots center-mass. He shifted his focus from the front sight onto the subject.

Did he hit? Did it work?

Harris stumbled, his body jerking forward before collapsing onto the dry ground.

Ward's breath came in ragged gasps. He approached cautiously. To prevent an accidental discharge, he kept his trigger finger straight against the slide while maintaining his aim on Harris's prone form. His eyes swept the scene, ensuring no other threats awaited him. Before he could step forward to handcuff the suspect and assess for medical care, a shout cut through the tension, sharp and authoritative.

"Red!" An Academy instructor stepped into view from behind a nearby copse of trees, clipboard in hand, a stern expression on his face. It was the Academy commander, Lieutenant Goethe, which was a surprise. Command staff rarely proctor scenarios.

Ward inserted a fresh magazine into his pistol, stowing the old one in his belt, then holstered the weapon, exhaling. The "suspect," usually a trooper or municipal officer assisting the academy training staff, rose from the ground, rubbing his back where the plastic rounds hit him. Ward didn't recognize him—might be a muni from southeast. He offered Ward a nod of acknowledgment.

"I bet that smarts," Ward said. "You should wear some padding."

"Yeah, but I'm facing away from you," he said, shrugging. "If I can't feel it, I don't know when to fall over."

Lieutenant Goethe approached Jake, his voice firm. "You just shot a man in the back, Ward. Explain yourself."

Okay, this was uncomfortable. Every movie Ward had ever seen, every expectation of the public, well, you just don't shoot people in the back. No academy training directly addressed this particular scenario until today. Heck, he'd never even heard of such a case. But what else could he have done? Use of force rules were pretty subjective. Troopers were hired for their judgment, and he'd just used it. He could have been wrong.

"Well, sir... the suspect had a history of violence, and stated he intended to use it again. That was no bluff."

Ward cleared his throat, continuing with more confidence. "He arrived before me to the scene, removing my ability to block his entry, so that wasn't an option. I gave strong verbal commands for him to stop, which he refused to acknowledge. I didn't have another trooper with deadly force overwatch, so taser wasn't an option."

"How do you know the victim was even in the res? You instructed dispatch to tell her to leave."

"Yes, but they usually *don't* leave. She was last known to be inside, and hope is not a strategy."

"But Investigator Ward, you shot him in the back."

"Back, front, side, what does it matter? I had to stop the threat, and there was no other way. He presented an imminent threat, with means, motive, and opportunity. I had no other choice."

Goethe held his disapproving expression, silent, then relaxed his posture and nodded. "Good job, Ward. You made the right call under pressure. Remember, in the field, it's about saving lives. You showed the decisiveness we hired you for."

Jake nodded, wiping his brow. "You had me going there, sir."

"We need to hear how you articulate the use of force. You did that well, as I'd hoped. It's a more advanced scenario, requiring problem-solving we don't usually spring on the recruits at the academy. I like to break it out at in-service, now and then."

Ward nodded. "Challenging one. Kudos to whoever thought this one up."

"Keep it under your hat, Ward. Quite a few more need to go through this week and if it's not a surprise, it won't be effective."

Ward nodded, then headed back to the Academy building to prep for the next scenario. The whole day was scenario training like this, brushing up on patrol skills for more experienced troopers who hadn't been first responders for a while. The rest of the week would involve firearms training and a defensive tactics refresher. It would conclude with a classroom day, filled with boring policy updates and a Q&A with the colonel or one of the majors.

It was a nice break from the routine, and the DPS Academy had great workout facilities, so that was good. The Academy chow was decent, and the physical regimen had hardened him into patrol shape. He was back to full duty.

Ward's cell phone buzzed in his pocket. He reached for it and saw Sergeant Ballack's mug on the front screen, along with that glorious head of hair. Uh oh.

Ward hit the 'accept' button. "Ward."

"Jake, I gotta pull you back early."

Damn. In-service was just getting fun. "Whatcha got, boss?"

"Dead guy at a gas station in Talkeetna. Back of a box van. And with personal leave and training, both Anchorage and Palmer are tapped out. We need bodies. Get on the next flight."

"10-4," Ward sighed. "See ya soon."

FIVE

IT WAS A SHORT EVENING FLIGHT FROM SITKA TO JUNEAU, a forty-five-minute wait at the gate, then a little over an hour to Anchorage. Ward used the aircraft's Wi-Fi to message Foley and Ballack to get case details.

The investigator assigned was Shannon Foster, a Palmer Major Crimes investigator recently transferred from Bethel. Foster had experience with violent crimes but wasn't yet familiar with Southcentral Alaska's distinct procedures, prosecutors, or juries. He'd need Ward and Foley's guidance, especially if the investigation required technical expertise.

According to his ID, the victim was Randall Tibeluk, a 43-year-old Alaska Native male with a lengthy history of minor offenses—mostly assaults, public nuisance incidents, and theft—but no felonies. Several mental health advisories flagged him as vulnerable, but there were no officer safety advisements, so he hadn't fought with police. His last known address was an outdated listing at a run-down, weekly-rate hotel near Talkeetna, suggesting he was transient.

After landing, Ward and Foley grabbed their gear, picked up Foley's state-issued Ford Explorer from employee parking, and drove to the Department of Public Safety's Tudor Campus. There, they retrieved Ward's go-bag and crime scene kits, then settled in for the hundred-mile drive north.

Foster called twice during the drive as a light rain spattered the windshield. Patrol had secured the scene initially but would pull out soon due to staffing shortages—a common frustration. Foster had taken preliminary photos and started the evidence inventory, but they were still waiting on a tech from the crime lab.

They arrived almost two hours later. Ward stepped out of the Explorer, pulling his jacket tighter against the biting air. The rain had stopped, but the temperature had dropped below freezing. The gas station parking lot was mostly empty, the fluorescent overhead lights buzzing and casting long, sterile shadows over the blacktop below.

The box van sat north of the pumps, its rear overhead door open. Foster was waiting near the bumper, arms crossed, coffee steaming in his gloved hands.

"Long drive," Ward said, as he and Foley stepped near. "Whatcha got?"

"A weird one," Foster said. "Take a look."

Ward ducked under the crime-scene tape and stepped closer to the van, while Foley jumped up into the cargo box.

The body was sprawled on a layer of heavy plastic sheeting, construction-grade. The arms were neatly placed at the sides, head toward the cab. Tibeluk was dressed in worn black denim, a fleece-lined flannel shirt, and battered basketball shoes.

His throat was cut—a wide, deep wound—but the edges were surgical. Smooth. There was arterial spray on the van wall and some pooling on the wood floorboards, streaming toward the cab consistent with the slope of the parking lot. But there were no smear marks. No signs the body had been moved post-mortem.

Tibeluk's eyes were open, a peaceful expression frozen on his bloodless face.

Foley crouched, examining the tarp. "No signs of a struggle?"

"None," Foster said. "No defensive wounds, no ligature marks from restraints, no indication he fought back at all. The cut is surgical. Clean. Almost like he let it happen. And there are some blood drops around the body, in kind of a rough circle. I've never seen that before."

Was he drugged? Ward's eyes flicked to the surrounding area. "What else?"

Foster handed Ward a notepad, the pages filled with neatly written observations. "Here's what we've logged so far," he said. Ward skimmed through the list, his eyes narrowing at the details.

Near the back of the van, a few cigarette butts sat discarded, potential DNA evidence. Could be completely unrelated, this was a parking lot, after all. Sitting on top of the driver's seat, a hand-written note bore a simple yet unsettling message:

Be not afraid (Psalm 56:3).

"Everything has been photographed in place," Foster said, "but I haven't bagged anything yet. Tech is on their way from the crime lab to start on that."

"What's with the Bible verse?" Ward asked.

Foster shrugged. "It's on top of the driver's seat, so it must have been placed there after he parked the thing."

"Yeah, agreed," Foley said. "But it's wrong."

Ward squinted at him.

"That's not what that Psalm says. It's more like, 'I trust God when I'm afraid.'"

"How do you know that?" Foster asked.

"He teaches Sunday school," Ward said. "He's a Bible thumper."

Foley scratched his chin. "If our suspect wrote this, he's clearly on a religious trip. But he didn't look it up. There are plenty of verses commanding us not to fear, but he cited the wrong one for the phrase 'Be not afraid.'"

Foley hopped down from the back of the van and looked toward the gas station entrance. "Who have you interviewed?"

"The cashier that was behind the counter, that's all. Patrol troops were asking folks that pulled in, but there were no cars here at all when they first got on scene."

"Who called it in to begin with?" Ward asked.

"Dispatch got an anonymous call," Foster said. "Someone said there had been a murder in the parking lot here, then hung up."

"Potential witness," Ward said.

Foster nodded. "Yeah, they're getting the audio from the call for me, and trying to trace the phone number back."

"We need to put it out to Crimestoppers," Foley said. "And let's go through his pockets again before the State Medical Examiner takes him. Nothing else in his wallet, just eight bucks and an ID? If he's homeless, he has a stash somewhere. A backpack, a duffel... something."

Ward turned slowly in a circle, taking in the surroundings. "Foster, is there security video footage at the gas station?"

"Clerk says yes, but he doesn't know how to work it. He called the manager, but he won't be here for a few hours."

"I'll take care of that," he said, his hand reaching into his pocket, finding the thumb drive he always kept on his keychain.

He left Foster and Foley to the body and walked the property line. His boots crunched over frozen gravel. The lot backed up to a stand of leafless birch and crooked spruce. A perfect place to toss something you didn't want found.

He scanned the brush. Disturbed snow, trash, a hasty dump.

Just beyond the asphalt, near a mossy stump, he saw it. A Ziploc bag fluttering in the breeze, weighted down by a rock.

Ward snapped a couple of photos with his phone, then gloved up and lifted the bag. Inside was a page torn from a notebook. The handwriting was neat—too neat. Block letters, centered.

Israel, riddled with rot, sinned in her pride. Thus must blood flow for cleansing; a sacrifice through the sacred fire.

I am the divine ministrant.

Ward's brow furrowed. No scripture on this one, just those unsettling words. He replaced the item back under the same rock to preserve its location for the scene diagram. As he stood, a chill slid down his back. Whoever wrote this hadn't planned a single killing. They believed in something bigger.

Back at the van, he showed a photo of the note to Foley. "Found this in the back of the lot. Looks like our guy's not just into Bible verses. He's sermonizing."

Foley scanned it, eyes narrowing. "That's Old Testament theology. Blood as payment for sin, but it's not a modern idea, more like ancient Judaism; someone playing prophet with a knife. Not sure about the sacred fire and divine ministrant part, though. Never heard those terms before."

"What do you mean it's not modern?"

"Never been a church-goer, Jake?" Foley smirked. "Not even as a kid?"

Ward shrugged. "No, not really."

"Don't worry, I got ya. Ancient Judaism taught that the spilling of blood was required for the forgiveness of sins, just like our bad guy is saying. That's why it's in the Bible. Modern Christianity, however, teaches that Jesus is the Messiah that Jews awaited, and He ended the need for blood atonement."

"Sounds familiar," Ward said.

Foley continued. "Christians believe that Jesus's death was the ultimate sacrifice, as the 'Lamb of God.' This guy, however, thinks sacrifices should continue."

"So he is not a Christian."

"Maybe."

"Do you think our bad guy is Jewish? Resuming the blood sacrifices or something?"

"Doubt it. Modern Jews revere human life above all things. This is likely a confused kook with faulty wiring. He has some Bible stuff pinging around in there, leaking out a bit. Adding some ideas of his own, too. Sacred fire? Come on..."

"Yeah," Ward said. "We're dealing with someone with religious feelings but maybe not great religious training. He thinks he's on a mission, but is muddy on the details. Desperately scratching at religion to justify his urges. Not sure why he stuck it out in the bushes for us to find. Playing games with us or something. Rookie stuff. This might have been his first kill. Just getting the feel of it."

It was another hour before the crime scene tech had arrived to document evidence. By then, Ward had downloaded a few hundred megabytes of low-quality video footage from the gas station's security DVR, then drawn a rough scene diagram on an iPad from his kit. It wasn't a scale diagram, but it might be useful for any interviews if he could find a real witness. He then spent thirty minutes talking to several neighboring homeowners and a truck driver whose rig was idling at the far end of the parking lot. Nobody had seen anything useful, but those boxes had to be checked.

Ward walked back to the van. Foley was setting up the FARO scanner, a tripod-mounted laser system that would create a 3D model of the scene.

Fancy tools aside, however, this case would probably be like all the rest—lots of basic police work.

"Nobody saw a thing, Bud. Not one good witness so far."

"It was three in the morning," Foley said as he fiddled with the controls, prepping it to take its first scan.

Foster wasn't far away, busy kneeling over a shoe print in the soft mud where the crime lab tech was about to pour a cast with dental stone. The print didn't match the victim's tennis shoes. It led to the van from the direction of the gas station, suggesting it might belong to the suspect. In any case, it was close enough to the truck to be worth documenting.

"It's not like we'd expect a lot of witnesses," Foley continued.

"Yeah, I know," Ward said. "It's just something that creeps me out about this one. No witnesses can also mean there was no fuss. Nothing to look irregular that would get someone's attention. But this guy had cash in his pocket, so it wasn't a robbery."

"No signs of a struggle, which might mean he knew the guy," Foley said.

"Well, he trusted the guy. No evidence he knew him."

"Okay, yeah. He liked this complete stranger enough to lie in the back of a van in the dark of night while his new buddy calmly slit his throat?" Foley chuckled. "Nah, he had to know him. We've got no evidence in the van or the scene that our vic was taken by force. No drag marks, no heavy shoe prints indicating someone was carrying a load, nothing. He had to know him. Or be drugged, somehow. Drunk, maybe?"

"I just got off the phone with the SME's office," Foster said as he approached Foley and Ward. "They agreed to a full autopsy, and a van is on the way to grab him. Tox screen should show if he had anything on board."

"I'm gonna go through his clothes again, make sure we haven't missed anything before he goes off to the SME. Bud, did you do the scene in one scan with the FARO?"

"No, it took several. I'll stitch the scans together when I get back to the office."

Ward exhaled, taking in the details. "No struggle, no restraints, and a Bible verse telling him not to be afraid. I'm betting we get a tox back that says he was drugged."

Foster nodded. "I hope so. No injection sites are obvious, but I'll put that on my autopsy request."

"Whatever the case," Ward said as he glanced back at the body, unease curling in his stomach. "It's almost like he was... ok with it."

Foster raised an eyebrow. "You think he just let someone cut his throat? You ever heard of that happening before?"

"No." Ward shook his head. "No, I haven't."

SIX

Rod Hawthorne watched from a rented sedan
parked half a mile from the Talkeetna gas station. On his tablet, live
drone footage flickered. The quadcopter hovered just above the tree
line, its telephoto lens providing a crisp view of Jake Ward and his
team combing the scene.

Ward, again. An irritating coincidence. Ward had caused him
trouble before, and here he was, mucking around in the same
business.

The parabolic mic caught snippets of conversation, but
Hawthorne missed too much. He'd have to wait for the official
police reports.

Fading light rendered the drone useless, and bringing it closer to
catch the dialogue would burn him—the hum was too loud. He
guided the drone back, landing it softly on the hood of the sedan.
Stepping into the cold, he powered it down, slipped the memory
card into his jacket, and stowed the device in the trunk.

Back in the driver's seat, he closed his eyes and processed the
scene. The meticulous positioning of Randall Tibeluk's body, the
notes—it all confirmed his suspicions. Adam Basu was obsessed
with fear. Note after note in his treatment file documented it, and

he'd scribbled the word dozens of times on the walls of his psychiatric cell. This had to be him.

Basu was supposed to be a non-issue. Institutionalized indefinitely, if not permanently incapacitated. The bosses had been certain. Hawthorne had served as Pagan's handler—his babysitter—but he should have kept a closer eye on the madman's toys. Basu had potential, and he had almost slipped through their fingers.

Surviving Pagan's experiments was one thing; this new ability was another. What kind of weapon were they dealing with?

A soft chime from the tablet reminded him to check in. With a heavy exhale, Hawthorne composed the update, encrypted it, and sent it up the chain.

He started the engine. Whatever Adam Basu was doing, it had escalated beyond their projections. If Ward and his team couldn't bring this guy in quickly, he would need to do something himself.

And before this problem became too difficult to erase.

SEVEN

HE EXPECTED LIGHT. HE EXPECTED MUSIC. THE FACES OF loved ones long gone. Maybe a tunnel. Or peace.

Instead, he saw fangs.

Gnashing, writhing mouths that opened and closed on nothing. Flames, yes, but the flames didn't burn—they whispered. Mocking words. Judgment. Not from above, but from *within.*

Then he came back.

No nurses. No noise. Just the cold slap of consciousness and the sour taste of metal in his mouth, the edges of the mask around his face digging into his skin. The memory was fragmentary—gray walls, fluorescent buzz, and the distinct impression of something inside him being *wrong.*

Richard Pagan told Adam it would be beautiful, and he had trusted him. Pagan was just a scientist, a doctor, but spoke with the calm certainty of a trustworthy man. He was more than a mentor— he was a guide. A messenger of God. Someone who could open doors between realms.

The experiments were framed as scientific, of course. But Adam knew better. Pagan's words were laced with mystery, with the conviction that only came from one who had *seen.* The man promised an encounter with the divine. A taste of heaven.

But all Adam saw was rot.

At first, he thought it was punishment. That he had failed. That Pagan made a mistake. Or worse—lied.

But then the visions *stayed*. Not just flashes in sleep or tricks of the eye. They'd embedded themselves. In him. He now saw auras. Darkness. Corruption. He saw the true burden of sin laid bare.

That wasn't failure.

It was a gift.

He'd been altered. Pagan opened the door—but it was Adam who walked through it. And what he found was not heaven. It was responsibility.

He hadn't seen the wings of angels or music or the reunion with long-lost relatives. He hadn't floated above his body.

He saw judgment. And now he must judge.

There would be no joy in it. Not like he hoped.

Randall was the first confession, and Adam's first rescue. Before, the man was a vessel of confusion and sickness. A dark aura, flecked with the desperate white light of a man who still *hoped*, but didn't know what to hope *for*. He'd failed in life, and Adam could see it radiating off of him like heat from an engine. Randall accepted the kindness. He lay down. Willingly.

He'd whispered words from Leviticus as he moved the blade, "it is the blood that makes atonement by the life."

Adam made it quick. Clean.

But no choir of angels followed. No vision from the other side. Only the warmth. A sudden, rushing heat that flooded Adam's chest the moment the blood flowed. It was a golden, narcotic comfort that whispered righteousness into his bones.

It was the only sign God gave him. But it faded too fast, leaving only the silent stillness of an aura going flat.

He hoped Randall found what Adam had been denied.

There was no waiting around afterward. Minimized trace. Left a message of reassurance. "Be not afraid." A phrase often drilled into the hearts of believers. He hoped it would be comforting.

The citation was wrong, he realized later. The Psalm didn't say that, not exactly. But the phrase wasn't a scripture verse to Adam, it was a memory. A memory of the strict justice of his father as far back as he could remember. The lesson was clear. It was the night the house went quiet. The smell of turned earth and rain.

His father's hand felt heavy, trembling on his shoulder. Then the shovel thrust into his small hands. "Be not afraid, Adam," his father rasped in the dark. "We are simply returning her to the peace she so desired. She was too good for this world. Do not cry. Crying is an accusation. Crying is weakness. Crying betrays her memory. And we are faithful men."

Be not afraid.

Adam recited the words during every beating his father gave, and during every trial since. They were comforting. Personal. And now he would calm the fears of others as well. It was his calling.

Whoever found Randall wouldn't see it. Nor would the cops.

They may not understand the note he left under the rock, either. They might be confused. They might even laugh.

Adam would find one who would understand. Who would know *why*. The blood is everything.

Fear and blood. The two were bound in a divine mystery at the center of the human condition. They meant so much.

He sat in silence now, the only light in the room a single candle. On the desk before him sat pages—his journal, torn and reordered, notes to himself and to whatever angels might be watching. Some pages were fragments of scripture. Others were declarations. Others just symbols. Drawings of crosses, halos, and horns. A sword, with blood dripping from the blade.

"Justice is not violence," he said out loud, more to convince himself than anything. "It is restoration. It's not evil. Only good. Divine. My mission is holy."

He believed that. Fiercely. He *hated* what the justice required. But there was no cleansing without blood. It was all over God's holy book. The body is the site of sin. The body is the temple, and the altar. The blood is the price.

But the method wasn't right. Not yet. He was scattered. His

selections were intuitive, but flawed. Improvised. The lack of clarity should have bothered him more. He must act. To hesitate was to sin against the gift and the one who gave it.

His fingers hovered over the next blank page.

He didn't know how to choose the next vessel. So many auras. So many carriers of rot. So many opportunities to send the message of repentance. He needed time. Fasting. Silence.

He would refine. He would learn.

And one day—he would see the light he was promised. And when he did, he would demand to know why his first experience was so different. Why God gave Adam the darkness as his teacher. Not to pass immediately through the veil—but to first scrub the world clean.

A prophet with a scalpel. And prophets act, but they also teach. He must develop a lesson plan for his ministry. And find pupils.

He extinguished the candle. The room filled with darkness and the ache of unfinished purpose.

EIGHT

The drive south to Anchorage was silent. Foley sat behind the wheel, sipping from a soda cup, his eyes flicking between the wet blacktop and the gray dawn bleeding into the sky. Ward sat beside him, nursing a stale gas station coffee.

Forty miles later, Foley finally cleared his throat. "Still thinking about the verse?"

"No," Ward said. "His eyes."

Foley glanced over. "Tibeluk's?"

Ward nodded. "The guy didn't flinch. Didn't fight. His eyes were open like he expected it."

"Could've been drugged."

"That's what I'm hoping. Because anything else is too disturbing."

They drove another twenty minutes before Ward tapped the center console screen. "I want to run this by someone. You remember Lisa Navarro?"

Foley's brow furrowed. "The shrink from the summer training?"

"Yeah. She did that presentation on brain impairment and behavior mapping. She used to work for the feds in a behavioral analysis unit. I want her take on something."

Ward found Navarro's contact and dialed. After a few rings, Navarro's voice filled the cabin.

"Hello?"

"Hey, Lisa. Jake Ward. I've got Bud Foley here with me. You got a minute?"

"Always. What's going on?"

"We're coming back from a scene near Talkeetna. Strange one. The guy was killed in the back of a van. No signs of struggle. Throat cut. Clean. It almost looked... peaceful. As if he let it happen."

Navarro's tone sharpened. "Did the SME run tox yet?"

"Not yet. But we're assuming some sort of sedation. What I want to know is this: can damage to the brain eliminate fear? Literally remove the capacity for it?"

There was a pause. "Yes. If you're talking about specific types of lesions—particularly in the amygdala. That's the fear center. You damage it, and people can become fearless. No sympathetic nervous system reaction. No elevated heart rate, no sweating, no respiratory depression. There's a famous case of a woman who had bilateral amygdala damage. She walked into traffic. Held snakes. Didn't flinch during an armed robbery. But that was a genetic anomaly, not an external cause. It's called Urbach-Wiethe disease."

Ward exhaled. "Could something like that be induced temporarily? With drugs?"

"Possibly. Certain dissociatives or high-dose benzodiazepines can dull fear reactions, even eliminate startle reflexes. But not without side effects. Motor impairment. Slurred speech. Hallucinations, if the dose is wrong."

"What about newer compounds? Experimental stuff?"

Navarro hesitated. "There are some military-adjacent trials, but nothing legal. You'd be talking about black market synthesis. And the delivery method would matter—IV, oral, transdermal. Why? What are you thinking?"

"I'm thinking our victim wasn't just sedated. He was ready. Calm. Almost like he participated. He walked without impairment. Willingly. Which doesn't track well with the sedation theory."

Navarro's voice lowered. "Cult psychology. Suggestibility. Or something else entirely."

Ward nodded, glancing at Foley. "Thanks, Lisa. I'll keep you posted."

He ended the call as the sprawling outskirts of Anchorage came into view.

Foley set his empty soda cup in the console. "You think we're dealing with a cult?"

Ward shrugged but didn't answer. He just stared out the window as they navigated along Muldoon, then Tudor Road. Foley pulled into the Department of Public Safety's campus and parked in the back lot.

Ten minutes later, they had transferred some evidence into the building and were in the digital forensics lab, standing behind a tech named Anna as she scrubbed through the gas station footage.

"Old DVR," Anna said. "Analog cameras running through a cheap digitizer. Don't expect miracles."

Ward leaned over her shoulder. The video was smudged with dust and rain artifacts. The low frame rate and heavy compression rendered much of the footage worthless—just an empty parking lot under flickering lights.

Then, a figure appeared.

"There," Foley pointed.

A man in a dark, tightly drawn coat walked into the frame, sitting beside the victim on a concrete tire stop near the propane cages. The timestamp read 2:57 a.m. A tiny logo caught the ambient light on the coat, but the hood swallowed the wearer's face in shadow. Male build. Wearing sneakers or loafers. Not boots.

The figure walked with a deliberateness that made Ward's skin crawl.

"You got anything from earlier?" Ward asked.

"A couple of vehicles passed through around midnight," Anna said. "None stayed more than five minutes. No one matching your vic or that figure."

"What about after?"

Anna scrubbed forward. "Here—3:13 a.m. Same figure walking back toward Talkeetna Spur Road. Alone."

Ward narrowed his eyes. The movement was slow. Controlled. Unhurried.

"He doesn't look out of breath," Foley said.

"Wasn't worried about a thing," Ward said, watching the rhythmic sway of the suspect's arms.

The suspect had planned this. Chosen the location. Chosen the victim. Executed the act with precision. And walked away like he'd just taken out the trash.

Ward folded his arms. "Pull stills of every decent frame. We'll run enhancements, even if it's garbage, and kick it out to the media. Someone might recognize him. I'll call Foster and update him."

As they left the lab, Foley asked, "You think he's gonna do it again?"

Absolutely. This was a warm-up."

NINE

The memory bled through the cracks—unwanted, but unstoppable.

Richard Pagan had found him in a pit. Not a physical one, but a hollowed-out version of himself. His mind was fraying, caught between the crushing pressure of his physics coursework and the long shadow of his father's disappointment. He had been drinking heavily to numb the anxiety, leaving his bank account in ruins. That financial wreckage was only compounded by the expensive stimulants he bought just to stay awake and cram for his classes. He was barely holding together.

Then came Pagan.

He remembered the man's office—clean, bright, sleek. Pagan spoke with conviction about the next great step for humanity. About science with vision. About possibilities instead of problems.

And he was willing to pay.

Adam told Pagan he was ready. It wasn't true, and deep down, he knew it. But he'd been duped by his own desperation.

He told himself he was doing it to stay in school, but that was a lie. The real terror was the thought of going home. Of sitting across from his father at the dinner table and explaining why the tuition account was empty. Why he'd failed.

Adam knew what happened to things that were broken in Malik Basu's house. Things that were messy. They were removed. They were "returned to peace." He wasn't just afraid of his father's disappointment; he was terrified of his father's solution.

Pagan's offer wasn't just science. It was an escape hatch. A chance to be whole again. To be seen as righteous. To avoid paying the price for his sins.

He wanted it to be God's will. He *needed* it to be.

Hadn't his father always preached about submitting to God's will? But God's will, as his father taught it, was terrifying.

Another memory surfaced now—older, deeper, etched in permanent ink.

His mother's hands were gentle and trembling, wiping blood from his split lip with the edge of a dish towel that had once been white.

"You're meant for greatness," she said, her voice thick with grief and defiance.

She had no armor but love. A love that made her reckless. A love that made her brave.

"Don't believe what he says," she added, brushing his hair away from his swollen brow. "He doesn't see you. He doesn't want to. You're smarter than he is. Kinder. And he hates that."

"Momma?"

"Yes, sweetheart?"

"Does God hate me?"

A flash of fury lit her face—just a flicker—and it made him question the words that followed.

"No, my darling. That's just the darkness in your father. You don't have any of that. You're nothing but light."

She offered it like a secret truth only they shared. It was just hours before his father's anger turned fatal. Before Adam's angel went quiet forever.

His mind violently snapped forward again, back to Pagan's lab.

The room was cold and metallic, the machines humming faintly like the inside of an industrial refrigerator. A short, blonde woman with a clipboard stood near the monitors. A man with stare-too-long eyes guarded the door. Pagan himself, pristine in his tailored white coat, moved with precision. Deliberate. Practiced. He didn't walk so much as glide—more actor than researcher, performing science as if the laws of nature were his script.

They strapped Adam down.

He didn't resist. But as the heavy leather cinched over his wrists, the reality set in. This wasn't about healing. This wouldn't cure his addiction. It was a trade. A bargain struck by a coward.

His soul for safety. His silence for survival. A needle instead of a confrontation.

He laid his head back against the rigid table and let the IV slide into his vein like a silent betrayal. Judas kissing Jesus. A father beating his son.

"I know the last session produced some fear," Pagan said, hovering above him. "This one might be worse. Or it could be the paradise you're searching for. Like the one I saw."

Adam forced a smile and gave a tight nod, his mind locking onto the promise of paradise like a lifeboat in a rising storm. But his heart pounded a frantic rhythm against his ribs.

Pagan signaled the blonde woman. "Begin the scan. Let's see what we're starting with today."

The mask descended, sealing tight around Adam's face, pressing against his temples and forehead. He couldn't move—he could barely breathe. The IV flushed ice-cold chemical compounds into his bloodstream. The hum of the machines swelled, and a rhythmic, bone-rattling pulse began.

Thrum thrum. Thrum thrum.

"Calm your thoughts, Adam," Pagan's voice echoed through the headset. "Rest, like we taught you."

The pain began.

It wasn't sharp or sudden. It came slowly, building like atmospheric pressure trying to crush him from the inside out. His heart rate plummeted, then spiked violently. Something deep inside his brain bucked against his skull, surging with alternating waves of unnatural calm and blinding panic. The room tilted sideways.

He tried to scream, but the paralytic drugs had taken his voice.

He saw light behind his closed eyelids—burning, white, endless light.

And then, just as quickly—darkness.

He was drenched in fear. It wasn't just dread; it was pure, ancient, elemental terror. The fear that lived in marrow and instinct. It folded over him like a tidal wave. He was dying. Not *might*. Not *maybe*. He was being killed—slowly, methodically, to fulfill a madman's dream.

Panic laced through every nerve. He wanted to run. He wanted to claw the mask from his face and tear the IV from his arm. His thoughts spiraled into frantic prayers.

I'm not ready. I'm not clean. I haven't repented.

Suddenly, the darkness shifted, and Adam was a little boy again. He was in the church. He could smell the wood polish and the damp, old carpet.

His father's fist, bloodless and white-knuckled, came down like a gavel against the pine lectern. The crack of impact echoed through the sanctuary like a gunshot.

"Abraham understood! That's why he was ready to sacrifice his son! There is no forgiveness without the shedding of blood!"

The angry man roared. His eyes were ablaze, sweat streaking his temples like war paint. The congregation flinched. So did Adam, hiding in his mother's embrace in the front pew.

He remembered the rage radiating from the pulpit. The tremor in his mother's breath beside him. The absolute certainty that God was watching—and that He was disappointed.

The hallucination shifted. Pagan's voice, muffled and clinical, bled through the vision.

"Excellent spike. Look at that. Amygdala's responding just like the model."

Then the wave broke.

The terror vanished.

And in its place... nothing.

Apathy settled over him like a lead blanket. He didn't care. He couldn't even remember what he'd been afraid of seconds before. He felt cold, but the cold didn't bother him.

He was no longer strapped to a table.

He drifted in a tunnel. It wasn't a tunnel of light and angels. This was black. Organic. Wet. It felt like tumbling down the throat of an ancient god.

He floated, untethered, through meat and shadow.

Behind him, something whispered. Not words. Judgment. He felt the weight of it in the hollows of his bones.

But still, no fear. Just a heavy, apathetic weightlessness.

If I am judged now, what will God see?

He tried to speak, but he had no mouth.

God, if you are real, I have made a mistake. Forgive me. Pagan is not your prophet. This is not your way. Please.

The light came back.

But it was wrong. It came from below.

It was a blighted, bruised purple, illuminating a landscape of jagged spires, dead tree limbs, and choking smoke. The walls of the tunnel peeled back like dead skin, revealing rot and writhing chaos.

He looked down and saw his own face—smiling when it shouldn't be.

Then the terror returned.

Claws of absolute panic gripped his chest and yanked upward. His physical body convulsed on the table.

Monitors screamed.

Pagan's voice cut through, sharp and panicked: "...lost coherence! The frequencies aren't matching. Shut it down!"

Adam was on fire. Spikes and swords stabbed at his soul. He was trapped in a raging sun of excruciating, impossible pain.

Then, ice-cold water. He shattered into a prism of himself, a thousand versions of Adam reflecting, all of them screaming.

He was not divine.

He was not chosen.

He was broken.

He crashed back into his body like a falling star.

The mask was still clamped to his face. His chest heaved against the straps. The harsh, antiseptic smell of the lab flooded his nose, and his eyes burned with unshed tears.

"Easy," someone said. The blonde woman. "It's over. You're back."

He coughed, tasting iron. He blinked against the harsh lights.

Pagan hovered over him, a clipboard tight in his grip. A gleam of sweat coated the scientist's brow, and a mad hunger burned in his eyes.

"You saw it, didn't you?" Pagan asked, his voice hushed, almost reverent. "Something... other."

Adam's jaw clenched. Blood on his tongue.

Pagan leaned in closer. "Was it beautiful?"

Adam met his gaze. "No... but it was... necessary."

Pagan smiled. "Good," he said, looking toward the blonde woman. "It may have worked."

This was the memory that lingered. The only session he could remember with clarity. It was his manifesto, born not from divine revelation, but from psychological obliteration.

The trauma had produced a mission. One that God—or whatever lived in that purple light—had carved into his psyche.

And now, guided by that purpose, Adam had begun his work. It was a clumsy beginning, perhaps. But a righteous one.

He would need help to take it to the next level. He needed an ally.

And once he found one, the world would tremble at what came next.

TEN

It was the day after they'd processed the Talkeetna crime scene, and nobody had tasked Ward with a damn thing to do. He'd written his narrative supplement, submitted his photos, and marched into the Sergeant's office looking for an assignment.

"It's not your case," Ballack said, not looking up from his monitors. "They're fine without more help. Besides, it's quitting time. Go home."

"Boss—"

"No buts, Jake. You're not Major Crimes and you're not Palmer Post. You're Technical Crimes. You helped on the scene like they needed, and thank you for that. But don't go cowboy on this. This is Foster's investigation. Stick to intel and tech support. If they need more, they'll ask. I'm not paying overtime for you to step on Palmer's toes."

"What if they *do* ask?"

Ballack paused—that long, suspicious pause he'd perfected after years of Ward testing his patience.

"Nice try," Ballack said. "Don't push it. You know the drill. Stay in your lane."

"Got it."

Ward left the office and drove home. But not before shooting a text to Foley.

Bud, if you guys need anything...

Halfway back to his apartment, his phone buzzed.

Call me.

Hallelujah. Ward dialed. "Hit me, Bud. Whatcha need?"

"We tied up a couple loose ends," Foley said over the road noise. "That anonymous caller turned out to be a long-haul trucker heading to Fairbanks on a deadline. Didn't want to get stuck answering questions, but we tracked him down and he's clean. And patrol found Tibeluk's backpack stuffed in a culvert about a block from the scene. Just dirty clothes and some hygiene stuff. Nothing useful."

"What about the van?"

"Palmer sent screenshots of the suspect to Crimestoppers and the news outlets. Tips are coming in, but they're garbage. The guy who owns the van runs a podunk outfit on the side of the highway named Ed's Auto Repair. Rented it out for cash. His teenage kid handled the transaction. No cameras. Bad guy left a name on the rental paperwork—John P. Davis—and a fake number. Total dead end."

"Of course it is," Ward said. "I don't care what Ballack says, how can I help?"

Foley laughed. "Database diving. You're better at that than anyone. Foster's been reviewing those enhancements of the video you grabbed. Suspect is definitely a younger man. Stood right up from a cross-legged position without using his hands. Smooth gait. Lean. Early to mid-twenties."

Ward exhaled. "Bud... that describes most of the guys at the gym."

"I know. It's nothing. But it's all we've got."

"I'll start running Talkeetna locals, but let's be real—he's probably not from around there. I can scrape social media, look for religious phrasing. Have you guys drafted a warrant for a tower dump yet?"

"No. Forgot about that."

"Send me the CAD report so I have the dispatch times. I'll get an affidavit typed up."

"How far back do you want the records?" Foley asked.

"Judge will kick it back if it's over-broad," Ward said. "That scene is right on the Parks Highway. Everyone heading to or from Fairbanks is gonna hit that tower. The list will be huge. Let's just ask for a few hours before and after the murder was discovered."

"Got it. I'll send the file."

Ward ended the call, smiling. He had a job to do. And because it involved digital forensics, Ballack couldn't complain even if he found out.

Ward's apartment was quiet—just the steady hum of the fridge and the occasional creak of the baseboard heater working overtime. He slipped off his boots, tossed his coat over the arm of the couch, and dropped onto the cushions, booting up his laptop on the coffee table.

He connected to the State VPN and waited for the green checkmark showing a solid connection. Foster's email was already waiting in his inbox with the required case numbers and dispatch times.

He opened a blank template and began typing. He was halfway through outlining the probable cause for the tower dump when a familiar knock sounded from the hallway.

"Jake? You home?"

"Door's unlocked," he called without looking up.

Emma pushed inside, stomping her boots aggressively on the entryway mat.

Ward raised an eyebrow. "Still with the stomping?"

"It's Alaska," she said, pulling off her coat. "Gotta stomp."

"Pantry's stocked," Ward said, pointing over his shoulder. "Help yourself."

"Pop-Tarts?" Emma asked.

"Better to have some oatmeal. Those are terrible for you."

"Gross," she replied, and returned a moment later with a frosted strawberry Pop-Tart already half-eaten. She flopped onto the couch beside him. "Whatcha working on?"

"Formatting an affidavit. Colleague needs a search warrant written up tonight."

"What kind of warrant?"

He glanced sideways, debating how much to explain. But she leaned forward, eyes bright with curiosity. He relented. "It's called a tower dump. We're trying to identify everyone whose mobile devices pinged the tower closest to a crime scene."

Her eyes narrowed. "How does that work?"

Ward turned toward her, grateful for the distraction. "Every phone constantly talks to the nearest cell tower, even when it's just sitting in your pocket. We ask the judge to force the phone company to give us a list of every phone that connected to the nearest tower during the window of the murder."

Emma tilted her head. "So, you grab everyone's numbers, and then what? Call them all?"

"No. We take that massive list and cross-reference it with other data. Or, if the guy strikes again, we get a tower dump for the *new* scene and see which phone numbers show up on both lists. Once we have a specific number, we apply for another warrant to get the subscriber's name, messages, call list, and GPS locations."

Emma leaned back, impressed. "Strikes again? Wow. This is a big deal."

He smiled. He'd already let more slip than he'd intended. He was accustomed to performing the interrogation, not being the subject of it.

"And the judge will just give you that?"

"Only if my paperwork doesn't suck."

She took another bite. "Better tighten it up then, Shakespeare. Public safety depends on you."

Ward chuckled and turned back to his screen. "Thanks for the pressure."

They sat in comfortable silence, accompanied only by the tapping of keys and chewing sounds. Then Emma leaned forward, pointing at a minimized window in the corner of his screen. "What's that?"

Ward clicked it open.

Tibeluk's lifeless face filled the screen, pale and oddly serene, the horrific wound visible just below his chin.

He scrambled to close it. "Yeah. Sorry, you shouldn't see that."

Her brow furrowed, but she didn't flinch. She'd always been a tough kid.

"That was the victim?" she asked.

"Yup." He opened up another photo, this one from far away, showing the entire scene by the roadside.

"Why pick a busy gas station?"

Ward paused, his hand hovering over the trackpad. He'd thought about the murder endlessly, but he'd written the location off as a crime of opportunity. "What do you mean?"

"It's wide open," Emma said, gesturing to the screen. "Anyone could've driven by. Why risk doing it there if he didn't want to get caught?"

Ward looked at her carefully, the implications of her question hitting him like cold water. It was an interesting line of thought.

"Maybe he wanted people to see," Emma said. "Maybe it wasn't just about the victim."

A chill crept down Ward's spine. "You think he's trying to send a message."

Emma shrugged, taking the last bite of her Pop-Tart. "Creepy, right?"

Ward finally closed the photo window, his mind racing. "Yeah. Good catch, kid. But seriously, no more looking at case files."

Her face twisted into a playful scowl. "I won't tell your boss.

Besides, how can I ever become a super-sleuth if you don't show me the ropes?"

The heavy thud of a door closing echoed through the wall from the neighboring apartment.

"That's Mom. Gotta go." She slung her backpack over one shoulder and headed for the door to put on her boots. "See you tomorrow, Mr. Ace Detective."

She disappeared into the hall, the door clicking shut behind her.

Ward sat in the silence, Emma's words echoing in his head. *Maybe he wanted people to see.*

She was right. The suspect hadn't dragged Tibeluk into the woods. He had positioned him in the back of a van, in a lit parking lot, right off the Parks Highway. It was a stage.

The bad guy wanted an audience.

Ward looked back at his affidavit. There was no doubt in his mind now. A man who builds a stage doesn't just put on a single show.

ELEVEN

Lena trembled beneath the thin, scratchy blanket, her body soaked in cold sweat. Her jaw clenched against the relentless throb pounding behind her eyes. Her stomach twisted with nausea, ribs bruised from hours of dry heaving, her muscles aching like she'd been thrown down a flight of stairs.

The Anchorage detox center was nothing more than a converted duplex—gray walls, flickering fluorescent lights, and the harsh smell of bleach failing to mask the tang of despair. Each second crawled, dragging fresh waves of panic and shame with it.

She didn't want to die. Not exactly. But she couldn't keep doing this, either.

The door creaked. Lena turned her face to the wall, bracing for another nurse with a clipboard or a patronizing counselor. But the footsteps were different. Slower. Measured. Intentional.

When she finally looked up, he was already standing beside her bed.

The man didn't belong in a place like this. He didn't wear a badge or scrubs, just plain clothes and an aura of absolute stillness. He was only a few years older than she was, but there was something in his eyes—deep and entirely too knowing. She shrank beneath his gaze, instinctively raising a trembling hand to cover her face. Shame boiled in her chest.

Then, he knelt.

He reached for her, slow and unthreatening. When his fingers touched her sweaty forehead, the atmosphere in the room shifted.

A wave of warmth rushed through her—real, almost electric. Her breathing leveled out. The violent hammering in her chest eased. The black wave of terror that had suffocated her since she stopped using began to unravel.

Her body still hurt—God, it hurt—but suddenly, the pain seemed survivable. Manageable. The phantom bugs crawling under her skin, the fear that made her want to tear her own hair out... it was gone. Not dulled. *Gone.*

She looked at him, her eyes wide with wonder. "Who... who are you?" she rasped.

Her voice sounded like someone else's. Weak. Hollow.

He smiled. His eyes were kind, but sharp with a purpose she didn't have the words to describe.

"I'm just a messenger, Lena," he said. "You don't have to be afraid anymore."

The words burrowed deep. They didn't feel like a rehearsed line from a counselor. They felt like a profound, absolute truth.

Tears welled, and she didn't try to stop them. He stayed, sitting by her bed while time bled into itself. She told him her name. Where she was from. How long she'd been using. How she used to sing— before everything went sideways. She told him how it had started with a prescription for painkillers and ended with her half-dead in a detox room nobody visited.

He listened. Not like a social worker or a cop waiting to check a box so they could leave. He listened like her pain actually mattered.

Like *she* mattered.

By the time he finally stood to leave, her fever had broken. Her mind was clearer than it had been in months.

"When you're ready, call me," he said, slipping a folded piece of paper into her trembling hand. "We have work to do."

He left her with a phone number. And hope.

TWELVE

WARD SAT AT HIS DESK IN ANCHORAGE WELL AFTER
everyone else had gone home, a steaming cup of reheated, too-
strong coffee sweating beside his keyboard. He'd spent the day
handling counter traffic and applying for warrants on an unrelated
Fairbanks homicide, and only now had the chance to dive back into
Foster's Talkeetna case.

He stared at the two oversized monitors on his desk. On one,
images alternated: a still from the FARO scan of the gas station van,
and a high-resolution close-up of the page he couldn't stop thinking
about.

> *Israel, riddled with rot, sinned in her pride. Thus must*
> *blood flow for cleansing; a sacrifice through the sacred*
> *fire.*
> *I am the divine ministrant.*

When Ward first found the note tucked under a rock at the edge
of the scene, he'd dismissed it as ego. But the phrasing gnawed
at him.

It sounded less like a threat and more like doctrine. A procedure rooted in pain. Twisted theology. It was the writing of someone who had seen something horrible and that ugliness had taken root in them.

A flicker of memory came to him—his father, years ago, on a park bench one Anchorage summer. Dogs running in the grass nearby.

"Jake," his father had said, a heavy hand resting on his son's knee. "The world can break you. And even if it doesn't break you, you'll meet those it has. Have a little mercy. They weren't always that way. Something, or someone, broke them."

Jake's mother had died when he was young. He had no siblings. His father had been everything to him, and the man poured everything he knew into Jake. He was patient, hardworking, and always quick with a gentle word of guidance.

That conversation was gold—some of the best insight Jake ever received. But, ironically, his father was "broken" by a drunk driver a few months later. Paralyzed from the waist down and riddled with pain, an opioid addiction finished him less than a year later.

The world had turned out to be too much for him, too. But the memory of that talk on the park bench stayed with Ward more than any other.

What, or who, broke this killer?

Ward leaned forward, his eyes flicking between the document and the scene photos. Randall Tibeluk rested peacefully, arms placed at his sides, eyes open. The blood pooled in a manner that suggested surrender, not struggle.

He mumbled the words from the note under his breath. "Not vengeance. Not rage. Cleansing."

On another monitor, a photo of the handwritten note from the driver's seat appeared.

Be not afraid (Psalm 56:3).

Wrong citation. Foley had caught that immediately. But misquoting a verse while using advanced theology elsewhere? That didn't track as mere carelessness. Not if the same man also used a term like "divine ministrant." It was more like he was reciting from memory, but had learned it wrong.

The suspect wasn't just trying to sound religious. He believed it.

Ward pulled up a plain-text document where he kept digital field notes—theories that might bite him in court if they never panned out and were found in any official documents. He typed:

Post-death positioning deliberate. Theology implied.
Cleansing as justification.

He stared at the screen, then pulled up a web browser and searched ritual sacrifices. The history was clear. Ancient Israelites, Romans, Greeks, Hindus, Mesoamericans—blood was seen as the source of life, and spilling it brought favor from the gods.

But as Foley had pointed out at the scene, the killer was heavily leaning on ancient Judaism. Giving up something of value—a blemish-free sheep, for instance—was how they paid for their errors.

But this killer hadn't picked a perfect sheep; Tibeluk was a transient with a record. He was anything but pristine.

Ward opened his field notes file and typed in the steps of an Israelite sacrifice found in his research:

1. Unblemished animal brought by the offerer. (Doesn't fit)
2. Offerer lays hands on the animal, transferring guilt. (No evidence)
3. Shechitah - Swift, precise throat cut by a priest using a shochet (knife). (Check)
4. Blood collected and sprinkled on altar. (Drops of blood around body)
5. Burning/Sharing – Offering is burned or shared. (No evidence)
6. Atonement – Brings forgiveness. (Check)

The steps didn't fit exactly. The ancient ritual had clearly influenced him, but he wasn't following it to the letter.

Ward clicked back to the autopsy photo of Tibeluk. The man's eyes, glassy and wide. His mouth slightly parted, almost in relief.

It wasn't just peace. It was absolution.

Maybe this wasn't about forgiveness at all, Ward thought. *Maybe it was a mercy killing?*

Now he was just guessing. Guessing is a bad idea in police work.

Foley knocked once on the doorframe and entered, holding a fresh cup of coffee. He wore the expression he always adopted when Ward plunged deep into conspiracy mode—half amusement, half worry.

"You're still looking at that note?" Foley asked, walking up behind Ward's chair.

"Yeah," Ward said. "I'm trying to make sense of his ritual. He's missing pieces. Specifically, the sacrifice is supposed to be unblemished to pay for the offerer's sins. Tibeluk wasn't unblemished."

"Yeah, he was a mess," Foley agreed, looking at the screen.

"Right. Which makes me think this isn't about the killer buying his own forgiveness. I think he's acting as the judge. He decides who needs to be clean."

"Ego?" Foley asked, sipping his coffee.

"Massive ego. But look at Tibeluk. He's calm. Cooperative. Why? Did he repent? Did he confess? Or did he just want peace so badly he'd take it from anyone offering?"

Foley tapped the doorframe. "You're going full theological profiler on this one, huh?"

"Can't help it," Ward said, staring at the screen. "I searched the terms from his note. Sacrifice, cleansing, blood, ministrant. You know what 'ministrant' means? It's not a common word. It carries weight. Age. It's the kind of thing you find in an old catechism or a dusty file in a seminary."

Foley set his coffee down on the edge of the desk. "You think someone groomed him for this?"

"Maybe." Ward let that sit for a moment. "His cadence, his vocabulary... it doesn't feel spontaneous. It feels taught."

"By who?"

"I don't know," Ward said.

Foley chuckled dryly and picked up his cup. "Well, I'm not a fan of his doctrine, so I won't be signing up. And I already have a church."

As Foley walked out, Ward minimized the browser and brought his notes file back up. At the bottom, he typed:

Hypothesis: Subject is replicating unknown/adapted ritual. Victims experience calm—then death. Phrases like "blood for cleansing" and "ministrant" indicate past exposure to rigid theological language. Authority-based conditioning? Language not spontaneous. Possibly taught.

He stared at the blinking cursor.

But who taught him?

THIRTEEN

The break room at the Alaska Bureau of Investigation smelled of coffee and pastries. Cops ate donuts. Troopers ate pastries. The distinction mattered.

Ward stood near the pot, staring at the sludge in the carafe, trying to scrub the Talkeetna crime scene from his mind.

"You gonna drink that, or perform an autopsy on it?"

Ward turned. Clint Galloway, the supervisor of the Aircraft Section, leaned against the doorframe. He held a bag of pretzels and wore a flight suit unzipped to reveal a faded "Salty Dawg Saloon" t-shirt.

"Thinking about it," Ward said. "What are you doing here, Clint? Shouldn't you be slipping the surly bonds of earth somewhere?"

"Was out running some hours on Helo 3," Galloway said, tossing a pretzel into his mouth. "Remembered I owed Marlowe twenty bucks. Figured I'd come over and pay up before he adds interest."

A siren screamed from the portable radio in the corner, followed by a garbled voice. Mat-Com dispatch. A siren meant a Troop was on a code run.

Ward turned up the volume.

1-B-44, Matcom, 10-60?

Dispatch checking status. Galloway leaned closer.

A pause. Then, a voice tight with adrenaline and road noise.

1-B-44. Still outbound on Knik-Goose Bay. Passing Mile 4. Speeds exceeding eighty. He's all over the road. Almost took out a minivan.

Vasquez. New guy, fresh off field training.

Speeds were too high for these conditions. If Vasquez was pushing this hard, the guy must have done something reckless.

Galloway's cell phone rang. He answered. "Galloway."

Ward could hear dispatch chatter coming through the cell.

"Yup." Galloway moved toward the door, then paused and turned to Ward. "It's the pursuit. I'm going up. You wanna be spotter? I'll be airborne in five."

"Absolutely."

Ward grabbed his go-bag and rifle from his car and sprinted to the pad.

Ward strapped into the front left seat, pulling the four-point harness tight.

Galloway hit the starter, the turbine's rising scream building fast into a tight, predatory hiss. He watched the temperature needle surge and safely settle, then rolled the twist grip forward. Above them, the rotor blades blurred into a single disc, sending a bone-deep tremor through the cabin.

Ward leaned forward, booting the FLIR system into a ghostly grayscale. He keyed his radio. "Matcom, 2-I-61 and Helo 3. Airborne in thirty."

Galloway eased in the collective. The AStar lifted cleanly into a tight hover. He gave the gauges a quick, disciplined scan—torque and temps in the green—and nudged the cyclic forward.

As they gained translational lift, the vibration smoothed. The helicopter bit into the clean air, the turbine's pitch deepening as Galloway fed in more power and the machine surged upward.

Power lines loomed near them, paralleling Tudor Road.

He held the climb steady—no wasted movement—nose slightly

down for airspeed, torque riding the edge without crossing it. The wires dropped beneath them with room to spare.

Only then did he bank.

The AStar rolled hard into departure, nose cutting toward the city as Anchorage opened beneath them in a sweep of icy asphalt, the helicopter clawing upward into the open sky.

Below, the city was a hustle of morning traffic. They climbed over midtown, heading west.

Pursuits on ice went sideways fast. Ward hoped this was still a pursuit and not a wreck by the time they arrived.

They rocketed across the water of Knik Arm, the churning gray waves blurring beneath them. As they approached the far shore, dirty blocks of ice littered the frozen coastline. Ward scanned the horizon. The Mat-Su side was a patchwork of birch, spruce, and frozen ponds.

"There," Galloway pointed. "KGB just north of Point Mac."

Ward nodded when he saw the plume of kicked-up snow that rose from the roadway less than a mile inland. Galloway clearly had eagle eyes.

Ward keyed his radio. "1-B-44, this is 2-I-61. We see you. Coming in from the northeast."

2-I-61? Ward?

"Directly overhead. Helo 3 has eyes on. Back it off a bit—drive safe. Let him see us. Maybe he'll realize it's over."

The suspect's Silverado fishtailed, drifting through corners and spraying snow and gravel from the road's shoulder.

Copy, Vasquez said. He slowed, opening the gap.

The truck turned right on Point MacKenzie Road and accelerated. Galloway positioned the helicopter well in front of the suspect and dropped altitude slightly, making sure the driver saw the helo.

But the idiot didn't slow. He hammered the gas, kicking up fresh snow in a near-loss of control.

He's back up to ninety, Vasquez called. *Road conditions degrading.*

"He'll run out of road eventually," Ward said through the headset. "Unless he knows the back way to Big Lake."

The suspect seemed to realize it too. A moment later, the truck braked hard and veered toward a side street. Kobuk Lane. A dead end.

"He's turning," Ward said. "Kobuk Lane."

But the truck was going too fast and hit the ditch. The nose plowed into the earth, sending dirt and snow everywhere, the rear end kicking up before slamming back down. Steam exploded from the radiator.

"10-50. Corner of Point Mac and Kobuk," Ward said. "Impact with the ditch."

The driver's door flew open. The suspect scrambled out—big, heavy dude, wearing a Carhartt jacket and knit cap—moving with the frantic energy of a man on the run. He sprinted toward the dense tree line. No weapon visible. Didn't mean there wasn't one.

Vasquez slid his Tahoe to a halt and bailed out.

Foot bail! Heading southwest into the woods! I'm in pursuit!

"44, wait," Ward said. "We can track with FLIR!"

With the forward-looking infrared imaging equipment on the helo, they could track the suspect until more units arrived. Set a perimeter. Let him get cold and desperate. Capture him later, when he was exhausted.

Negative! Losing visual!

Vasquez disappeared into the trees.

Damn it. Vasquez was going solo against a desperate criminal. Ward knew the feeling—adrenaline and prey drive overriding logic.

Ward released the mic. "Put me down, Clint. Close as you dare."

Galloway flared the AStar, bringing it to a shaky hover three feet above the snowy road behind the idling Tahoe. Ward popped his harness and stood on the skid, the rotor wash threatening to peel him off. "Stepping off in three... two... one... clear!" Ward launched himself. Behind him, the AStar bobbed violently as Galloway fought the sudden weight shift, the engine screaming as it fought for balance.

Ward racked the charging handle on his rifle, activated the safety and sprinted for the treeline.

The shoe prints were easy to follow.

"You're under arrest!" Ward heard from the trees ahead.

Then, a sound that chilled Ward to the bone: a dull thud and a grunt of pain.

Ward tore through the brush, leaping through shallow snow. He burst through a copse of black spruce, his rifle sling snagging a branch. He spun, ripping it free, and emerged into a small clearing.

Vasquez was on his back, nose bleeding. The suspect straddled him, one hand gripping the trooper's holster, the other wrenching at the weapon. Vasquez bucked, fighting, but the big man had leverage. Thank God for triple-retention holsters.

Ward had a clean shot. Justified. But they were so close...

He launched at the man, hitting him like a linebacker. The impact was audible—a wet meat-slap. The force tore the suspect off Vasquez, sending both him and the man tumbling into the snow beyond.

They scrambled to rise. The suspect was big—six-three, two-fifty—eyes bloodshot. Drunk?

The man roared and swung a heavy boot. It caught Ward square in the left ribs.

Crack.

Something snapped. A jagged edge shifted inward, a spike of white-hot fire dropping Ward to his knees. He gasped.

Stupid. Stupid.

His brain registered the damage, acknowledged the pain, and then—endured it.

Adrenaline surged in his veins, and the pain in his side dulled slightly.

Ward looked up. The suspect's eyes were wide. He had just landed a brutal kick and didn't get the reaction he expected.

His ribs were on fire, but he had endured far greater pain. Cancer treatment. Torture on a madman's table.

Ward rose to his feet and took a step back, holding his rifle at the guard position.

"Don't move!" Vasquez bellowed. He'd regained his feet and was standing, his pistol leveled at the suspect. "On your knees!"

The suspect dropped to his knees, defeated.

"On your belly!" Vasquez boomed. "Arms out!"

The suspect complied. The fight had left him the moment guns came out. Drunk maybe, but not dumb.

Vasquez holstered, approached, and cuffed the man. The clicks of the handcuffs were music to Ward's ears.

"Mat-Com, 2-I-61," Ward said, breathing steady, despite the pain. "One 10-80. All 10-60."

He looked at Vasquez. The young trooper sat in the snow, wiping blood from his nose. Above, the thump-thump-thump of Helo 3 grew louder as Galloway circled back.

Ward helped Vasquez guide the man to the Tahoe.

A few minutes later, the suspect was secured. Ward snapped photos of the scene for the DA.

"You okay, Ward?" Vasquez asked, eyeing his side. "He crushed you with that kick, didn't he?"

Ward rubbed his ribs.

"Nah," he lied, his lungs still struggling to breathe through the pain. "Must have glanced off."

Vasquez frowned, then shrugged. It was an uncomfortable pause. "If you say so."

The pain was lancing across Ward's torso this very minute. But to support Assault on a Police Officer charges, Ward would have to be checked out by a physician. Photos of the injury. Documentation.

That couldn't happen. Not when the injury would be healed so soon. It took the fear out of it, leaving only the pain. Pain he could handle.

Besides, with the bad guy fighting over Vasquez's holster, they had a felony assault charge anyway—putting the trooper in fear of imminent serious physical injury by means of a bullet from his own gun. Plus the Hit and Run. DUI. Eluding. This was a big case for Vasquez. Extra charges were unnecessary.

But damn did his ribs hurt right now. The adrenaline was fading and breathing would soon be torturous.

Ward walked toward the helo that was just now landing on the roadway, the thrum-thrum of the helicopter blades reminding him of the machines in Pagan's lab.

What an odd career. Messy. Desperate. And freakin' exhilarating.

Mat-Com, 1-B-44, Vasquez called over the radio. *10-19 to Mat-Su Regional for medical clearance. One 10-80.*

Ward climbed into the helicopter, rubbing his side as he buckled in. The pain had faded slightly in the last few minutes, even without directed meditation. In a day or two it would be no more than a minor ache, reminding him that he was different from others wearing the badge.

He suspected he would need every bit of that edge for the path ahead.

FOURTEEN

The air on the park strip was brittle, a sudden cold snap having moved over Anchorage during the night. Leaves clung to the frozen grass in scattered clusters, their veins dark with frost. A thin rime crusted the birch bark behind Lena as she huddled near its base, her arms locked around her knees.

She hadn't slept. Her body ached with the ghosts of withdrawal, but the worst of it had passed, just like Adam promised it would.

She hadn't used since the day he touched her forehead in the detox center and whispered, *You don't have to be afraid anymore.*

No one had ever said that and made it feel true. But with him, it was. Long ago, her drug of choice had ceased to offer pleasure; her habit had become so powerful that even eighty milligrams of OxyContin left no more than a warm buzz in her head. She had used merely to avoid the agony of withdrawal. But Adam had changed the game. The horrible stomach cramps over the last few days had been torture, no doubt, but without the suffocating blanket of fear, they'd been bearable. She had found the courage to let go of the pain.

Life had changed.

Now, she followed him. She didn't understand what came next, but she knew what wouldn't: sleeping in strange rooms, dodging dark-eyed hustlers with razors in their smiles and violence in their pants.

Adam offered something different. Something pure.

She watched him now, standing near the trailhead, speaking to a man whose eyes looked bloodshot and hollow. The man swayed on his feet, his lips cracked, skin flushed. He was obviously drunk, but more than that, he just looked exhausted. Lena recognized that look. End-stage. The point where dying felt like a relief.

Still, the man listened. Adam had that effect. One hand rested on the man's shoulder, steady and unyielding. Even from where Lena sat, she could feel the warmth radiating from their contact.

The man kept glancing her way, uncertain, before looking back to Adam. It was early enough that the park was mostly empty—just a jogger in the distance and a truck idling near the edge of the lot. The sun hovered low behind a heavy blanket of clouds.

Adam turned and waved her over.

Lena stood, her joints stiff, and crossed the distance. Her boots crunched over the frozen leaves. She kept her arms wrapped tight around her ribs, unsure if it was the cold or something else making her shiver.

"Lena," Adam said, his voice warm. "This is Eric."

Eric gave a weak nod, his eyes darting. "She gonna... she's gonna watch?"

"She's already walked through the sacred fire," Adam said calmly. "And come through healed."

Lena stepped closer, meeting Eric's eyes. "A week ago, I stood where you are. Sick. Shaking. Wanting to die." Her voice was hoarse but steady. "Then he found me, and the fear just... stopped. I haven't used since. No dope. No booze. Just peace."

Eric blinked, his eyes wet.

"I don't know what he is," Lena said, her voice cracking. "But he gave me my life back. That's real. That's what matters. And that's why I'm here."

"Eric," Adam said, stepping closer to the man. "Do you believe you need to be cleansed?"

Eric swallowed hard, nodding. "I... yeah. I done stuff. Bad stuff. My kid—I left her in the car. It was cold outside. I just... forgot she was with me."

Adam didn't flinch. "But you remember now."

"Every day."

"You've confessed," Adam said, his hand tightening slightly on the man's shoulder. "You've repented. Now comes the peace."

Lena felt it—a sudden, heavy shift in the air, like the pressure dropping before a storm.

Eric crumpled to his knees without prompting. He offered no resistance. No bargaining. His eyes went glassy and wide. Total surrender.

Adam reached into the bag at his side and pulled out a folded piece of plastic sheeting. He spread it over the frosted grass with gentle precision, as though laying out linen for a sacred rite. Then he stood beside Eric, placing one hand over the man's forehead and the other across his back. He guided Eric to lie down, and Eric followed blindly, like a child being tucked into bed.

Lena's breath caught. Somehow, she knew what would come next.

Adam knelt beside the plastic.

"You matter, Eric. You are valuable, beyond imagining. Close your eyes now. The hard part's done. The struggle is over."

A small blade slid from Adam's coat. The edge caught the weak light from a street lamp. Lena thought she might flinch, but she didn't. The suffocating peace radiating from Adam held her perfectly still.

There was no scream. No spasm. Just the knife, then the blood, then the faint hiss of breath leaving lungs.

Silence.

Tears rolled down Lena's cheeks. Not from horror, but from a strange, terrifying reverence. Eric's face was slack and calm—nothing like the overdose deaths she'd witnessed in dirty flophouses. There were no twisted limbs. No foaming mouths. Just release.

Adam sat beside the body for a long time, his head bowed, his eyes closed.

Lena wanted to speak, but her throat was tight.

Eventually, Adam rose. He seemed to have absorbed something from the act. He stood taller, the weariness replaced by a sharp, terrible confidence.

He knelt to wipe the blade on Eric's pant leg with practiced care, then retrieved a folded square of paper from his coat. He knelt once more and tucked it beneath Eric's folded hands.

Lena caught a glimpse of the neat, handwritten letters:

Be not afraid, for the blood has made you clean.

A light snowfall began. Soft. Weightless. It landed on the plastic like grace.

He drew a small flashlight from his coat, its tight beam cutting through the predawn gloom as he meticulously checked the scene. He looked for stray fibers, footprints, dropped items. His hands moved with a clinical, almost obsessive certainty. Lena watched him, realizing this wasn't just caution. This was ritual. Every movement had to be perfect. Cleanliness was part of the holy act.

When they finished, they walked in silence to the car they'd "borrowed" earlier.

At the doors, Lena finally found her voice. "Was he bad?"

Adam rested a hand on the door handle and stared across the roof of the car. "He carried his sin like a millstone around his neck. But he wanted release. He needed the light."

Lena exhaled, releasing a breath she didn't know she'd been holding. "And you gave it to him."

She looked at Adam across the roof. The glimmer of absolute confidence had faded slightly, leaving behind something... wanting.

"Why didn't you release *me*?" she asked, her voice barely a whisper over the wind. "Why did I get to live?"

Adam didn't respond right away. He just looked into her eyes.

His brow furrowed in genuine curiosity, as if he were asking himself the same question.

"I don't know," he finally said. "Maybe because... I need your help." He nodded, almost imperceptibly, solidifying the thought. "Your words help them accept the peace."

"Do *you* suffer?" she asked.

He offered a gentle smile. "Not anymore."

She hesitated, a knot tightening in her chest.

Adam's gaze lingered on her. The snowfall dusted his shoulders like ash.

"You're not like them, Lena," he said, looking back toward the park strip. "You weren't spared. You were chosen. Your wounds are your altar now. You were injured, but you now stand. That's what makes you holy. And perfect for your mission. You can tell them. You can testify."

She stared at him, her breath fogging the air between them.

"I don't feel holy."

"You will," he said. "In time. Pain is how we learn the shape of God."

Something in his voice chilled her, even as his radiated peace continued to soothe her frayed nerves. It sounded like the calm of a man who had stared into a roaring fire—and decided it belonged to him.

They climbed into the car. The city was waking up around them.

Lena turned to the window and whispered a prayer—not to the God of steeples and psalms, but to the one who had pulled her from the pit.

She didn't know what Adam really was.

A prophet? A madman? Or a savior?

Maybe he was all of them.

But one thing she knew for certain:

She would follow him into the abyss.

FIFTEEN

Ward's phone buzzed on the edge of the desk. It was a call. Foley.

"Yeah," Ward said.

"You at your desk?"

"Yup."

"Good. I need you sitting. Gotta share something that's been bugging me."

Ward rolled his eyes. "What is it?"

"The Pagan case file. In ARMS."

Ward's stomach tightened. "Yeah. The access control list locked us out."

"Yeah, well, about that. Before they ACL'd it, while I was finishing my narrative supplement for the case file and I was still on the access list..."

"You made copies? The sealed stuff?"

"Technically, it hadn't been sealed yet. Not for me... cuz I had to—"

"—write your supplement. Yeah, I get it. But you're just now telling me?"

A heavy pause hung on the line. "I'd catch an administrative investigation if anyone found out," Foley said. "I was gonna tell you, eventually. But you haven't exactly told *me* everything, either, so I was keeping it close. And besides... I think it might help with this case."

Ward opened his mouth to say something, then closed it.

What could he say? That he died, a couple times, saw the other side, and it was amazing? That he came back, and for a while, he did things that didn't make any sense?

"Well, Jake?"

"So... I tell you—you tell me."

"It's fair. I was waiting for you to open up about what happened in that lab, but that's not how you operate. You bottle it up, move on, and pretend the ugly stuff never happened."

"Don't we all do that? At least a little?"

It was true, and the point would hit home with Foley. You can't do this job, see the evil humans do to one another and remain unaffected. Some of it has to be dealt with, or more often, swept under the rug. It's the only way to keep functioning.

And that ugly stuff adds up.

"Okay, Bud, here it is. I had a couple near-death experiences. There wasn't any fear, it was beautiful, and it changed me. In more ways than one."

"Not surprised. That stuff was all over Pagan's notes. Seems like he was *trying* to kill you guys. That was the whole point of his research. But how did you escape the goons?"

Ward took a deep breath. "That's hard to explain. It's like, for a while, I saw what they were going to do. I saw options, possible futures, and I just had to pick the one that worked best for me. Not full visions, but snapshots. Enough to see what was coming."

"That's... messed up." Foley's voice carried a tone of incredulity. "So you're telling me you were reading one of those 'choose your own adventure' stories and you picked the path that had you defeat the bad guys, find the treasure and save the girl? Really?"

"Yeah, except I didn't save the girl, did I?"

"Oh, yeah. Sorry, Jake. I didn't mean—"

"It's okay. I know what you meant."

A long pause. Foley probably thought he was insane.

"Can you still do that?"

"No, I've tried. Whatever he broke in me has since healed, I guess."

Another pause.

"I don't know what to say. You kind of surprised me with that."

"I don't blame you, it sounds crazy. I wondered if my noodle was scrambled. Then, I thought it was the adrenaline. Or the drugs they gave me. But Belle Anderson had experiences too—fragments of intuition. It's like she sensed emotions. It wasn't just trauma. It was... something else."

Foley exhaled. "Jesus, Jake. I don't blame you for not sharing. If you're not nuts, Pagan was unlocking something that should have stayed hidden."

Ward chuckled. "But I could be nuts."

"Yeah, you could." Foley sighed and Jake almost heard him smile through the phone. "Well, Jake, you and Belle aren't the only ones Pagan messed with. Last night I was reviewing those notes I pulled—just trying to make sense of it all. I found a file about a male subject—identified only as 'AB.' Said the guy was erratic, hard to sedate. 'High resistance to consciousness suppressants.' I suppose that means anesthesia. Pagan called this guy 'unpredictable and unresolved.' Lots of anxiety, and such."

"AB?"

"That's all it says. But listen to this—he describes a session where AB was coming out of sedation. Delirious. And he kept repeating: 'There is no forgiveness. No forgiveness. Blood must be shed.' Over and over again."

Ward's throat tightened. "That's the phrase," he said.

"This AB subject—he wasn't just drugged. Pagan had him dosed with radiation, too. I guess he used that on most of you guys. Something about 'neurological openness' and 'cellular decay thresholds.' All that crazy mad scientist stuff he was doing to y'all's heads."

Ward's mind wandered to Belle. He thought she was a mind

reader, but she'd said, 'Not thoughts. Feelings, but often with the same result.' Those words stuck in his head.

Feelings, not thoughts. And fear is a feeling.

Now they had found another freak—this one detected fear. Or maybe not detected it, but... suppressed it. Which was worse.

"Bud, do you think AB endured the same experimentation as Belle? The same kind, I mean?"

"That or something similar. Pagan only referenced a few long-term survivors in the files. AB... he may have survived. Long enough to leave a mark."

"And he's still out there?"

"That's the thing. Some of the other files end with the subject dying. This one seems to show they let him go. You'll have to read it for yourself."

"Maybe they kicked him to the curb. Burned out his brain and left him for dead somewhere. He must have been damaged enough they weren't worried about him surviving to rat them out."

"Then how is he now killing people, Jake?"

Ward took another deep breath. "There's something else I didn't tell you."

Foley chuckled. "Big surprise."

"Yeah. Well, Pagan taught me how to heal. Fast."

"What?"

"Yeah, he unlocked something, and I'd go into this trance, and heal quickly. Like a bullet wound in just a couple days. Even works a little when I'm awake. He needed us to heal to endure the damage he was inducing."

"Can you still do that?"

"Why, wanna shoot me and see if I live?"

They endured an awkward silence.

"That's sick," Foley said.

"Yeah, tell me about it. Keep this under your hat, Bud. Not a word to anyone."

"Of course! They'd think I was as crazy as you." Bud paused, clearly taking it all in before continuing. "So this AB character, with a burnt-out brain, maybe he recovers from it? Maybe he *is* our guy, Jake."

"Could be."

Pagan's darkness hadn't ended in that lab. It had just gotten loose.

"Bud, you're gonna have to give me copies of those files."

"I know, I know…"

SIXTEEN

The evening air was brittle, carrying the sharp scent of evergreen mingled with the dampness of a light, intermittent snowfall. Lena led Thomas along a narrow path that twisted through a dense stand of spruce and birch. Their trunks shone silver in the moonlight, branches brushing against their coats. The sun had already surrendered to the night, leaving only a bruised violet glow hovering on the horizon.

Thomas stepped cautiously, his eyes darting through the shadows as though expecting violence to erupt from the tree line. Lena had grown familiar with his guarded nature since finding him shivering outside a downtown shelter. He was just a kid, really—no older than Adam—but the dirty, unshaven scruff shadowing his jaw gave him the worn, slumped posture of someone accustomed to betrayal. His eyes held a hollow exhaustion—the look of a stray who had stumbled through a life of bad decisions and was desperate for a way out.

He was looking for redemption. And Lena knew Adam could provide it.

At last, the woods parted into a small clearing illuminated by the warm, snapping glow of a modest campfire. Adam sat in a weathered folding chair, gazing into the flames. He stood as Lena and Thomas approached, offering a quiet smile that softened the severe angles of his face.

Thomas hesitated, glancing at Lena before meeting Adam's steady gaze. "Lena said you can help people," he said, his voice thick with skepticism. "I've trusted people before. It never ends well. How do I know you're different?"

Adam's smile deepened with understanding, untroubled by the doubt. "Trust is not given, Thomas. It must be earned. Sit with me."

Reluctantly, Thomas took the empty chair near the fire. Lena stood a few paces back, her heart picking up pace.

Adam settled back into his seat and slowly rolled up his left sleeve, exposing his pale forearm. Lena felt a familiar rush of awe, knowing what was about to happen.

Adam reached into his coat pocket and retrieved a small knife. The blade caught the flickering firelight.

Thomas stiffened, leaning back, the panic instantly returning to his face. "What are you doing?"

Without blinking, Adam pressed the steel to his own forearm.

The blade sliced a deep, clean line through the flesh. Dark blood welled instantly from the wound, spilling over his skin and dripping with a steady, rhythmic tap onto the frozen soil.

Thomas's eyes widened in horror. His breath caught in his throat, but he remained frozen in his chair, transfixed by the violence.

Lena moved closer, resting a gentle hand on Thomas's trembling shoulder. "Watch," she whispered.

Adam set the bloody knife aside. He closed his eyes and let his breathing settle into a slow, perfectly measured cadence. Despite the severe laceration, his posture never wavered.

Minutes passed. The clearing was hushed, broken only by the crackle of burning wood and the hiss of the winter breeze. Thomas shifted uneasily, but Lena squeezed his shoulder.

"Wait," she said.

Time seemed to stretch. Then, the bleeding slowed. Gradually

—almost imperceptibly at first—the torn edges of Adam's flesh crawled inward. They knit together with a grotesque, miraculous patience, guided by an unseen force. It wasn't a sudden flash of magic; it was methodical repair happening in real time.

They sat in reverent silence as the tissue bound itself and the wound sealed shut. What should have taken weeks of stitches and bandages was completed in ten minutes.

Adam wiped the blood away with a cloth, leaving nothing but a thin, silvery scar and the quiet certainty that they had witnessed something holy.

Thomas exhaled a shaky, ragged breath. "How... how is that possible?"

Adam opened his eyes, regarding Thomas with absolute compassion. "The flesh knows how to purge the rot. Pain is merely the fire that purifies us, Thomas. Sacrifice paves the way to redemption. And the blood always flows before the healing. I endured my own trials in the dark to prove that even the deepest wounds can be closed."

Thomas stared at Adam's arm, struggling to process the impossible reality sitting in front of him. "I want to believe. But I've seen so much ugly in this world... trusting is hard."

Adam nodded. "The world is noisy. It is harsh. Men hurt each other because they are drowning in their own pain. That confusion is why you need a guide. Someone to lead you out of the static and into the quiet."

Thomas bowed his head, his voice cracking. "I've stumbled my whole life. I've made so many mistakes. I'm just... I'm tired of the darkness."

Adam leaned forward, extending a hand. "Then step into the light. Allow me to guide you. Together, we can grant peace to others who are lost, just as you were."

Thomas looked up. He glanced at Lena for confirmation. She met his gaze with a fierce, unwavering nod.

Taking a deep breath, Thomas sat up straighter. The nervous

tremor left his shoulders, replaced by a desperate resolve. "I want to help. Show me how."

Lena stepped around the chair and looked down at the recruit. "Not everyone will accept the help, Thomas. Some will resist. Their hearts are hardened by the rot. Those souls must find their peace in a different way. Do you understand what that means?"

Thomas looked at Lena, his gaze hardening. "I understand. I'll do whatever is necessary."

He fell silent, staring into the flames.

Lena turned back toward Adam. He was watching the fire, his eyes reflecting the orange glow, utterly calm and assured. Standing near him, Lena felt the suffocating blanket of his peace washing over her, keeping her own demons at bay.

Yet, looking at the fresh scar on Adam's arm, a question lingered in her mind. What horrors had he witnessed? What unimaginable suffering had he endured in his past to be gifted with such a power? No one could have known just by looking at him, but she felt the weight of it: the ache beneath his calm, the quiet nobility of a man who had survived what should have broken him.

The awareness didn't unsettle her. It bound her to him.

Nothing he asks of us, she thought, *is something he wouldn't bear himself.*

Lena wrapped her arms around her ribs, suddenly hyper-aware of her own hidden wounds—the trauma she had buried deep, the unseen scars of her addiction. The hurt she had caused her family. She looked again at Adam and a quiet, desperate hope bloomed in her chest.

Maybe someday, he could teach her how to heal the wounds inside her heart.

SEVENTEEN

The rain had returned to Anchorage by nightfall, sluicing down the windshield in silver rivulets. Hawthorne sat in a nondescript Subaru half a block from the low-rent motel where Adam Basu had checked in hours earlier. The heater hummed against the October cold, but his coffee had long since gone lukewarm.

He kept the binoculars low, sweeping between the room's second-floor window and the parking lot. No movement. No shadow against the curtains. He'd endured worse stakeouts, but impatience was creeping into the cab like a physical draft.

On the passenger seat, his tablet streamed the feed from a city traffic camera positioned down the block. The camera wasn't aimed directly at the motel, but it caught enough of the sidewalk to be useful. It meant he didn't have to stare unblinking at the building for twelve hours straight—not when Basu had an uncanny knack for noticing eyes on him.

When the motel room door finally opened, Hawthorne immediately lifted the binoculars.

Adam stepped out first. He was dressed for the weather but moved completely unhurried, the hood of a black rain jacket pulled low over his brow, covering the stocking cap on his head. A woman followed, her shoulders hunched against the chill, hands buried deep in her coat pockets.

And then came a third figure.

It was a man, taller than Adam but walking with a subservient, nervous slump. He hovered close to the woman, his head on a swivel. A new addition to the cadre. Hawthorne's jaw tightened. Basu wasn't just hiding; he was recruiting.

The trio walked side by side toward the street, passing under a streetlamp that washed their skin in a sickly, paper-thin yellow.

Hawthorne's thumb hovered over the door handle. He fought the urge to pursue on foot, but his orders were clear: *Watch. Report. Don't engage.*

He tapped the tablet's record button instead, capturing the grainy feed from the traffic cam.

Halfway down the block, Adam slowed. His head tilted slightly, like a hound catching a distant scent on the wind. He stopped and glanced back over his shoulder—not directly at the Subaru, but scanning Hawthorne's general direction.

A cold prickle worked its way down Hawthorne's neck.

He had tailed spies, cartel traffickers, and seasoned killers who had never once clocked him. But Basu? He never made direct eye contact, yet Hawthorne felt entirely exposed.

Adam leaned toward the woman, murmuring something Hawthorne had no hope of hearing through the rain. She glanced back once, briefly. The new man flinched, looking around anxiously before Adam placed a steadying hand on his back and guided him forward.

They crossed the street and disappeared into a narrow alley between a pawn shop and a boarded-up diner.

Hawthorne cursed under his breath. It was too tight to follow in the car without drawing attention. He abandoned the vehicle at the curb, cutting across the wet asphalt on foot.

The alley was empty. Just overflowing dumpsters, a row of sagging chain-link fence, and a rusty fire escape leading nowhere.

There were no footprints in the shallow puddles. No sound of retreating steps echoing off the brick.

Hawthorne stood in the cold rain, scanning the deep shadows, knowing they were already gone.

Adam didn't speak again until they were three blocks away, tucked safely beneath the deep overhang of an abandoned service station.

"He's been watching us for a while," Adam said.

Lena frowned, wiping rain from her face. "Who?"

Thomas shifted his weight, his eyes darting frantically toward the street. "Cops?" he asked, his voice tight with rising panic. "Did they track us?"

"No," Adam said, his tone entirely matter-of-fact. "The man in the Subaru. Gray jacket. Disciplined... likely ex-military."

Lena glanced back the way they'd come, but the driving rain had erased the city behind them. "Do we need to leave town?"

"No. He's cautious. That means he's not ready to do anything." Adam looked past her, his eyes narrowing as if searching the horizon for something unseen. "But it's... distracting."

"Distracting how?" Lena asked.

Adam didn't answer immediately. The truth was harder to admit—even to himself.

Since leaving Talkeetna, the city felt crowded. Too many people. Too many auras.

Every block radiated with the rot, flecks of corruption layered over strangers's faces like invisible, suffocating grime. It was usually background noise, a static he could filter at will. But now, with Thomas's lingering guilt adding to the chorus, it pressed against him in heavy, suffocating waves, each pulse sharper and more demanding than the last.

He told himself it was the watcher in the Subaru throwing him off balance. But deep down, he knew it was more than that. The gift was expanding, demanding more of him.

"I'm seeing too much," he said finally.

Lena's brows drew together. "Too much what?"

"Everything."

For a long moment, the three of them stood in the wet hiss of the cold rain. Thomas looked at his boots, clutching his coat tight. Lena wanted to ask if that meant her, too, but the words wouldn't come. She was too afraid of the answer.

Adam straightened, the vulnerability suddenly shuttered away behind a mask of rigid certainty. "We're leaving. I need to go somewhere safer. I need to pray."

EIGHTEEN

THE CALL CAME JUST AFTER DAWN, THAT HOUR WHEN the world still hadn't decided what it wanted to be yet. Ward had been awake for most of the night, dozing in fragments on the couch with the TV muted, the gray Palmer morning leaking into his apartment around the edges of the blinds.

His phone vibrated on the coffee table, the screen lighting up with Foley's name.

He answered before the second buzz. "Ward."

"Got another one," Foley said. "Anchorage. Coastal trail near Ship Creek. APD's all over it, but Foster's tied up on something else and can't make it."

Ward sat up, swinging his legs to the floor. "Same deal?"

There was a pause. Long enough to matter.

"Kinda," Foley said. "But the victim seems... different."

The scene sat just off the trail, tucked into a pocket of trees where the creek bent hard against the embankment. Dozens of early joggers must have passed within fifty yards of it without seeing a thing, their breath steaming in the cold air, headphones sealing them into their own private worlds.

Ward and Foley flashed their badges at the Anchorage Police patrol officer and ducked under the yellow tape. Ward felt the familiar, cold narrowing of focus as he gathered in the surrounding scene. APD had marked a clear path over the frosted grass to avoid contaminating the area. A crime scene tech was busy photographing the periphery as Ward approached the body.

Male. Mid-forties. Reasonably well-groomed. No obvious signs of homelessness this time. He wore a clean jacket and decent boots.

The body was positioned on heavy plastic sheeting—new, not scavenged—the edges weighed down with stones. The throat wound was just as precise as the Talkeetna murder. Surgical. No hesitation marks. No defensive injuries.

Ward crouched on the grass near the victim's head, careful not to disturb the plastic, and studied the man's face. It was impossibly peaceful.

"You see it too," Foley said, standing over him.

Ward nodded. "Yeah."

Dead people just didn't look like this, unless they were old and died in their sleep. In the field, troopers were accustomed to bodies in car wrecks, suicides, and violent homicides. Bodies were deformed, broken, and displaced in the desperate fight for life. This scene defied everything Ward had learned in over a decade of law enforcement work. It rankled his sense of order.

The tech from the crime lab stepped past them, her camera clicking rapidly. The creek murmured nearby, water sliding over rock, indifferent to human tragedy.

"Wallet's still on him," Foley added. "Cash untouched. Phone and car keys still in his jacket pocket."

Ward exhaled, a plume of white breath rising in the chill. This wasn't rage. This wasn't theft. It wasn't even punishment, not in the traditional sense. This was... consent.

He stood and took in the broader scene. No signs of a struggle anywhere along the approach path. No broken brush. No gouged earth. The victim walked here willingly.

"Any witnesses?" Ward asked.

"Two joggers passed by around 0500," a voice said from behind them.

Ward turned.

Standing just outside the perimeter tape was a woman in a dark woolen coat, her breath steaming in the air. She ducked under the tape and approached them, her movements efficient, her dark, assessing eyes tracking Ward.

"Detective Vanessa Miller, APD," she said. She didn't offer a hand, just a curt nod. She held a small notepad, tapping it rhythmically against her thigh. "The jogger heard voices. Nothing urgent. No yelling. Said it sounded like a quiet conversation. Two, maybe three people. Then he saw a flashlight beam cut out, and that was it. Called it in almost an hour later as something suspicious. No idea it was a murder."

"Quiet conversation," Ward repeated, the words landing heavy.

"Like friends catching up," Miller said, her gaze shifting to the body. "That's what the jogger said. 'Polite. But kinda weird.' Those were the words he used." She looked back at Ward. "Which one of you is Foster?"

"Foster is stuck in Palmer," Foley said. "I'm Bud Foley. This is Jake Ward."

"Right. Well, thanks for coming. Inter-agency cooperation and all that," she said, her tone dry. "Don't mess up my scene."

She pointed toward the ground near the victim's left hand. "We found a note in the victim's hand."

She motioned to the tech, who hurried over with the camera.

"Show 'em the note," Miller ordered.

The tech thumbed through the digital display until she found the image. A piece of paper, tucked beneath the victim's fingers. No quotation marks this time. No citations. Just a single sentence, written carefully in neat block letters:

Be not afraid, for the blood has made you clean.

Ward stared at the small screen.

"That phrase is from the book of Hebrews," Foley said.

Miller raised an eyebrow at Foley. "You got a concordance in your back pocket, Investigator?"

"I've been brushing up. For obvious reasons."

"Handy," Miller said. "Similar to what Foster found at his scene, no?"

Ward nodded. "Yup."

Foley's extracurriculars were useful, but something else bothered Ward. It wasn't the citation. It was the confidence. The way the words stood alone, unframed, and unapologetic. The killer didn't even bother to write a scripture this time. The earlier notes seemed to borrow authority from the Bible. This one claimed its own.

"His language is changing," Ward said. "Stripped down. Simple."

"And more arrogant," Miller added, her eyes narrowing at the screen. "He's not quoting now. It's like he's preaching."

Ward raised his eyebrows at her. She'd clearly been briefed on the Talkeetna murder.

She shrugged. "Foster and I have been chatting a bit."

Ward nodded, scanning the perimeter again. His mind was already fitting this new piece into the larger shape he'd been sketching the night before. Different victim profile. Same ritual mechanics. Same absolute calm. *He's refining.*

He turned back to Miller. "You have a victim ID yet?"

"Preliminary," Miller said, flipping a page in her notebook. "Eric Nolan. Local contractor. Driver's license says he lives in South Anchorage, but an officer contacted him a couple nights ago near here, and Nolan admitted he'd been sleeping in his truck on and off for a week. We've got patrol out looking for the vehicle now."

She looked up from her pad. "He's been spiraling. Divorced recently. He caught a child neglect charge last winter—left his toddler in a freezing car outside a bar for three hours. Kid ended up with frostbite. Office of Children's Services got involved, his wife kicked him out, and he's been going downhill ever since."

"Any substance abuse?" Ward asked.

"Just alcohol. A couple DUIs. License was suspended last year, but he got it back," Miller said.

Foley leaned in, examining the dead man's face and hands up close. "He looks clean. No dirt on his face or hands. Fingernails are even trimmed. He probably showered recently at a gym or a shelter."

Ward winced inwardly. This wasn't a man living completely on the margins like Randall Tibeluk. Not someone society had quietly agreed not to see. Eric Nolan was a recently functional man who had endured a setback, but wasn't quite street-level yet.

Which meant whatever happened before the blade came out had been powerful enough to shatter whatever was holding him together.

Ward walked a slow circle around the scene, keeping to the flattened grass. His eyes moved methodically, noting what wasn't there as much as what was. No LED lantern. No scattered blood drops like the first scene. The ritual was becoming leaner, more efficient.

"State Medical Examiner is en route," Miller said. "We'll do a full autopsy and a tox screen, but there are no track marks on his arms. If he was high, he hid it well. Maybe just drunk."

Ward nodded. It fit the pattern. But if Eric Nolan was like Tibeluk, he hadn't been drugged into submission. He'd been talked into it.

And that shouldn't be possible.

Back at the Anchorage Trooper headquarters, the morning chaos had kicked into high gear. The large ABI classroom had been commandeered as a task force center, with investigators from both the State Troopers and APD working in tandem. It made sense.

Before the press got wind of a serial killer operating across jurisdictions, the brass wanted to show they were running a full-court press.

Phones rang. Whiteboards filled with timelines and victimology. Command staff wandered the aisles, their voices low but urgent.

Ward bypassed the war room and retreated to the Technical Crimes Unit, taking a seat at his quiet desk. He began updating his working file, fingers moving rapidly across the keyboard as he drafted his supplementary report from the latest scene. Then, he opened his digital notebook.

> Second victim confirms pattern. Victim cooperation now unmistakable. Ritual streamlining. Language evolving toward authorship.

He paused, staring at the blinking cursor, then added a line he'd been resisting all morning:

> Killer offers something victims desire.

He didn't like the phrasing. It felt slippery. But he couldn't think of a cleaner way to articulate it. Was it fearlessness? Or maybe just total relief? Whatever it was, it carried enough power to overwhelm men who hadn't yet shown any suicidal ideation.

Ward leaned back and stared at the ceiling tiles, tracing the water stains that mapped years of unnoticed leaks in the old building. It would be easy—tempting, even—to label this the work of a charismatic religious extremist and apply the usual psychological tools.

Maybe this suspect could smell when someone was nearing their breaking point and knew how to give them that final, fatal push.

But to get them to lie down on a plastic tarp in the freezing dark? To ensure they didn't fight, didn't even *flinch* while a blade sliced their throat? That required a level of calm that defied reason.

His phone buzzed on the desk. A text from Foster:

> Press got wind. APD wants a joint statement.
> Need to control the narrative. Ideas before I call
> the PIO back?

Ward grimaced. *Narrative.* There it was again. The desperate urge to frame, to simplify, to declare understanding before it had actually arrived. The Public Information Office would work over-time to give the public a sense of safety, even if true safety was an illusion.

It brought Ward back to something his Field Training Officer had told him, many years ago: *"If you can't make 'em safe, Recruit, at least make 'em feel safe."*

He typed back:

> Dunno. We don't have the whole picture yet.

The reply came quickly:

> That doesn't stop the reporters from asking.
> We're a joint task force now. Send me
> something.

Ward set the phone down without answering. He wasn't in the practice of inventing fiction to smooth over ruffled feathers. He'd let the bosses spin the media while he stuck to the evidence.

But the press coverage would inevitably breed a new problem. He opened a new document and typed a bold heading: BRAIN-STORMING.

Then, beneath it:

Possibility of imitation. Copycat(s). Escalation potential high.

He saved the file and closed it, violently resisting the urge to keep speculating. Notes were good. Guessing was dangerous. He had learned the hard way that forcing conclusions was just another form of vanity. The meaning would reveal itself when it was ready. But writing things down helped him think.

For now, his job was to watch. To listen. To help. Foster was working the Talkeetna case, and Foley and Miller were running Ship Creek. Ward didn't have case responsibility, but he'd stay as close as he could to provide tech support and monitor things. Ballack and the command staff would bench him the moment he overreached, just like they always did.

He stood up, grabbed his jacket, and headed toward the briefing where voices would already be rising in debate. As he walked down the hall, a single, unwelcome certainty settled heavy in his chest.

This was going to get worse before it got better.

NINETEEN

Ward preferred the building after midnight.

Not because he romanticized the quiet—he didn't—but because silence stripped things down to their essentials. During the day, trooper posts were full of voices competing to be heard: detectives arguing theories, supervisors pushing timelines, administrators measuring progress in neatly boxed metrics. At night, all that noise fell away.

What remained were facts.

Ward sat alone in the Technical Crimes bullpen, his jacket draped over the back of his chair, sleeves rolled up to the elbows. A half-empty mug of coffee sat forgotten near his keyboard. Two monitors glowed in front of him, bathing the desk in pale light.

On the left: data.

Names, dates, locations. Causes of death. Scene characteristics written out in prose. It was a familiar layout—one he'd stared at more times than he cared to count—but something about this case resisted comprehension. The facts lined up, but refused to settle.

On the right: images.

Photographs telling the stories where words failed. Ward didn't linger on the bodies themselves. That part of the job, grim as it was, no longer demanded his primary attention. What he studied instead were the edges of the scenes. The hidden spaces.

Randall Tibeluk. Talkeetna. Back of a box van. Eric Nolan. Downtown Anchorage near the coastal trail.

Same wound. Same positioning. Same absence of struggle.

Ward tapped a pen against the desk, slow and deliberate, letting the rhythm anchor his thoughts. He toggled between photographs, zooming in on the handwritten notes recovered at each scene. The ink strokes were careful. Measured. No hesitation marks. No pressure tremors. But he had written over each character multiple times, as if once wasn't enough. He'd wanted emphasis, and had taken his time to ensure it.

The first note quoted scripture—incorrectly. The second note was a manifesto of sorts. The third was a scripture quote, but uncited.

He opened a blank document and typed a single word at the top in bold:

MINISTRANT

He stared at it for a heartbeat before adding notes beneath.

Not common usage. Liturgical. Suggests service within an established system.

Ministrant. You didn't choose a word like that unless you wanted it to mean something. It suggested someone active in a ministry, serving an important role. A role of service, but also of substance, which fed a narcissist's ego.

But this didn't feel like narcissism. It felt like devotion.

Ward pulled up the security footage from the Talkeetna gas

station. Grainy. Low resolution. Analog converted to digital. He scrubbed forward frame by frame, watching the hooded suspect sit beside Randall Tibeluk on a concrete tire stop. No urgency. No dominance. Just presence.

The suspect stood, beckoned with a hand, and Randall followed.

They paused, side by side, illuminated by the harsh glare of the halogen canopy lights.

Ward froze the frame.

He clicked over to his browser window, pulling up Tibeluk's full APSIN entry.

Height: 5'9".

He looked back at the video. The suspect was taller.

Ward grabbed a clear plastic ruler from his desk drawer and leaned in, holding it flat against the screen to measure the difference between the tops of their heads. Then he measured the total height of the suspect's figure for a baseline comparison.

He opened the calculator app and crunched the numbers, adjusting for the lens distortion at the edge of the frame.

Two inches taller. Maybe a shade more, depending on the angle and the footwear.

Ward did the mental math. The suspect was about 5'11". Give or take an inch. Quick and dirty guess. Far from precise, but a great starting place.

He opened his notepad and typed it in bold. It wasn't great, but it helped narrow the pool.

He moved forward in the video, stopping when Tibeluk walked out of the lights and toward the waiting van.

No resistance. No hesitation.

Ward stared at the frozen frame.

"Preparation," he said to the empty room.

The word fit.

He turned back to his notes and typed:

Victims appear psychologically prepared. No overt coercion. Fear response completely absent. Not consistent with chemical sedation.

Ward rubbed his burning eyes and leaned back, the chair creaking beneath him.

He thought about the sheer power of fear and the massive effect it had on the human condition. It was the great, unseen driver. Too much of it, and a person was crippled by anxiety disorders. It was so potent that every political speech and television commercial was soaked in it, weaponized to manipulate the masses into buying a product or casting a vote. People spent their whole lives being controlled by it.

But fear was also an alarm bell. It was the primal armor that kept people alive. If someone could truly take all the fear away, they weren't offering a gift. They were stripping away a person's only defense. Without fear, a human being was entirely vulnerable, unable to protect themselves against the wolf at the door.

He'd experienced suppression of fear once before—not in a criminal context, but in a sterile lab near Knik River Road.

The memory rose unbidden: the moment when terror should have been overwhelming, and instead... there was only stillness.

Beyond the thick leather straps binding his wrists and ankles to Pagan's table, something else had held him down.

Resignation.

Not during the first session, no. He'd fought like a cornered animal that time. But the second session? Did he fight?

There had been curiosity. Just a little. A dark, quiet wonder at what lied beyond the pain. And a feeling that maybe his race was done, and that the absolute peace we all yearn for would finally be his.

Maybe Tibeluk and Nolan experienced that same resignation. That yearning to be beyond the pain.

Ward forced the memory back into its box, returning his attention to the screen, lining the notes up side by side. Here was the danger no one on the command staff wanted to talk about. Not because it was implausible, but because it was terrifyingly inconvenient. Once they figured out how he pacified them, a killer could be hunted. But a belief system? A theology? That wouldn't be so easy.

He stood and walked to the window, resting his hands on the cold sill as he looked out at Anchorage. The houses on the hillside stood quiet beneath a low ceiling of clouds, their lights diffused into soft halos by the mist. Somewhere in the distance, he heard a city plow scraping half-heartedly at the icy pavement.

It was a dangerous temptation, watching a narrative take shape and wanting to cast himself in the lead. A quiet trap. It invited him to declare a personal crusade against the dark, to charge headlong into the fire just to prove his worth—that he had survived Pagan's table for a grand, cosmic purpose. The lone investigator against the fanatic. Reason holding the line against madness.

The temptation to assign personal meaning to tragedy was a powerful one. To decide that enduring something extraordinary meant *he* was extraordinary.

But it was all vanity. Selfish ambition.

The truth had been humbling and, strangely, comforting: He wasn't special. Nobody was.

He was just one moving part among countless others, no more important than anyone else. And that meant his role wasn't to impose his grand theories on the case, but to pay attention. To measure heights on a grainy screen. To document the data. To learn. And to serve.

That's how he would matter.

He returned to his desk and shut down the monitors. The day was over, and his eyes were burning. Whatever this was, it was far from finished. And it wouldn't end cleanly.

But he knew his place in it.

And for now, that was enough.

TWENTY

Their safe place was a basement apartment in a run-down section of Spenard, a neighborhood that wore its exhaustion like a second skin. One of Lena's old high-school friends had loaned the place to them for a few days—after some "encouragement" from Adam, of course.

The walls of the apartment were thin, barely keeping out the cold, and the rooms smelled of stale cigarette smoke and the poor hygiene of a dozen prior tenants. But it was better than the streets.

Adam rested on the sleeper sofa, buried beneath three layers of wool blankets.

Thomas sat in the corner, a silent sentinel in a plastic folding chair, watching the shallow rise and fall of the Ministrant's chest. For twenty-four hours, Adam had rested. He looked drained, his pale skin almost translucent in the dim light of the single floor lamp.

Lena knelt beside the sofa, wringing out a washcloth over a plastic bowl. The water turned pink.

"His nose is bleeding again," Thomas said.

Lena didn't look up. She dabbed the cloth against Adam's upper lip, wiping away a trickle of blood that refused to clot. "He should be healing," she said. "It's the burden. I think he takes it all into himself. The fear. It has to go somewhere, doesn't it?"

Thomas shifted, the folding chair creaking beneath his weight. He looked down at his own hands—clean, steady, strong. He remembered what he used to be: a man paralyzed by the memory of his failures, shaking with the tremors of withdrawal and self-loathing. Adam had taken that away. Adam had touched his forehead, and the wracking agony of his guilt had simply vanished.

But at what cost?

He looked back at the sofa. Adam looked broken. Mortal.

"The cleansings. They weigh on him," Thomas said, his voice low and gravelly. "He started this mission all by himself. But he can't keep doing this alone. Look at him, Lena. He's dying."

"No, he is healing," Lena said, though her voice lacked its usual certainty. She smoothed Adam's dark hair back, her hand trembling slightly. "He told us it would be like this. The fire burns the vessel."

"The vessel is cracking," Thomas insisted. He stood up, the small room suddenly feeling too tight for the energy coiling inside him. "He needs help. Real help. Not just us sitting here watching him wither away."

"We are helping. We pray, and we keep watch while he rests."

"We could do more. He's told us about the first two, and how it is to be done. There are so many who need release."

Lena stopped wiping Adam's face. She turned slowly, her expression hardening. "What are you going to do, Thomas? You're not him."

Thomas stood there, letting the silence stretch. No, he wasn't Adam. But if Adam spoke the truth, and God was now working His cleansing over this city, then why couldn't God work through Thomas, as well?

He walked toward the kitchenette, where Adam's coat hung over a chair. He stared at it, knowing exactly what was in the inside pocket: the journal, the folding blade, the notes written in that careful, block script.

Be not afraid.

The words echoed in Thomas's mind, not as a memory, but as a command. One he insisted on obeying.

He turned back to Lena. "I know the liturgy. I've listened to him. I know where he keeps the knife. I've felt the peace he brings. I can do it."

"Thomas. No."

"Why not?"

"Because you aren't him."

"I am his disciple," Thomas said, his voice rising with a strange, frantic conviction. "He cleansed me. He made me holy. Why would he do that if he didn't intend for me to carry the load? Moses had Aaron. The work is too big for one man."

"It's not about the words, Thomas," Lena said, glancing anxiously at Adam's sleeping form. "It's *him*. It's what he is. You can't do what he does."

"How do you know? Have you tried?"

Lena stared at him, her eyes wide with a mixture of fear and pity. "Sit down, Thomas. You're talking crazy. Just wait for him to wake up."

Thomas looked at her, then back at Adam. The exhaustion was eating the Ministrant alive. Thomas loved Adam with the fierce, desperate loyalty a drowning man holds for the one who pulls him onto the raft. He couldn't watch his savior drown in return.

"I'm going for a walk," Thomas lied.

He didn't wait for permission. As Lena turned back to murmur something soothing to Adam, Thomas reached toward the counter, ripping a blank sheet of paper from the notebook and swiping a black pen from the table. From the inside pocket of Adam's coat, he grabbed the folding hunting knife.

"Thomas, don't!" he heard from behind him.

He moved toward the sink, snatched a bundle of plastic sheeting from the cabinet beneath, grabbed his parka from the hook by the door and slipped into the biting cold of the morning.

The air outside was thick with ice fog, a rare thing in this part of town. The streetlights bloomed into hazy orange spheres that illuminated nothing but swirling show. Thomas walked with purpose, the snow crunching loudly under his boots.

He didn't feel the cold. He felt heat—a burning in his chest he recognized as righteousness.

For years, he had existed as a pathetic spectator to his own life, a victim of circumstance and weakness. But Adam had changed the physics of his world. Adam showed him that pain wasn't a punishment—it was preparation. And death wasn't an end, but a release.

I can help him, Thomas thought, his pace quickening. *I can bring him a harvest. When I come back, and he sees that the work continued while he rested, he will know that I am a true disciple. He's not alone.*

He headed toward downtown. He knew where the lost ones gathered. He knew where the pain was thickest.

He found his target twenty minutes later, huddled in the deep alcove of a shuttered souvenir shop. The man was half-wrapped in a filthy sleeping bag, clutching a half-empty bottle of cheap vodka like a holy relic. He rocked back and forth, a string of curses and mumbled pleas vaporizing in the freezing air.

He squinted, trying to discern the darkness Adam spoke of. But he saw no aura, only the grime on the man's skin, the yellowing of his eyes, and the tremble in his hands.

Rot, Thomas told himself. *It is the rot of fear and regret. Sins unwashed.*

The man's misery radiated off him like heat from a furnace. That was enough. Faith was believing in what you could not see.

He stepped into the alcove, stopping a few feet away from him.

The man looked up, his eyes bleary and red-rimmed. He flinched, pulling the sleeping bag tighter around his shoulders. "I ain't got no cash, man. Leave me be."

Thomas smiled. He tried to mimic Adam's expression—beatific, calm, all-knowing.

"I don't want your money, brother," Thomas said.

The man squinted, suspicious. "Then what? You a cop?"

"No. I'm a friend." Thomas crouched, ignoring the sharp odors of urine and alcohol. "You're hurting. I can see the weight you're carrying."

The man produced a wet, hacking cough. "Hell yeah, I'm hurting. It's below zero. You got a smoke?"

"I have something better," Thomas said. "I have peace."

The man let out a sharp, bitter laugh. "Peace? Unless you got a warm bed or whiskey, you can keep your peace."

"The bottle only stops the noise for a moment," Thomas said, reciting the liturgy Adam had used on him. "I offer a silence that lasts forever. A cleansing of the soul."

He reached into his pocket, his fingers brushing the cold steel of the folding knife. He held it there, letting the power of the impending ritual anchor him.

The man's eyes flicked between Thomas and the empty sidewalk, suspicion sharpening into raw hostility. "Serious, man, what do you want?"

"Be not afraid," Thomas said. He reached out to place his hand on the man's forehead.

This is the moment, Thomas thought. *I touch him, and the fear goes away. The connection is made.*

He pressed his palm against the man's grime-streaked skin.

"You are chosen," Thomas declared, waiting for the current to flow. For the surrender.

But the man didn't surrender. He slapped Thomas's hand away with surprising, violent strength.

"Get your hands off me, you freak!" the man shouted, scrambling backward and tangling a foot in the sleeping bag.

Thomas blinked, the spell breaking instantly. "No, you don't understand. I'm here to help. I'm here to minister to you."

"Get away!" The man kicked out blindly. His boot connected hard with Thomas's shin.

Pain shot up Thomas's leg. He stumbled back. It shouldn't happen like this. The others hadn't fought. They had welcomed it.

He's just confused, Thomas reasoned, panic fluttering in his chest like a trapped bird. *The rot is too deep. I have to push through it.*

"Stop fighting," Thomas hissed, his voice losing its practiced calm. He ripped the knife from his pocket, flicking the blade open with a loud *clack*. "It's for your own good! The blood is the cleansing!"

The man saw the blade and screamed—a raw, terrifying sound that bounced off the brick facade of the storefront. He slipped on the icy pavement, his eyes wide with animal terror. "Help! Help me!"

Panic flared in Thomas—not for his own safety, but for the ritual. The man was ruining it. He was making it ugly.

He doesn't know, Thomas thought frantically. *He doesn't know he needs it.*

Thomas lunged.

He didn't move with Adam's fluid grace, but with clumsy, violent desperation—grabbing the man's coat, hauling him back. The man swung the empty vodka bottle, smashing it against the side of Thomas's head.

Glass shattered, and the alcohol burned Thomas's eyes. Warm blood trickled down the side of his face.

Thomas roared, tackling the man onto the hard porch. They rolled together on the concrete, a desperate tangle of limbs and heavy coats. The man bit, scratched, and clawed, fighting for his life.

"Be not afraid!" Thomas screamed, pinning the man's arm with his knee. "Accept it! Accept the peace!"

He drove the knife down.

It wasn't a surgical, precise cut across the throat. It was a messy, frantic slash at the side of the neck.

The blade caught on a tough band of muscle before sinking deep, shearing through vessels and sinew. The man's frantic thrashing stopped cold, his body collapsing into a heavy, wet slump. Thomas scrambled backward on the slick concrete, his chest heaving as his wild gaze swept the frozen street. Empty. No witnesses.

He grasped the man's limp arms and pulled him straight, arranging him on the icy concrete, setting his hands at his sides. The man's breathing was wet and shallow, his eyes blinking rapidly in shock as he gazed up at the barren branches of a tree nearby.

The blood pumped out in erratic spurts, staining the concrete beneath.

The sacrifice went still. The cleansing was complete.

Thomas stood up, wiping his face with the back of his sleeve.

But as he looked down at the red slush spreading near his boots, something felt horribly wrong. He'd botched it. He saw no peace here, not like he'd planned. There was only the hot chaos of a dirty struggle, the smell of cheap liquor, and the throbbing pain in his head and shin.

It felt less like a sacrament and more like a mugging.

He reached into his pocket to retrieve the note he had written, intending to leave it by the body. As he did so, his hand brushed the bundle of plastic sheeting he should have spread on the ground.

He bit his lip in frustration. In the chaos of the moment, he'd forgotten all about it. It was a ruined ritual, tainted by his own incompetence.

I need to pay better attention, Thomas told himself, stepping over the body. *I'll do better next time.*

He pulled the note from his pocket, preparing to drop it, when he heard a sharp gasp.

He snapped his head up. Two women were standing on the street, nearby. One was holding a cell phone to her ear; the other was pointing a trembling finger straight at him.

Thomas dropped the note and ran.

TWENTY-ONE

THE AIR IN THOMAS'S LUNGS BURNED LIKE INHALED glass, the subzero temperature turning every gasp into a struggle as he fled the scene. He scrambled over a chain-link fence, the metal biting into his palms through his gloves, and dropped into an alleyway slick with ice and garbage.

He slipped, his hip slamming hard against a dumpster, but he didn't stop. He couldn't.

Behind him, the wail of sirens cut through the heavy ice fog, growing louder, multiplying. They were close. Too close.

I failed him, Thomas thought, the shame hotter than the cold. *I made it ugly.*

He had meant to bring a harvest. He had meant to be a good ministrant, a hand of the divine just like Adam. Instead, he was a mugger running from a messy kill, leaving a trail for the world to follow.

He turned the corner onto 5th Avenue and skidded to a halt.

Blue and red lights strobed against the brick facades of the buildings, fracturing in the swirling mist. A cruiser skidded sideways across the intersection two blocks down, blocking the road. Another screeched to a halt behind him.

He was boxed in.

Panic flared, raw and animalistic, threatening to buckle his knees. But then, a sudden, clarifying thought pierced the chaos.

The vessel is cracking.

Adam couldn't be found. If Thomas led them back to the basement in Spenard, to Lena and the Ministrant, the work would end. The cleansing would stop.

He looked at his hands. They were trembling, but not from the cold.

I can still serve, he realized. *I can be the distraction. I'll tell them it's me.*

If they caught him, they would stop looking for anyone else. They would think the monster was caged. Adam would be safe. He could rest. He could heal, like Lena said.

Thomas straightened his spine. He reached into his pocket for the knife. Empty—he must have dropped it.

It didn't matter. The message was his weapon.

"Be not afraid!" he screamed into the blinding lights of the approaching cruisers. "There is no forgiveness without the shedding of blood!"

It was another cold morning, and Ward was sipping a fresh latte and walking across the icy pavement of the ABI parking lot. Some sliding tires announced APD Detective Miller as she pulled up in her unmarked Taurus and skidded to a halt.

"We've got him cornered at 5th and C Street. Get in."

Ward threw his coffee into a snowbank and hopped in as Miller slammed the accelerator, the tires fighting for purchase on the icy asphalt. He grabbed the handle above the passenger door as the back end fishtailed before straightening out. It was a special treat for a Trooper Investigator to get this close to the developing action in a case. Usually they were miles away when it all went down. City detectives certainly worked in a different world.

"Patrol is already on scene, perimeter established. Two scenes—a body near 4th Avenue, throat cut. Two witnesses."

Wow.

"Second scene is the subject himself, surrounded by patrol on 5th Avenue. They were roping off a couple streets for a community event and he ran right into them, covered in blood. Subject is being erratic, screaming about forgiveness and all that jazz."

Ward stared out the frosty windshield. "Erratic? That doesn't fit."

Miller kept her eyes locked on the road. "Desperate men get crazy when the walls close in, Ward. Doesn't matter how cool they are when they're in control. When the cage rattles, they shake. And we caught him red-handed, running from his latest kill."

A few minutes later, they passed the park strip, several patrol officers visible in the far distance. Another five blocks and around a corner, they screeched to a halt behind a wall of patrol cars. The air echoed with the aggressive barking of a K9 unit and the commands of officers.

Ward was out of the car before it fully stopped moving. He forced himself past bystanders, Miller right on his heels.

Chaos dominated the scene.

In the center of the intersection, illuminated by a dozen spotlights, a man stood alone. He was lanky, his face a mask of manic terror and ecstasy. Blood stained the side of his head and his hands. He wasn't hiding. He wasn't running.

He was preaching.

"The blood is the cleansing!" the man screamed, his voice cracking. He spun in a circle, arms wide, gesturing to the officers with empty hands. "I bring you peace! I bring you the silence that lasts forever!"

Ward narrowed his eyes.

He watched the man's movements. Jerky. Uncoordinated. Frantic.

This can't be him, Ward thought. *Can it?*

He had watched the video from Talkeetna a hundred times.

Despite the fact that the suspect's face was unclear, he had moved with a fluid, terrifying grace. That suspect sat calmly beside his victim. He walked like he was strolling through a park.

This man was about the right height, but he moved like a meth-head looking for a fight.

"Get on the ground!" a patrol sergeant bellowed over a PA system. "Drop to your knees!"

"You don't understand!" Tears streamed down the suspect's face. "I did this for you! I am a Divine Ministrant! I am the hand!"

He took a step toward the nearest officer, reaching into his jacket.

"He's reaching!" Miller shouted, her hand flying to her holster.

But the man didn't pull a gun. He pulled an empty hand out, pointing a finger to the sky.

"Be not afraid!"

Taser probes hit him in the back a second later.

The man's body went rigid, unbalanced by the seizing of his muscles. He uttered a guttural cry of pain and collapsed onto the ice, twitching uncontrollably.

A K9 barked furiously, straining against its lead. Officers swarmed the downed man, knees pressing into his neck, cuffs ratcheting tight.

Ward walked forward slowly, ignoring the adrenaline-fueled shouts of the officers securing the scene. He stopped ten feet away as they hauled the suspect to his feet.

The man sobbed now. Snot ran from his nose, mixing with the grime and blood on his face. He looked at Ward, his eyes wide and dilated.

"Did I do good?" the man said, his voice trembling.

Miller holstered her weapon and walked up beside Ward, a grim smile of satisfaction on her face.

"Got him," she said. "Same rhetoric. Same MO. Confessed right here on the street."

Ward looked at the suspect.

"Yeah," Ward said, the cold settling deep in his bones. "But look at him."

"I'm looking at a killer, Ward."

"You're looking at a mess." Ward shook his head. "The guy in Talkeetna? The guy at Ship Creek? A surgeon. This guy? This guy is just a nut."

TWENTY-TWO

THE INTERROGATION ROOM AT THE ALASKA BUREAU OF
Investigation—conveniently located just down the hall from the
task force's war room—was a ten-by-ten box lined with sterile gray
acoustic foam. It smelled of musty, short-pile carpet and anxiety.

Safely down the hall in the viewing room, Ward stood with his
arms crossed, his eyes locked on the live monitor. Beside him, Bud
Foley methodically chewed on a piece of fried chicken, while Foster
sat quietly in the corner.

On the screen, Detective Vanessa Miller sat at the scarred metal
table, her posture rigid, a file open before her. Across the desk,
Thomas Dillon was cuffed to a padded folding chair, a bandage on
the side of his head where medics had attended to him. He couldn't
sit still, constantly shifting his weight and frantically scratching the
back of his left hand. The manic energy that had fueled his street
sermon had completely curdled into a twitchy, vibrating desperation. He looked less like a hardened serial killer and more like a live
wire stripped of its insulation.

"Let's go back to the scene in Talkeetna," Miller said, her voice
level, devoid of judgment.

Good. No details, Ward thought. But she gave him space to offer
them, if any were to be had.

"Tell me how you got there."

Thomas licked his lips. His eyes darted around the room, fixating on the camera in the corner, then back to Miller.

"I drove," Thomas said quickly. "I drove the van."

"What type of van?"

"Box van. White, if I remember right."

"And the victim? What about him?"

"He needed release," Thomas said. He sat up straighter, trying to summon a dignity that his grime-streaked face couldn't support. "He was heavy with sin. I saw it on him. The rot."

Ward narrowed his eyes. *The rot.* It was the specific language from the notes.

"Did he fight you?" Miller asked.

"No," Thomas insisted. "No one fights the peace. They welcome it. I told him... I told him not to be afraid."

"And then?"

"And then I cleansed him," Thomas said, his voice dropping to a harsh whisper. "I used the blade. I let the blood flow. It has to flow to wash them clean. There is no forgiveness without it."

"Did you leave anything at the scene?"

"I left a message. That's all you need to know."

"No, I need a good deal more than that."

"I am the Ministrant. Without the shedding of blood, there can be no forgiveness. That's what you need to know."

Miller glanced at the video camera, her eyes locking briefly. It was a look of triumph.

Inside the room, she slid a photo of Eric Nolan across the table.

"And this man? At Ship Creek?"

Thomas stared at the photo. He blinked rapidly, a bead of sweat tracking through the dirt on his temple.

"Him too," Thomas said. "He was... he was spiraling. He forgot his children, I think. He needed to be purified."

"How did you get him to the woods, Thomas?"

"I led him," Thomas said. "I walked with him."

"Did you drug him?"

Thomas hesitated. His eyes flickered. "The peace... it's a drug, in a way. The words are the drug. The connection."

Miller leaned back. "You killed Randall Tibeluk. You killed Eric Nolan. And you killed the man in the alley, today."

"I am a Ministrant," Thomas declared, his voice rising, cracking with a frantic, theatrical fervor. "I am a hand that cuts the thread! I did it all! I bear the burden so others don't have to!"

"So again, I'm asking. When you say you did it all, you killed Tibeluk, yes?"

"Yes."

"And Eric Nolan."

"Yes."

"And the man today."

She didn't have a name because they hadn't identified him yet.

"Yes, him too." His relentless scratching appeared to be drawing blood on the top of his left hand.

Miller closed the file. She stood up and left the room, signaling to the Court Services Officer in uniform outside to watch the prisoner.

She walked down the hallway, then into the observation room, closing the heavy door behind her.

"Slam dunk," Miller said, exhaling a long breath. She looked tired. "He knows the details, Ward. He knows the locations, the method, the rhetoric. We have the weapon, and we have a blood-stained note he dropped. *Be not afraid.*"

Ward didn't move. He kept his eyes on the screen, watching the enigma scratch his bloody hand. He was rocking back and forth now, muttering to himself, his lips moving in a rapid, silent prayer.

"He's reciting," Ward said.

Miller frowned. "What?"

"He's reciting lines," Ward said, turning to face her. "He's not telling you a story, Miller. He's parroting. *The rot. Ministrant. The peace.* It sounds like he memorized it."

"Serial killers have manifestos. They have rituals. This is his."

"No," Ward said, shaking his head. "Look at him. Look at his hands."

Miller looked at the video feed. Thomas's hands were shaking violently, rattling the chain of the handcuffs against the table. "He's nervous. And probably going through withdrawal," she said. "He's a junkie. We knew that."

"The guy in the video at the gas station wasn't shaking," Ward said, his voice hard. "The killer at Talkeetna and Ship Creek cut those throats with surgical precision. No hesitation marks. No jagged edges." He pointed at the trembling wreck in the chair. "You think *that* guy could hold a blade steady enough to sever an artery without making a mess? Look at the butcher job he did today."

"Adrenaline dumps are real," Miller countered, crossing her arms. "He botched the one today because he got spooked. Maybe he was sloppy because we were closing in. It happens."

"Closing in? We weren't closing nothin'. We had no idea who he was and today we just got lucky. Compare today's scene with the last two. Do they even look remotely similar? They found the plastic sheeting at today's scene, but he didn't use it. Why? Today was a brawl, nothing like the other scenes."

"I know, but..."

"And the victims?" Ward said. "Tibeluk and Nolan didn't fight. They lay down. They were calm. You seriously think this guy, vibrating like a tuning fork, talked two grown men into letting him slit their throats? You think he exudes peace?"

Miller's expression hardened. She stepped closer, invading Ward's space.

"He knows about the box van."

"White box van. How many times did the news plaster that scene on TV? It's not exactly privileged info."

"Okay, what about 'the rot' and screaming about the blood?"

Jake didn't have an answer for that yet.

"So what's your theory then, smart guy?"

Ward looked at Foley and Foster. No help at all.

"Maybe this guy hung out with our real killer? Um..." Ward

said, stumbling over his words. "I mean the first killer. There's little doubt that he did the deed today."

Miller harrumphed. "Hung out? That's your theory."

It was a stretch. "Maybe he witnessed it? An accomplice?"

"Okay, tell me this, Jake. And I'm not actually letting you have any say in this—heck, you play a support role and don't even have case responsibility. But you're here, and you're no dummy, so let's hash this out."

She looked pissed. As she should be, he was basically trying to steal her victory.

"Let's say you're right. Someone out there, the *real* killer, as you would have it. And we somehow get enough to charge him with the first two murders. How hard would it be for even an average defense attorney to use today to create reasonable doubt?"

She did have a point. He looked to Foley, who just shrugged and took another bite of chicken.

"I'm all about catching the right guy, but your phantom defendant would just have to point to this idiot. He knows details about the other scenes and admitted to both of them. He used a knife to slit a throat and screamed the same phrases your 'real' murderer wrote down—details the news never broadcast."

"Yeah, I know, but—"

"He was found a couple of blocks from a fresh crime scene with blood on his clothes that is almost surely today's victim's. What jury is going to have any issue finding reasonable doubt about the guilt of your *real* killer? Forget a jury, what DA would ever charge them when they know they couldn't win?"

She poked a finger at him so close to his face it almost jabbed him in the chin.

"I know you Troopers like to overthink things, you're freaking legendary about it, but sometimes a bad guy is just a bad guy. We caught him. Anchorage can sleep tonight. Do you really want to rob my city of that?"

Ward looked back at the video feed of Thomas. The suspect had laid his head on the metal table, sobbing now. It wasn't the wail of a monster in a cage. It was the weeping of a child who had lost his mommy.

"Well, for the record, I think he's protecting someone," Ward said. "Do what you're gonna do. I'm sure your bosses are gonna love you. Mine too, probably."

The door to the hallway opened, and Sergeant Ballack stuck his head in. His face was flushed with the ruddy hue of administrative victory.

"Good work, Miller," Ballack said, beaming. "Colonel is happy. Your Chief is happy. Heck, the Governor even called. Press conference is being set up."

"He's not the guy, Sergeant," Ward said.

The room went quiet. Ballack's smile evaporated and Miller scowled.

"Excuse me?"

"He's a copycat," Ward said, holding his ground. "The psychology is wrong."

Ballack stepped fully into the room, the heavy door clicking shut behind him. He looked at Ward with the exhaustion of a man who just wanted a win.

"We have a suspect in custody who says, 'I did it.' Do not rain on this parade. You are here to assist, not to undermine this win."

Ward shot back. "If the real guy is still loose—"

"The real guy is in that chair!" Ballack snapped. He pointed a thick finger at the video feed. "That is the face of the Anchorage Slasher, or the Ministrant, or whatever the hell he calls himself. And he is off the street."

Ballack turned to Miller. "Our guys will write up everything they have so far and it will be in the DA's hands before arraignment tomorrow." He turned to Ward. "That includes you, Jake. And shut the hell up."

"Thank you, sir," Miller said. She shot Ward a smirk—and followed Ballack out.

The three remaining just stared at the video screen.

"You're not wrong," Foster said from his chair.

"Thanks for sharing when I needed it, Shannon. Real helpful."

"Well, I just didn't see the point. Miller got her 'Ministrant.' Bosses had some closure. Sometimes you just gotta read the room. You weren't gonna win that fight."

"Yeah," Ward said and looked back at the screen. "For the record, he also said '*a* Ministrant,' not '*the* Ministrant.'"

"You're reaching," Foley said. "But if you're right," he added, still eating his fried chicken. "We'll see soon enough."

They watched Thomas Dillon for a long time. The man had stopped crying. After a while, he lifted his head and looked straight at the video camera, and smiled. It was a broken, jagged thing, absent a few teeth, but his visage held a terrifying clarity. From crying to smiling in just a few minutes. What a disaster of a human being.

Ward turned and walked out of the room and back toward his desk.

It was wrong. He knew it in his bones. A familiar chill moved down his spine and for a brief moment, he felt as helpless as being strapped to a metal table while a madman injected poison into his veins.

TWENTY-THREE

WARD SPENT THE LAST HOUR AT HIS DESK IN THE TCU, trying to swallow the idea that Thomas Dillon was the serial killer; the mastermind of both the Talkeetna and the Ship Creek murders.

It would have been easier to swallow a toothpick.

If they stopped looking, and another innocent human being was killed, Ward wouldn't forgive himself. Not if he could have kept fighting. Ballack and Miller were doing a happy dance, and would not be deterred, but maybe someone else would listen.

He charged down the hall toward the task force headquarters.

The room was suffocating on unearned victory.

Uniformed lieutenants clapped each other on the shoulder. A trooper captain assigned to the Commissioner's Office was on his phone, likely coordinating the press release with the Anchorage Mayor's office. The air smelled of cheap coffee and false bravado.

Jake Ward placed himself near the back wall, watching the celebration with nausea growing in his stomach.

After a short time, Foley appeared next to him, sipping something from a foam cup, looking like he wanted to be anywhere else.

"Dude, what are you thinking?" Foley asked.

Ward said nothing.

Sergeant Ballack was standing near a snack table, nibbling on a cookie, deep in conversation with Lieutenant Kincaid, one of APD's detective brass. Kincaid was a tall, broad-shouldered man with a flattop haircut that hadn't been in style since the Cold War and a demeanor that suggested he viewed questions as insubordination.

Ward moved straight toward them.

"Jake, don't—" Foley said, reaching out a hand, but Ward was already out of range.

Ballack saw him coming. The smile on his face vanished, replaced by the weary tightening of the jaw that appeared whenever Ward went off-script.

"Investigator Ward," Kincaid said, his voice booming. "Hell of a job on the assist. Miller says you've been a big help working this guy."

"He wanted to be caught," Ward said. "We need to talk."

Kincaid's smile didn't drop, but it grew colder. "We're debriefing in about an hour. You can add your notes then."

"Not notes. Problems," Ward said. "Huge ones. You can't book this guy as the sole actor. It doesn't wash."

Ballack stepped in, physically positioning himself between Ward and the APD commander. "Ward, take a breath. We have a confession. We have the murder weapon. The suspect recited the exact nonsense found in the notes. Heck, he dropped a note. It's a closed loop."

"It's a performance," Ward said. "Did you see the footage from Talkeetna? How the suspect moved? Controlled. Calm. He sat with the victim for ten minutes in the freezing cold and talked him into dying."

Ward gestured back toward the interrogation room.

"That idiot? Dillon? He's vibrating so hard he's going to shatter his own teeth. He acts like a junkie in withdrawal. You think he has the patience to sit still for that long? You think he has the steady hand to cut a throat without making a jagged mess? Look at the botched job on the latest victim, for crying out loud."

Kincaid crossed his arms. "Adrenaline changes motor control. He got sloppy tonight because we were breathing down his neck."

"That's the party line? Sloppy?" Ward laughed, a harsh, humorless bark. "He attacked a homeless guy in an alley with a knife, got injured by his own victim, and then ran straight into police screaming Bible verses. That's not 'sloppy.' That's a suicide run. He's either a complete idiot or he was *trying* to be caught."

"Why would he want that?" Ballack asked, his patience thinning.

"I dunno, maybe to stop us from looking for the real one," Ward said. "He's a disciple. A patsy. He's taking the fall so the real 'Ministrant' can escape."

"The 'Ministrant' is the name Dillon called himself," Kincaid pointed out.

"Exactly. He's reciting lines. He memorized the script, but he didn't write the play." Ward looked from Ballack to Kincaid, pleading now. "Look at the psychology. The first two victims were calm. Resigned. They participated in their own deaths. Tonight? That victim fought for his life. He was terrified. The *peace* wasn't there. The *calm* wasn't there. Because Dillon can't do what the real killer does. This isn't the guy."

Kincaid stepped forward, looming over Ward.

"We have a confession," Kincaid said, enunciating each word like he was speaking to a slow child. "We have physical evidence. The District Attorney is happy. The public is terrified, and today, we're going to tell them the monster is in a cage. That restores order. That stops the panic."

"It's a lie," Ward said.

"It's what we have!" Kincaid roared, the veneer of politeness vanishing.

The room went dead quiet.

"And unless you have a photo of someone else holding the knife, Investigator, you are speculating. And we don't submit speculation for prosecution."

Kincaid turned to Ballack. "Control your man, Ballack."

Kincaid turned and made for the exit.

Ward watched him go, his hands balled into fists. He felt a hand on his shoulder. Ballack.

Ward turned, ready to fight, but the look on Ballack's face stopped him. It wasn't anger. It was finality.

"You're done, Jake," Ballack said.

"Boss, you know I'm right."

"Jake, it matters what we can prove. And right now, Thomas Dillon is the only suspect we have. He fits the box."

"The box is wrong."

"Then maybe we'll have to build a better one," Ballack said. "But not you. And not on this case. You're Technical Crimes, remember? You were assigned to help on a few things. You took it further, like you always do, but that's over. The suspect is in custody. The task force is dissolving."

"You're pulling me. Big surprise."

"I'm ordering you to stand down," Ballack said, his voice hardening. "Go back to your desk. Work on your device exams and agency assists. Leave the serial killers to major crimes and APD."

"If I'm right," Ward said, his voice low, "and we stop looking... he's going to improve. And the next time he kills, it's on us."

Ballack sighed, rubbing the bridge of his nose. "Go. Now. That's an order."

A few moments later, Ward stood alone in the hallway outside the TCU. The fluorescent lights hummed, a monotonous droning.

Foley walked up beside him, silent. He didn't say 'I told you so.' He just stood, a solid presence in the chaos of the moment.

"They're going to do a little public happy dance," Ward said. "They're going to tell the world it's over."

"That's the job, Jake," Foley said. "We catch the ones we can. We close the files."

"It's not over."

Ward turned and walked toward the building's back door, pushing through the exit into the cold Anchorage air. It was the end of the work day, and the sun had slipped down over the horizon.

The ice fog was gone but the air still felt thick, swirling around streetlights, hiding everything.

The 'real' bad guy was free. Maybe even watching. An enigma who had shown himself to have such charisma that his follower, or followers, would gladly take the heat for his actions. Ward had investigated many crimes, but he never found an adversary who could inspire such loyalty. Criminals usually turned on each other, like panicked, starving animals fighting over food.

This guy was different.

For someone who could remove all fear, this killer was terrifying.

TWENTY-FOUR

Few sounds polluted the apartment, save for the low murmur of the television in the corner.

Lena sat on the floor, her knees pulled tight to her chest, staring at the screen. The volume was turned down to a whisper, but the images screamed.

Blue and red lights strobing against the ice fog. Yellow tape fluttering in the wind. And then, the banner at the bottom of the screen, bold and red: BREAKING NEWS: 'MINISTRANT' SUSPECT IN CUSTODY.

They showed a grainy clip of Thomas being shoved into the back of a cruiser. His face was pressed against the glass, his eyes closed, his mouth moving in a frantic rhythm Lena recognized. He was praying.

"Oh God," Lena said, rocking back and forth. "Oh God, Thomas, no."

She looked over her shoulder at the sleeper sofa.

Adam hadn't moved in hours. He looked small beneath the heavy wool blankets. Mortal.

The familiar itch of panic crawled under Lena's skin—the violent urge to run, to find a needle, to find a dark corner and disappear. They'd caught Thomas. It was only a matter of time before he broke. Before he told them about the basement in Spenard, about the man who spoke of cleansing, about the woman who scrubbed the blood from his clothes.

They were coming. She knew it.

She stood up, her legs shaking, and moved to the window. She peeled back the edge of the blackout curtain. The street outside was empty, just snow swirling in the amber light of the streetlamp.

But for how long?

"We have to go," she said to the quiet room. She turned back to the sofa. "Adam. Please. We have to leave."

He didn't stir.

She crossed the space between them, her trembling fingers smoothing the dark hair from his brow. His skin was slick and unnaturally cold. *Is he dying?* The possibility paralyzed her. Adam anchored her against the chaos; he was her only source of light. Losing him meant more than loneliness—it meant the cage door opening, leaving her defenseless against the addiction waiting to devour her.

Her fingers brushed the wool blanket.

Adam drew a sudden, ragged breath, like a drowning man breaching the surface. His eyes snapped open.

Lena recoiled, stumbling backward against the coffee table.

He carried no confusion in his gaze. No grogginess. His eyes, usually dark and heavy with the weight of the things he saw, were now clear and bright. Terrifyingly sharp.

He sat up in one fluid motion, the blankets falling away as vitality returned to his face.

"Adam?" Lena said.

He didn't answer immediately. He looked at his hands, turning them over, flexing the long fingers. Then he touched his nose, his fingertips coming away with flakes of dried blood. He wiped them on the sheet.

"The noise," he said, his voice rasping but incredibly strong. "It's gone. I am healed."

"Adam, look at the TV," Lena said, pointing with a shaking hand. "The news says that they caught Thomas. He's... he's in jail."

Adam turned his head slowly. He watched the footage playing on the screen—the replay of Thomas screaming in the intersection, the Anchorage police swarming him.

Lena waited for the anger. She waited for Adam to rage at Thomas's failure, at the sheer clumsiness that had endangered them all.

Instead, he smiled.

It wasn't a smile of amusement. It was the smile of a fever breaking.

"He did it," Adam said. "He actually did it."

"He got caught!" Lena cried, her voice rising in panic. "He's going to tell them everything! We have to run!"

Adam stood up. He seemed taller than he had yesterday. The heavy stoop in his shoulders was entirely gone. He walked to the television and placed his hand flat against the glass, covering Thomas's frantic face.

"He won't tell them anything that matters," Adam said. "Don't you see, Lena? It wasn't a failure. It was an offering. He was bold. He had faith, he moved forward, and he made a sacrifice."

He turned to face her. The room felt charged with the intense, static electricity of his presence.

"For days, the city has been screaming," Adam said, stepping closer. "The fear was everywhere. It hunted me. A weight I couldn't carry anymore. I was drowning in their panic."

He gestured to the television.

"But now... look. The panic has a target. The fear has a name, and that name is Thomas. He took it. He took all of it onto himself."

Adam closed his eyes and took a deep breath, savoring the stale, cigarette-tinged air of the apartment like a crisp mountain wind.

"He became the lightning rod," Adam said. "The police, the press, the people... they are all looking at him. Their eyes are fixed on him alone. And that means..."

"...they are no longer looking at you." Lena stared at him, fully absorbing the implications. "So... we're safe?"

"We are unburdened," Adam said. "The static is gone. I can see clearly again."

He looked around the room, his gaze drifting over the peeling wallpaper, the stained carpet, the dark water rings on the ceiling.

"The rot," he said. "It's quiet. It's not pressing in."

He walked to the kitchenette. He opened the fridge, took out a carton of milk, and drank directly from it, swallowing in long, hungry gulps. He wiped his mouth with the back of his hand.

"Thomas is suffering for us," Adam said. "He is in the belly of the beast. He is scared, Lena. But he is holding the line."

"So we leave him?" Lena asked, a desperate hope flickering in her chest. "We get out of Anchorage while they're distracted?"

Adam paused. He set the milk down on the counter with a heavy thud.

"Leave him?"

He looked at her with genuine confusion, as if she had just suggested they stop breathing.

"He is my disciple," Adam said. "He is the first fruit of the harvest. He took the fall so I could rest. You don't abandon a gift like that."

He walked over to the chair where his coat hung. He shrugged it on, the movement sharp and kinetic. He checked the inside pocket. His knife was gone.

"We aren't running, Lena," Adam said. "Running is for the guilty. We are the righteous."

"Then what are we doing?"

Adam walked to the door. He paused, his hand resting on the brass knob, and looked back at her.

"Come. We need to learn about the enemy. Thomas is in the lion's den," Adam said, his voice dropping to a resonating register that made the fine hair on Lena's arms stand up. "And the lions think they have won."

TWENTY-FIVE

The fluorescent lights of the diner hummed, a
low, relentless frequency that felt like it was drilling directly into the
base of Ward's skull. It was late—or early, depending on the shift—
and the place reeked of old bacon grease and wet mops.

But the real discomfort was the dense, radiating heat in his chest
—a deep, maddening itch in the marrow of his fractured ribs. He
had spent a couple of hours meditating in his apartment, using the
focus he'd learned on Pagan's table to trigger the process. Now, his
body was knitting bone at a terrifying speed, and that kind of rapid
healing required fuel. His metabolism was redlining, burning
through calories like a wildfire.

Spread across his booth were the decimated remains of a
chicken-fried steak, four eggs, a double order of hash browns, and a
stack of pancakes. He had eaten with a grim, mechanical efficiency
until the frantic trembling in his hands subsided. Now, with the
furnace fed, Ward sat nursing a black coffee that had gone cold
twenty minutes ago. He watched the door.

He had been benched for six hours. Six hours of sitting in his
apartment, staring at the walls, watching the local news cycle churn
out a victory lap for APD. They had the suspect. Alaska was safe.
The nightmare was over.

It was all a lie, but it was a comfortable one. And comfortable lies were the hardest to kill.

The bell above the door jingled.

Bud Foley walked in. He didn't look like the jovial investigator Ward knew. No dress shirt, no tie. He wore a dark beanie pulled low and a jacket Ward didn't recognize—civilian clothes, entirely nondescript. He scanned the room, his eyes lingering on a couple of rough-looking guys at a booth before locking onto Ward.

Foley slid into the booth opposite him. He didn't take off his coat. He glanced at the wreckage of empty plates covering Ward's side of the table, his eyebrows rising slightly, before meeting Ward's eyes.

"You look like hell, Jake," Foley said. "And apparently, you eat like a grizzly bear coming out of hibernation."

Ward pushed the plates aside. "You ordering?"

"Not hungry." Foley kept his hands buried in his pockets. He glanced out the dirty window, then back at Ward. "Ballack asked about you. Wants to know if you're going to be a problem."

"I'm always a problem, Bud. That's why they keep me in a dark lab with the computers."

Foley managed a tight smile. "They finalized the charges on that Dillon character. Coordinated it with the Palmer DA. Three counts of first-degree murder, evidence tampering, assault... the list is a mile long. The DA is talking multiple life sentences."

"He'll take a plea deal," Ward said, leaning over his cold coffee. "He *wants* to take it. That's the whole point. He's the fall guy."

"Maybe. But he definitely committed at least one of those murders."

Ward exhaled, the truth of it souring his stomach. "He did."

The admission hung in the air between them, heavier than the odor of frying grease.

"You agree with me, though," Ward pressed.

Foley sighed—a long, ragged exhale that seemed to deflate him entirely. He leaned in, lowering his voice to a bare whisper over the clatter of silverware from the kitchen.

"I watched the interview, Jake. Dillon... he was reciting. You were right. He got the words right, but the music was wrong."

"Then tell Ballack. Tell Kincaid."

"And say what?" Foley shook his head. "They have all they need. Or close enough. Thomas had the victim's blood on his hands. He had the note. The handwriting isn't an exact match, but it's close enough. It's a wrap. If I stand up now and say 'wait a minute,' I'm not just fighting APD. I'm fighting the Governor and our entire command staff."

Ward sat back, the disappointment tasting bitter in his mouth. "So that's it? We just let the real guy walk?"

"No," Foley said. "We don't. *You* don't."

Foley pulled his right hand out of his pocket and laid a closed fist on the formica table. His knuckles were white.

"I knew you'd need a pick-me-up. So I brought you something."

Ward raised his eyebrows.

Foley opened his hand.

Sitting in his palm was a small silver thumb drive.

"Like I promised. Everything," Foley said. "All the incident reports from the lab raid. It's mostly state and local stuff from the search warrants we executed while you were in the hospital. Nothing from the Feds, but Pagan's personal notes and logs? They're on there. It should keep you busy for a while."

Ward stared at the drive. It was small, innocuous. It looked like something used to store family photos, not the dark secrets of a shadow agency.

"You stole classified data," Ward said. "The Feds would crucify you."

"Technically, I preserved evidence gathered by the Alaska State Troopers from an active file while I still had legal access to it," Foley said, though the lawyer-speak lacked conviction. "But yeah. If they catch me with this... I'm in trouble."

He slid the drive across the table.

Ward covered it with his hand. "Why give it to me?"

Foley looked down at his empty hands. "Well, because I said I would. And because I have three kids, Jake. I have a mortgage. I have a wife who worries every time I walk out the door. I can't go down this rabbit hole. I can't fight whoever covered that up." He looked up, his expression pained but resolute. "But you... you were there in the lab. You're the one with the scars. And let's be honest—you don't know when to stop."

"Is that a compliment?"

"More of a diagnosis," Foley said. "You're the only one crazy enough to read what's on that drive and do something about it."

Ward slipped the drive into his pocket. It felt heavy, like a loaded magazine.

"What's on it, Bud?"

"Answers, hopefully," Foley said, sliding out of the booth and buttoning his coat. "Enough to cure your nightmares. Or summon new ones. There's the stuff about 'Subject AB.' About the conditioning. It wasn't just fear removal, Jake. It was... I don't know, about removing the roadblocks to human evolution. Freaky stuff."

Foley hesitated, standing over the table.

"Be careful, Ward. The people who locked that file? They aren't local PD. They aren't troopers. They play by different rules."

"I know," Ward said.

"Do you?" Foley looked at him with a mixture of pity and respect. "I hope so. Because once you plug that in, you're on your own."

"Thanks, Bud," Ward said, offering a genuine smile. "Distance yourself from me for a while. Just to be safe."

"I'll say a prayer for ya, my friend." Foley hesitated, the heavy silence proving he meant it. He then nodded, pulled his beanie tight, and walked out of the diner without looking back.

Ward sat alone in the booth. He reached into his pocket, his thumb tracing the metal edge of the drive.

He threw cash on the table to cover the meal and stood up. Anchorage was celebrating a victory, sleeping soundly under the illusion of safety.

But he was wide awake.

TWENTY-SIX

The press conference was a masterclass in political theater—a formal victory lap designed to confirm what the local news channels had already been broadcasting for hours.

Inside the Anchorage Police Department's downtown headquarters, the podium was flanked by state and city flags. Lieutenant Kincaid commanded the center microphone, bathed in the strobelight flashes of cameras, looking every inch the victorious general. Sergeant Ballack flanked him on the right, in full uniform, while the Mayor and the Anchorage Police Chief hovered on Kincaid's left, practically radiating relief.

Ward watched from the back of the room, leaning against a structural pillar with his arms tightly crossed over his chest.

"Today," Kincaid boomed, his voice echoing off the glass walls, "the citizens of Alaska can finally breathe again. The individual responsible for the heinous murders in Talkeetna and Ship Creek— the self-styled 'Ministrant'—is in custody. He was apprehended this morning, caught in the very act of taking the life of a third citizen."

A murmur of somber approval rippled through the press corps.

"Thomas Dillon has confessed to these crimes," Kincaid continued. "He has provided details known only to law enforcement. We have recovered the murder weapon. The threat has been neutralized."

"Lieutenant!" a reporter from the *Anchorage Daily News* shouted over the din. "What about the motive? Why did he do it?"

Kincaid paused, offering a grave, practiced nod. "Mr. Dillon is a disturbed individual struggling with substance abuse issues and religious delusions. He believed he was 'cleansing' his victims. It is a tragedy, but let me be clear: this was the work of a lone actor. There is no cult. There is no wider conspiracy. The monster is in a cage."

Applause. Actual applause broke out among the people in the room.

Bile rose in the back of Ward's throat. It was a perfect story. Simple. Linear. Easy.

He looked at Miller, standing near the front row of reporters. She met his eye, then looked away.

Ward pushed off the pillar and turned toward the exit. He couldn't watch anymore.

In the basement apartment in Spenard, the television cast a flickering blue light over the peeling wallpaper.

Adam sat on the edge of the sleeper sofa, his elbows resting on his knees as he watched Kincaid speak. His face was unreadable—smooth, still, and terrifyingly calm.

Lena sat on the floor near his feet. She didn't look at the screen. She watched him.

She had her knees pulled tight to her chest, rocking slightly. The air in the room felt thick, heavy with the supernatural peace Adam projected. It carried a physical sensation, like a warm, leaden blanket draped over her shoulders. It muffled the sounds of the traffic outside. It muffled the scratching of the rats in the walls.

Most importantly, it muffled the screaming in her own head.

For years, Lena's mind had been a jagged, unforgiving landscape of regret and craving. Every waking second had been a brutal negoti-

ation with pain. But since Adam found her, the pain had simply…
stopped.

It was better than heroin. Cleaner than oxy. The peace was
absolute.

But today, for the first time, Lena felt a tremor in the
foundation.

She looked at Adam's hands. They were clean now, but she'd
seen what they could do. She'd seen the blood.

Thomas was gone. Locked away in a concrete box where the
peace couldn't reach him. Was he screaming right now? Was the
noise rushing back into his head, tearing him apart?

The thought made Lena's stomach twist. She realized, with a
jolt of cold terror, that she wasn't afraid *for* Thomas.

She was afraid of *becoming* Thomas.

If Adam left… or if they caught him… the blanket would be
ripped away. The cold would come back. The noise would return.
She looked at him, desperate to keep him safe. Not just because he
was holy. But because he was her supply.

"They think it's over," Adam said. He didn't look angry. He
sounded disappointed. "They are celebrating a lie."

"Let them," Lena said. "It keeps us safe, Adam. If they think it's
Thomas, they won't look for you."

Adam turned his head slowly. His eyes were dark voids in the
dim light. "Safe? Is that what we are here for? Safety?"

"We can't do the work if we're locked up," Lena said.

"We will not be locked up, and neither will Thomas,"
Adam said softly, his gaze drifting back to the television screen.
"But we cannot strike the lion inside its own cage. The jail is
too fortified, too crowded with their panic. The law demands
they move him. He must be arraigned at the courthouse, then
returned to the jail. When they bring him out into the open,
that is when they will be vulnerable. We wait for the
transport."

She reached out, resting her hand on his knee. The contact sent
a jolt of pure warmth up her arm, soothing the tight knot in her gut.

She leaned into it, greedy for the relief. "We should leave Anchorage. Go north. Like you said. To the Valley."

"Not yet," Adam said.

He stood up. The warmth pulled away from Lena, and she shivered.

Adam paced the small room. "The noise is still here, Lena. Can't you hear it? The police... the mayor... they are loud. But there is a specific frequency cutting through all of it. A rot I recognize."

He stopped at the window, peering through a crack in the blackout curtain.

"Dr. Carter," he said.

Lena froze. "The psychiatrist? From the hospital?"

"She saw me," Adam said, his voice tightening. "Every day for six months. She looked right at me, scribbled in her little notebook, and called me 'cured.' She looked at a spiritual awakening and called it 'recovery.'"

He turned back to the room, his expression hardening into something jagged and cruel.

"She is proud, Lena. She is sitting in her high tower, probably drinking a glass of wine, thinking she fixed the broken toy. Her pride is a beacon. It's polluting the air."

"So?" Lena asked, her voice rising slightly. "Let her be proud. What does it matter?"

"It matters because it is a lie," Adam said. "And lies are the soil where the rot grows. I need to show her. I need to cleanse her."

"That's not cleansing," Lena blurted out.

Adam stopped pacing. He looked at her, his head tilted. "What did you say?"

Lena scrambled to her feet. Her heart hammered against her ribcage, the old, familiar anxiety clawing at her throat. She needed him to understand. She needed him to be careful. If she lost him...

"The man in Talkeetna," she said, her voice shaking. "The one downtown. They wanted it. You said you were saving them from their pain."

"Yes."

"But Dr. Carter?" Lena took a step closer, pleading. "She isn't asking for it, Adam. She isn't suffering. She's just... annoying you. She's just wrong. Killing her isn't a mercy. It's... revenge. It's personal."

The words hung in the air, dangerous and sharp.

Adam didn't strike her. He didn't yell. He just looked at her with a profound, terrifying pity.

"You still think like a human, Lena," he said. "You think in terms of punishment and reward. Revenge is for the petty. This is different. She is infected. I am the surgeon. Would you hate the surgeon for cutting out a tumor, even if the patient didn't know it was there?"

"It's too dangerous," Lena pressed, desperately switching tactics. "Thomas is in jail. The police are everywhere. If you go to her house... if you get caught..."

I will die, she thought. *I will wither and die without you.*

"If you get caught," she said again, "who will save the rest?"

Adam smiled. He walked back to her and placed both hands heavily on her shoulders.

The wave hit her again—massive, narcotic, overwhelming. Her knees buckled. She slumped against him, breathing in the scent of his old wool coat. The fear vanished instantly. The crippling doubt dissolved into a golden, euphoric haze.

"Oh," she breathed, her eyes fluttering shut. "Okay. Okay."

"Do not fear," Adam whispered into her ear. "I will not be caught. They are blind."

He released her.

Lena swayed, suddenly cold again, but the heavy residue of his touch kept her upright.

"I have to go alone," Adam said, pulling his coat tight. "This is a private session. Just doctor and patient."

"Will you come back?" Lena asked, her voice small and fragile.

"Of course," Adam said.

He walked to the door. "Wait for me," he said. "And pray."

He slipped out into the hallway.

The deadbolt clicked shut.

Lena stood alone in the center of the silent room. The television droned on—the APD Lieutenant was shaking hands with the mayor now, smiling for the cameras.

Without Adam's presence, the apartment was just a dirty basement. The odor of stale cigarette smoke and mildew returned. The distant wail of a police siren bled through the thin walls.

Lena wrapped her arms tightly around herself, digging her fingernails into her own skin until it hurt, desperately trying to hold on to the fading warmth of his hands.

"He's coming back," she said to herself in the empty room. "He has to."

But deep down, buried beneath the thick layer of supernatural calm he had plastered over her mind, a small, frantic voice was screaming.

It's not holy, the voice said. *It's just murder.*

Lena reached for the remote and turned up the volume, drowning out her thoughts with the sound of their lies.

TWENTY-SEVEN

WARD'S APARTMENT FELT LIKE A BUNKER. THE BLINDS were drawn tight against the morning light, and the only illumination came from the harsh, blue-white glow of his laptop screen.

He sat at his small kitchen table, the silver thumb drive plugged into the side of his machine. It hummed, or maybe that was just the blood rushing in his ears.

He expected some sort of file encryption. Passwords or biometric locks. But Foley was right—a bulk export, a raw data dump grabbed in panic before the feds slammed the door on the state investigation. It was messy, unorganized, and terrifyingly accessible.

Simple file structure. A single folder with a series of PDF files containing supplementary reports in various stages of completion. Troopers were there, along with a few APD guys, and the APD case officer, Sergeant Paddock. Most of the events were in Anchorage, so it's understandable they had the lead. One of the supplementary reports documented an exam in the TCU lab by Anna on an Apple MacBook found in Pagan's Lab. She'd imaged the drive, copied the entire thing bit by bit, to the TCU server, then begun an exam. But she hadn't completed it. Those things take time, and they'd yanked the case before she was done.

But, just like Foley said, she'd found a treasure trove of research.

A couple of clicks later, and there it was—a .zip archive labeled, "From Pagan laptop."

Ward double-clicked the icon. A password dialogue popped up —probably secured by Anna with standard unit encryption. He typed in the default TCU passcode and hit enter. The directory decrypted, spilling its contents across the screen.

He saw it immediately.

A sub-folder titled: *WET, WARM, AND NOISY.*

Ward stared at the words. They triggered a memory of a conversation he'd had with that grad student at the university. What was her name?

Amy Doherty. That was it. She said the human brain was too warm and noisy for quantum... something.

Pushing the thought aside, he double-clicked a PDF inside the folder.

He didn't expect a government header.

The document was crisp, official, and terrifyingly lucid. It wasn't the raving of a madman; it was the cold, calculated logic of scientists doing the impossible. And it had been partially redacted.

PROJECT: ██████ // SUB-PROTOCOL: ██████
DOCUMENT ID: ███████████
DATE: 14 NOV 2012
AUTHOR: Dr. Richard Pagan
CLEARANCE: TS/SCI - NOFORN
SUBJECT: META-ANALYSIS OF QUANTUM COHERENCE IN BIOLOGICAL SYSTEMS (REBUTTAL TO THE "WET, WARM, AND NOISY" HYPOTHESIS)
I. EXECUTIVE SUMMARY
For decades, the established consensus of the neuro-scientific community—backed by the standard model of physics —has been that the human brain cannot sustain quantum processing. The argument, popularized by ██████ and

the conservative faction at MIT, is that the brain is a thermal bath: too "wet, warm, and noisy" to allow for the delicate state of quantum superposition. They argue that environmental decoherence occurs within 10^{-13} seconds, rendering any quantum effects on consciousness impossible.

They are incorrect.

Following a review of classified data from Project ███████ (DIA), Project ████ ████████ (INSCOM), and the unpublished biological assays from the ████████ sub-projects, we have isolated the mechanism of failure in previous studies. They were looking at the neuron as a switch. They should have been looking inside—at the scaffolding.

He kept reading, dumbfounded. There were hypotheses about how to disturb the "framework" that maintained quantum coherence in the brain. These theories included using radiation, manipulation of brain waves, theories about oxygen deprivation, and carefully-dosed anesthesia.

Then they were no longer theories. The data documented experiments that began in "Phase Zero," a series of crude trials conducted on rhesus macaques.

The outcomes had been "known" as scientifically impossible—yet the results were consistent. The macaques that served as experimental subjects achieved a state of "quantum malleability," with some exhibiting precognitive behaviors—reacting to threats seconds before they materialized and predicting randomized automated feeding schedules with statistical significance.

But the neurological price was absolute. The treatment deadened the brain's pain centers on some of the monkeys, stripping the animals of physical sensation, followed by bizarre behavior. The logs noted a rapid descent into hysteria and catatonic depression, culminating in unprovoked suicidal ideation. Many of the subjects would violently hurl themselves against their enclosures, seeking an end to a suffering they could endure no more.

Ward felt a chill unrelated to the weather outside.

He clicked through the files, his eyes scanning clinical descriptions of torture masked as therapy. Sensory deprivation tanks. LSD derivatives. Induced hypothermia to slow metabolic rates during "reprogramming."

He found a folder marked *Subject Manifest*.

He hesitated, his finger hovering over the trackpad. He knew what it contained. He didn't want to see it.

He clicked, anyway.

SUBJECT JW.

Ward opened it, his hand shaking. A few clicks later, his own face appeared before him—a photo taken while unconscious, strapped to a steel table. His skin was pale, his eyes sunken.

SUBJECT JW: Prior exposure to platinum-based neuropathic agents (chemotherapy) effectively prepped the neural pathways. The induced erosion allowed us to introduce significantly lower dosages of the catalysts, minimizing damage while maximizing the likelihood of detachment during the session. Physiologically, he is the ideal research subject, however, he retains distinct ego strength. Risk of escape and exposure is high. Recommendation: Terminate participation.

He closed the file, his hands shaking. The word, "terminate," lingered in his mind. But despite the recommendation, Pagan persisted with his experimentation on Ward. He just couldn't resist the science, and it led to his end.

He wanted no more of this walk down bad memory lane.

He closed the file and scrolled further down the list. One of the other files was marked *DECEASED. Another marked TERMINATED.*

And then, near the bottom:

Subject AB.

He opened the file.

It showed a photo of a young man. Early twenties, white with Asian heritage—dark eyebrows, a bit of stubble on his upper lip and chin. A dense wall of text followed the photo.

SUBJECT AB: ███████ Age 22. Admitted via voluntary protocol.

OBSERVATION: Subject initially proved resistant to intervention, failing to achieve the painless detachment observed in most other subjects. Instead, AB followed the specific degenerative trajectory of the Phase Zero primate trials. Sessions 1 through 10 resulted in extreme physiological distress, weeping hysteria, and two confirmed attempts at self-termination within the containment cell.

ADAPTATION: Resilience achieved only when the subject began integrating the trauma into a rigid teleological framework, possibly learned from previous religious training. He stopped fighting the pain and began accepting it as "cleansing." He interprets the continued exposure not as experimentation, but as, "...divine revelation necessary to purge his own corruption and prepare him for his mission."

Ward scrolled down, his stomach tightening as the clinical notes described a mind shattering and then gluing itself back together.

SESSION 12: Neural degradation is accelerating. The subject's capacity for meditative reconstruction is failing to keep pace with the synaptic scarring. Catatonia is projected within days. However, a new anomaly manifested. As the subject's integrity collapses, his external influence expands. He exhibits profound control over the amygdala activity of research members within a three-meter radius. He is no longer just suppressing his own fear; he is broadcasting the suppression.

SESSION 13: Subject is leaning further into the delusion. Subject believes he is no longer being cleansed but instead being *sanctified*. Neural damage is excessive, with reduced cognitive clarity, slurred speech, and impaired motor function. Catatonia imminent.

Sanctified.

Pagan hadn't just broken AB's mind; he had tortured him until he retreated into a religious labyrinth of his own making. He took a terrified young man and twisted him into a maniac. The mental stillness AB honed to endure the pain became a weapon. The very mechanism that allowed him to survive hell was now being used to unleash it on the innocent.

Ward opened a video file attached to the log.

The screen flickered to life, low-quality black-and-white footage of a small room. A shiver went down his spine as Ward recognized the bed and the small window from his own captivity.

The subject, presumably AB, sat on a metal chair in the center of the room. It was the same person as the photo at the beginning of AB's file, but he now looked exhausted, skeletal, eyes sunken and rimmed with dark bruises.

Pagan's voice came from behind the camera.

"Adam. How do you feel?"

The man looked up. His eyes were wide, the pupils large, desperate.

"I feel... heavy," Adam said. "But the noise is quiet now. I made it quiet."

"And the fear?"

"There is no fear in love," Adam recited, his voice shaky. The words were slurred.

Adam continued. "Perfect love casts out fear. I have to love them. I have to take it from them."

"Good," Pagan said. "I'm glad you're coping with the challenges of the research. You're doing well."

Adam smiled. Not a smile of joy, but instead the resolved, beatific smile of a martyr stepping onto the pyre.

"There is no forgiveness," Adam said, a tear tracking through the grime on his cheek, "without the shedding of blood."

"Yes," Pagan encouraged. "Find that peace. You're doing great work, Adam. Great work."

The video ended with a still frame of Pagan's face looking oh so pleased with himself.

Ward slammed the laptop shut. What the hell?

How could Pagan—a man who claimed to have had a beautiful near-death experience as a child—be capable of inflicting such profound horror? Was it truly in the name of science, or had he simply been blinded by his desperate search for paradise?

Did it matter?

Ward pushed the chair back and stood up, pacing the small length of his kitchen. He felt sick to his stomach.

Adam was his name. Pagan called him exactly that. And Adam wasn't evil. Pagan tortured a young man, a kid, really. And transformed him into a killer.

Ward wielded a front-row seat to a horrifying experiment gone awry, in which what used to be a perfectly good human being now believed murder was holy work. He used a power he'd developed because it was the only thing that stopped his own screaming.

Now, this young man could project an induced calm. It was so potent that victims thanked him for the knife—just to feel his relief. Relief he himself had relished. Relief he needed to survive.

Ward looked back at the closed laptop. A question gnawed at him. One of the other subjects in the manifest was marked TERMINATED. If Adam was this damaged—catatonic, suicidal, his brain turning to mush—how could he now be walking around Anchorage cutting throats instead of rotting in a shallow grave near the lab?

Ward sat back down and pried the lid open.

He scrolled past the video file and found another document in the folder. A memo, dated three weeks after the last session. The header differed—standard internal correspondence—but the subject line chilled Ward's blood.

FROM: Dr. Richard Pagan TO: ████████ Security Chief,
Site B SUBJECT: DISPOSITION OF ASSET AB
CURRENT STATUS: Subject has entered full fugue catatonia. Synaptic responsiveness is nil. Containment recom-
mends Protocol 3 (Liquidation).
DIRECTIVE: Request denied.
Asset AB represents a unique biological anomaly. With his
current neural architecture collapsed, we do not have
resources to house the subject, but there is value in
measuring his capacity to regenerate brain tissue. Viability
for future research remains non-zero.
ACTION PLAN:
1) Insertion: Stage narcotic overdose to induce moderate
respiratory depression and abandon subject near Providence
Alaska Medical Center to ensure high likelihood of
discovery.
2) Narrative: Subject will be processed as a John Doe overdose with resulting hypoxic brain injury. History of drug
abuse should quell any investigative efforts by authorities.
3) Monitoring: State placement in long-term psychiatric
care is likely. If regeneration occurs, subject will be regath-
ered for analysis.

That was it. Nothing more on SUBJECT AB. But Pagan or his
bosses, perhaps in error, failed to redact the video file, and Ward
knew Subject AB's name.

Adam.

Ward leaned back, the air leaving his lungs in a rush.

They hadn't released him. They hadn't killed him. They threw
him away like a broken thing, but kept a watch in case he fixed
himself. Pagan parked his experiment in a state hospital, waiting for
the day the engine might turn over again.

But Pagan didn't come back. Ward saw to that.

Adam, however, did recover. And now, Pagan's murderous
weapon walked free.

TWENTY-EIGHT

Ward couldn't go to Ballack, or APD, or anyone else with this. If he disclosed how he knew the killer was named Adam—and where he'd come from—Foley's act of sneaking the classified data out of ARMS would be revealed. Foley had a family, and he had surrendered the data as a favor. Ward couldn't reward that with a federal indictment.

He grabbed the mouse and opened a secure browser, choosing to avoid the state's ARMS database entirely. ARMS kept rigid, subpoena-ready logs of every search query. If the Feds were monitoring the digital footprint around Pagan's files, a sudden inquiry into a former test subject would trip a silent alarm.

Instead, he navigated to ACCURINT, a private, pay-to-play public records aggregator that often saved his bacon. No state oversight. No federal tripwires.

He typed in his login credentials and set the search parameters: *First Name: Adam. Last Name: B. Age Range: 18 to 25. Location: Alaska.*

The system churned before returning a few dozen hits. He thanked his lucky stars he lived in a state with a tiny population; if he were in California or New York, this search would have returned hundreds of results.

He started scrolling. Many of the ACCURINT files lacked associated photographs, so he began cross-referencing the names with standard web and social media searches. It was an inexact, frustrating science.

An hour passed, and he was only on his eighth subject.

He typed another last name into the search engine. The cursor blinked for a second, and then the results for 'Adam Basu' populated. Most were useless social media returns, but halfway down the page, a link from the *Anchorage Daily News* archives caught his eye.

Headline: *Future Einsteins—Local Students Shine at 65th Alaska Science and Engineering Fair.*

The dateline was six years old.

Ward clicked the link. The page loaded a gallery of high schoolers in ill-fitting dress shirts sporting nervous smiles, standing proudly in front of their science projects at the UAA Student Union.

He scrolled until he found it. Image 4 of 12.

Caption: Adam Basu, 17, demonstrates his project on 'Flux Pinning in Superconductors.' Basu earned the Grand Prize and will represent Alaska at the international competition in May.

Ward stared at the boy in the photo.

This wasn't the skeletal, haunted figure from Pagan's video. This Adam was vibrant. He stood next to a glass tank where a small, silver disc appeared to be floating frozen in mid-air above a magnetic track. He smiled—not the creepy, beatific smile of a serial killer, but the genuine, toothy grin of a kid who loved his life. His eyes were bright, sharp, and unmistakably alive.

He had the world by the tail.

"You had no idea..." Ward whispered to the glowing screen. "...what was waiting for you."

Ward tabbed back over to ACCURINT, plugging in the full name.

Adam Basu, age 22. Anchorage, Alaska. The file was minimal. A couple of old residence addresses in East Anchorage. A single moving violation from APD: 54 in a 35 MPH zone.

Ward pulled up the digital copy of the ticket. It listed Basu's occupation as *Student*.

The word hung on the screen like a neon sign pointing down a dark alley. He was a student. Just like Belle Anderson.

It was the same pattern. Pagan hunted for brilliance, but he preferred it fractured. He wanted genius that was desperate, isolated, and pliable.

Ward needed to know more about Basu's time at UAA. His teachers. A connection to Professor Mueller—and by extension, Richard Pagan—was likely.

Ward grabbed his personal cell phone and dialed Darin Hatch.

The University Police officer picked up on the third ring. "Ward. To what do I owe the displeasure? You ready to get destroyed on the pool table?"

"Not today. I need a favor."

"You always need a favor. You never call just to tell me I'm pretty."

"You're hideous, Darin. Now, listen. I need you to check your internal university RMS. Not APSIN, not the shared stuff. Just the local campus files."

Hatch's tone shifted instantly, dropping the banter. "This off the books?"

"Way off. Deep freeze. If anyone asks, we didn't talk."

"Jake. You in trouble?"

"Not yet. But I'm trying to avoid getting there. Name is Adam Basu. B-A-S-U."

"Hold on." The muffled clatter of a keyboard came through the line. It was a familiar, comforting sound—the steady rhythm of police work happening in real-time. "Basu... Basu... Okay, I got him. You sure about this kid?"

"What do you have?"

"He was a baby, Jake. Admitted to UAA at seventeen. Early enrollment program."

"Major?"

"Physics. Another Einstein."

Ward closed his eyes, the cold air biting at his face. Physics. Just like Belle. The trap was set in the classroom. "Any contacts with your department?"

"Yeah. One incident, about two years ago. Patrol found him passed out in a study room in the science building at three a.m. They woke him up, searched his bag and found a small bottle of pills. Adderall. No prescription."

"Speed," Ward said. "Trying to keep up with the workload?"

"Exactly. Looking at the interview notes, he was terrified. Apparently, his dad—Pakistani guy, very old school—was a rough dude. Basu broke down, said his father would disown him or worse if he failed or got caught with drugs. The kid was cracking, Jake. Total meltdown. He feared for his life."

"Did you charge him?"

"We seized the Adderall, but we didn't charge him. But here's the interesting part. The Dean of Students was ready to drop the hammer. Zero-tolerance policy on controlled substances in these cases. He could have stayed in school, but would have lost the scholarship."

Hatch paused, and Ward heard a mouse clicking.

"Didn't happen, though. Someone went to bat for him. A heavy hitter from the faculty submitted a formal letter to the conduct board. Claimed Basu was a 'once-in-a-generation intellect' and that losing him would be a tragedy for the scientific community. He volunteered to take personal responsibility for the kid. Placed him on academic probation under his direct supervision. Basically took him under his wing."

Ward gripped the phone tighter. He already knew the name before Hatch said it. "Who was it?"

"Professor Jan Mueller."

"Of course it was," Ward said. A chill ran up his back that had nothing to do with the Alaskan winter. Mueller didn't just teach these kids; he curated them. He found the ones desperate for a kind father figure, and he stepped in as their savior.

"Mueller became his faculty advisor," Hatch continued, oblivious to Ward's realization. "And get this—Basu's transcript shows he immediately transferred into Mueller's upper-division 'Directed Research' course. The kid went from being on the brink of expulsion to being the teacher's pet overnight."

"He wasn't a pet, Hatch," Ward said, his voice grim. "He was livestock."

"What?"

"Nothing. Just... thanks. You've been a lifesaver. Keep this buried."

"Always. Watch your six, Jake."

Ward ended the call and stared at the little goldfish in his over-sized aquarium.

It was a pipeline. Mueller scouted the talent at the university—brilliant minds like Belle and Adam who were struggling with personal demons. He groomed them, gained their trust, and then fed them directly into Richard Pagan's meat grinder.

Adam Basu hadn't just stumbled into that lab. He had been hand-picked.

TWENTY-NINE

Ward stared at the glowing screen of his laptop, the classified PDF of Subject AB open in front of him. The face of Adam Basu—young, terrified, and tortured—burned into his retinas.

He knew the name. He knew the origin. He knew the motive. He knew that the trembling man sitting in the APD interrogation room was just a pawn sacrificed to buy the young king time to move.

People had died. More would, surely. And Ward couldn't do a damn thing about it.

He leaned back, rubbing his temples where a migraine was digging in with spurs. In the eyes of the law, everything he had just learned didn't exist. The thumb drive Foley gave him was stolen property, yanked from a restricted database. If Ward kicked down Basu's door right now, even a first-year public defender would use the court's exclusionary rule to have the case thrown out before the handcuffs were cold.

Fruit of the poisonous tree. Basu would walk, and Ward and Foley could be fired. Or worse.

Ward needed a bridge.

He needed to build a pristine, legally defensible path to Adam

Basu without stepping on the landmine of the stolen drive. He needed to find a legal way to discover what he already knew.

How do I put him at the scene?

Ward looked at the notes scattered on his kitchen table. Talkeetna. The white box van. The isolated gas station at three in the morning.

The warrant.

Ward sat up straight. Back in the heat of the investigation, before Ballack pulled the plug, Ward had authored a search warrant affidavit for Foster and Foley. A cell tower dump. It compelled the carrier to provide the identity of every device that pinged the tower nearest to the Talkeetna crime scene during the exact window of the murder.

The judge had signed it. It was legal. It was perfectly clean.

If Adam Basu had been at that gas station—and if he hadn't been wise enough to turn his phone off—his number would be buried in that data.

Ward grabbed his mouse and minimized the stolen files. He opened his agency email application.

He held his breath as the inbox refreshed. One unread message stood out:

**Subject: Warrant Return - 3AN-26-402SW - AT&T Received: 4:12 AM

The data had arrived yesterday morning. He had been so busy fighting with APD and command staff that he'd missed it entirely.

He opened the email. Attached were instructions to download a zipped CSV file from the carrier's secure portal. It would be a massive spreadsheet containing thousands of rows of raw data: time stamps, durations, tower sector azimuths, and subscriber numbers.

He shouldn't touch it. Ballack had explicitly ordered him to stand down.

But Ballack wasn't here. And Ward was still the Technical

Crimes investigator who authored the warrant. Reviewing the return was just... follow-up.

He forwarded the email to Investigator Foster in Palmer. He kept the tone light and bureaucratic.

> Foster, I just got an alert from the carrier that the Talkeetna tower dump is available for download. I know the task force is winding down with the Dillon arrest, but I'm going to run through the data just to close out the file and make sure we didn't miss any co-conspirators. I'll let you know if anything interesting pops. -Ward

He hit send before he could talk himself out of it. Now he had a paper trail. He wasn't hunting a ghost; he was conducting due diligence on an open case.

Ward downloaded the attachment and opened it. The screen filled with a chaotic wall of text—a comma-separated value file containing thousands of rows of data headers and telecom acronyms.

IMSIs. MSISDNs. Tower Sector Azimuths.

The cell tower in Talkeetna covered a massive stretch of the Parks Highway. Every trucker, tourist, and local who drove past that gas station in the twelve-hour window was on this list.

He stared at the blinking cursor.

He knew exactly what he was looking for. Adam Basu's cell number burned a hole in his memory from the traffic ticket he'd pulled up earlier. *907-555-0199.*

But he couldn't just search for it.

If he hit Ctrl-F and typed Basu's number directly into the spreadsheet, he would leave a forensic artifact on his machine. If an investigator or a savvy defense attorney imaged his laptop before he wiped it, they'd find a targeted search. They'd see he was hunting a specific suspect long before he had a legal reason to know the man existed.

They would ask: *"Investigator Ward, why did you search for Mr. Basu's number specifically among thousands of other entries?"*

And he would have no good answer.

He needed to make it look like he found the needle by searching through the haystack, one piece of straw at a time.

Ward cracked his knuckles and opened a terminal window.

He wasn't just a cop; he was a TCU investigator. He spoke the language of the machine.

He began typing, the rapid clatter of keys the only sound in the silent apartment. He wrote a Python script that took the raw data from the tower dump and parsed out only the phone numbers that were active between 02:00 and 04:00 AM—the exact window of the murder.

He hit Enter.

The script churned for two seconds, stripping away thousands of irrelevant entries. When it was done, it spit out a clean list of sixty-two phone numbers.

This was the grunt work. If anyone asked, he wasn't targeting Basu; he had narrowed the time frame and was manually running down the remaining leads.

Ward opened the state ARMS database. He cracked his neck, settled into his chair, and began manually typing the sixty-two numbers into the search bar, one by one.

He worked methodically, letting the server logs record his human pace. He dumped the results into a new spreadsheet, building columns for *PERSON*, *BUSINESS*, and *NO RECORD*. For the individuals, he added *AGE*, *SEX*, and *HEIGHT*.

It took over two hours of tedious, mind-numbing data entry.

When he was finished, thirty-five of the numbers returned to actual people; the rest were local businesses or unregistered phones with empty fields. Of the thirty-five individuals, twelve were female. He deleted their rows. Of the twenty-three remaining men, he screened for height, eliminating anyone under five-foot-nine or over six-foot-two.

Eleven more dropped out, leaving twelve.

He screened for age, restricting the parameters to men between eighteen and thirty. It was a rough guess based on the gas station video, but it was a legally defensible parameter.

The spreadsheet reduced to four names.

Adam Basu was one of them.

Thank God.

Ward paused, a sudden wave of skepticism cutting through his relief. Adam Basu was a brilliant physics wunderkind who had been meticulous regarding forensic evidence. Why would he take an active cell phone to a murder scene?

It didn't fit.

Ward looked at the tower dump spreadsheet again, tracing Basu's specific row of data. The entry wasn't an incoming or outgoing call. It was a small, automated data transfer.

Maybe Basu thought turning the screen off was enough. Maybe he kept the device on because he had a compulsion to follow the news cycle to see if his message had been received. Or, more likely, the kid simply didn't realize that mobile devices don't have to make calls to connect to a network. Background applications constantly fetch data and update location services, silently pinging the nearest tower.

The kid might be a genius with quarks and bosons, but he was a novice at operational security. Plus, his mind had been shattered by Richard Pagan, so there's that.

Whatever the reason, Ward would take the win.

The other three men on the list could be eliminated with basic interviews and alibis. If he looked deeper at the cell data, he'd probably find that none of their phones lingered at the gas station as long as Basu's had. It didn't matter.

He had his guy.

It looked like persistence. To some, it might look like luck.

Most importantly, it would hold up in court.

Ward sat back and opened the full ARMS record for Adam Basu. Minor criminal history. Anchorage address.

He checked the *Case Involvement* tab and found a listed relative:

Malik Basu. The notes identified Malik as the pastor of a small, independent church near Big Lake in the Mat-Su Valley.

Ward opened a web browser and searched for the church. He found a simple website and clicked on the *About Us* tab.

A photo loaded. It showed a stern, older man of Indian or Pakistani descent standing behind a modest wooden pulpit. Standing next to him, looking uncomfortable in a stiff suit, was a boy in his late teens who looked terrifyingly familiar.

"Gotcha," Ward said.

He had built the bridge. Now he was going to cross it.

THIRTY

Two hours later, Ward was driving north. The Parks Highway stretched like a ribbon of gray asphalt through the heart of the Mat-Su Valley, flanked by leafless birch forests that stood like skeletal sentinels against the overcast sky.

Ward drove his personal truck, an older Chevy pickup that blended perfectly into the Valley traffic. Where he was going, he preferred to keep a low profile; even an unmarked Trooper rig would stick out like a sore thumb. Besides, today was his regular day off. He wasn't on the clock.

Technically, he wasn't even on the case.

Ballack had been clear: *stand down*. But Ballack would get over it. When things hit the fan, the Sergeant usually had his back. More importantly, Ballack wasn't the one who had suffered inside Pagan's lab. Ward had promised himself he would play a humble support role in this investigation, but walking away now was a bridge too far. He knew things nobody else did. One good interview might be enough to force command to change course and save lives.

Or, it might spook the prey.

On the passenger seat, Ward's portable radio hummed with the usual morning traffic—welfare checks, civil problems and minor collisions. Then, a transmission from Mat-Com cut through the static.

1-B-77, Matcom, be advised, we have a complainant from Nelchina. Hunter was found tied to a tree. He claims a 'ghost' in the woods ambushed him. No vehicle tracks. Suspect stole his extreme-weather gear and all his food, then vanished on foot. Complainant has a history of wildlife-related charges.

Ward reached over and twisted the volume knob down a notch. Interesting as it was, a crazy poacher near Glennallen wasn't his problem today.

Near mile 52, he took a left onto Big Lake Road. The two-lane blacktop wound past frozen lakes and scattered, off-grid homesteads.

The Mat-Su Valley was a world away from Anchorage. It was quieter, fiercely independent, and heavily dotted with churches ranging from majestic log cabins to humble storefront chapels.

The Church of the Sanctified Spirit fell somewhere in between.

It sat at the end of a long gravel driveway—a rectangular building with aging white vinyl siding and an ill-fitting fiberglass steeple that looked like an afterthought. The dirt and gravel lot was empty, save for a late-model Nissan sedan parked near a side entrance.

Ward parked, taking a deep breath to center himself. He had his cover story. He had his badge. Most importantly, he had the truth.

He stepped out into the biting air, the gravel crunching loudly under his boots. The faint odor of wood smoke drifted on the breeze. He slipped his hand into his pocket, activating his digital voice recorder, and walked toward the front double doors.

Locked.

He circled around to the side entrance near the Nissan and knocked on the metal security door.

Silence.

He knocked again, harder. "Hello? Alaska State Troopers."

The deadbolt clicked, and the door swung open.

The man standing in the doorway was taller than Ward

expected. Malik Basu wore a simple black sweater and gray slacks, but he carried himself with the rigid, exacting posture of a military officer. His skin was light brown, his thick hair graying at the temples.

But it was his eyes that stopped Ward cold.

They were Adam's eyes. Not just in shape, but in their terrifying intensity. They burned with a dark, unblinking focus.

"Can I help you, Officer?" Malik's voice was deep and thickly accented—a cultured British clip layered over something older.

"Investigator Ward, Alaska State Troopers," Ward said, flashing his badge. "I'm looking for Malik Basu."

"I am *Pastor* Basu," Malik said, emphasizing the title.

Ward paused. "I'd like a word, sir. It concerns your son, Adam."

For a split second, a flicker of something passed behind Malik's eyes. Not fear. Calculation.

"Adam?" Malik stepped back, pulling the door wider. "Has something happened? Is he hurt?"

"No, sir. Nothing like that. Just a routine inquiry regarding a case we're closing out. Do you have a few minutes?"

Malik studied him for a long beat, then nodded. "Come in. It is cold out here."

The small sanctuary smelled of lemon pledge and old paper. Rows of wooden pews faced a simple, raised platform. There was no ornate cross, no stained glass. There was only a heavy wooden pulpit and a large white banner hanging on the back wall.

Ward's eyes locked onto it as he walked down the center aisle. The text was painted in stark, bold block letters:

PURIFICATION THROUGH SACRIFICE

A chill crawled up Ward's spine. "A bit severe, isn't it?" he asked, gesturing to the banner.

Malik didn't look back. He walked to the front row and sat, motioning for Ward to do the same. "We believe in the literal truth of scripture, Investigator. The modern church has become soft. They preach comfort. We preach cleansing."

"Cleansing," Ward repeated. "That's an interesting word."

"It is a biblical concept," Malik said. "Now, what is this about Adam? I haven't seen my son in... some time. We didn't part on the best of terms."

"How long is 'some time'?"

"Over a year. Maybe two. He... struggles. He prefers solitude."

"What kind of car is he driving these days?"

Malik frowned. "Adam does not own a vehicle. He walks. He finds walking meditative. Why do you ask?"

"We're following up on some data from a cell tower dump," Ward said, watching the man's face closely. "Near a crime scene in Talkeetna. Your son's phone number popped up in the area during the specific timeframe of a homicide."

Malik went absolutely still. "A homicide?"

"Yes."

Ward expected shock. He expected a father's denial. Instead, Malik let out a slow, measured breath. He looked down at his hands —large, capable hands resting motionless on his knees.

"And you think Adam did this?" Malik asked.

"We have a suspect in custody, actually," Ward said. "A man named Thomas Dillon. He's confessed."

"Then why are you here?"

"Because the data puts Adam near the scene. We need to clear him. If he was just passing through, or if Dillon stole his phone... we need to know. We're just dotting our i's and crossing our t's."

Malik looked up. A strange, serene smile touched his lips. "Thomas Dillon," he said. "I do not know this name. But if he confessed, then justice is served, is it not?"

"Perhaps," Ward pressed. "Unless your son was part of it."

Malik stood up abruptly. The movement was so sudden and violent that Ward almost reached for his weapon.

"My son is a scholar, Investigator. A scientist. He was... unwell for a time."

"Drug use. Yes, I know about his university records."

Malik froze. A church leader would naturally be uncomfortable having a son with a documented drug problem, Adderall or otherwise.

"Then you know he is fragile," Malik said, his jaw tight. "He is not a killer. He is a boy, broken by the world."

And maybe by you, Ward thought.

Malik turned away and walked up the short steps onto the stage, taking his place behind the heavy wooden pulpit. He placed his hands on the wood, instantly reclaiming his authority.

"I raised him to fear God," Malik said, his voice taking on a booming, resonant tone. He was giving a sermon now. "To understand that sin is a weight. A noose around our necks. That it must be removed through sacrifice. Through penance. Maybe he took those lessons too far in his own mind. But murder? No. He took no part in this."

"You talk about removing sin," Ward pressed, walking slowly up the center aisle toward the pulpit. "How exactly do you teach that, Pastor? The shedding of blood?"

Malik's brows furrowed, his dark eyes blazing. "Indeed, under the law almost everything is purified with blood, and without the shedding of blood there is no forgiveness of sins!"

Ward fought to keep his face neutral. It was the exact verse from the notes left on the bodies.

"Do you teach that in church?" Ward asked.

"I teach the Bible!" Malik raised a fist into the air. "We live in a world of filth, *Investigator.*" He spat Ward's title with obvious disgust. "Rot. It is everywhere. In the streets, in the homes, in the hearts of men. People carry it like a disease. They beg for release. They beg to be clean."

"And who decides who gets cleaned?" Ward asked.

"God decides," Malik hissed, leaning forward in the pulpit. "We are simply... His ministrants."

The air left the room.

Ministrants.

This wasn't just a church. It was a training ground. Adam hadn't hallucinated a new theology in the isolation of Pagan's lab; he had brought it with him. Pagan had shattered the boy's mind, yes —but Adam had poured the broken pieces back into the terrifying mold cast by his father.

Ward had come here to find a lead. Instead, he had found the source.

"Where is he?" Ward asked. "If he's not with you, where would he be?"

"I told you," Malik said, his manic energy suddenly evaporating. His arms dropped to his sides, and he retreated a half-step behind his pulpit. "We parted ways. We haven't spoken."

"If you hear from him," Ward said, standing and pulling a business card from his pocket and dropping it on the front pew, "call me."

Ward turned his back on the man and walked out. He felt Malik Basu's intense eyes boring into his spine every step of the way down the aisle.

Just as Ward pushed through the double doors into the freezing afternoon air, he heard Malik's voice one last time, echoing through the empty sanctuary.

"Be not afraid, Investigator!"

Ward practically ran to his truck. He slammed the door, keyed the ignition, and killed his voice recorder. His hands were shaking.

Holy crap.

He grabbed his phone. He needed to call Foley right now.

Command had it all wrong. Thomas Dillon was indeed a distraction. Adam was the killer.

And Malik Basu might be the key to tracking him down.

THIRTY-ONE

Dr. Elizabeth Carter poured the Pinot Grigio until it kissed the rim of the glass, the red liquid shivering as she set the bottle down on the granite island in her kitchen.

Her luxury condo was silent, sealed against the Anchorage winter. The in-floor heating radiated a gentle warmth, and the recessed lights were dimmed to a soft, amber glow. It was a sanctuary of beige tones and expensive abstract art—a space designed to soothe, to neutralize, and to reassure.

She took a long sip of wine, closing her eyes as the cool acidity hit her tongue.

On the television in the living room, the late local news was replaying the APD press conference. Lieutenant Kincaid's voice, deep and triumphant, drifted into the kitchen.

"*...monster is in a cage... Thomas Dillon... confessed to all counts...*"

Elizabeth exhaled, but her shoulders didn't drop.

She had spent the last twenty-four hours in a low-grade state of panic, checking deadbolts she knew were secured, flinching at the mechanical hum of the elevator in the hallway.

When the news had first broken about the "Ministrant"— about his religious delusions—a cold knot had tightened in her stomach. The psychological profile seemed familiar. Too familiar.

She had thought of Adam Basu.

She had reviewed his discharge file three times today, frantically searching for something she might have missed—a red flag, a hidden crack in the façade of his miraculous recovery. But her own clinical notes remained stubbornly consistent:

Patient exhibits profound spiritual breakthrough. Anxiety manageable. No lingering violent ideation.

She had signed his release. She had unleashed him on the world.

Now, the man on the television screen was screaming about the "rot" and the "cleansing."

Elizabeth took another sip of wine, larger this time, but the alcohol provided no relief. Thomas Dillon was a junkie. A stranger. But the words he was shouting... they were words Adam had used, early in his treatment. Dillon was mimicking his exact pathology.

Adam wasn't a success story. He was a contagion. And she had let him out.

The doorbell rang.

Elizabeth froze, the wine glass hovering halfway to her lips.

It was 9:30 p.m. Her luxury building was highly secure; you needed an RFID fob to get into the lobby and another to operate the elevator. Only the concierge or security could get this far without being buzzed in.

What could they want?

She set the wine down. The crystal clinked loudly against the stone island.

She walked to the front door, her thick socks sliding silently on the hardwood, and pressed her eye to the peephole.

The blood drained from her face. The world tilted on its axis.

It couldn't be. Not him.

"Dr. Carter?"

The voice was soft, muffled slightly by the heavy wood, but terrifyingly familiar.

"It's Adam."

Elizabeth couldn't breathe. She backed away from the door, her heart slamming against her ribs. "How..." She couldn't finish the sentence. *How did you get in?*

"I need a session, Doctor," Adam said through the door.

"Go away," she said, her voice trembling as she retreated toward the kitchen counter.

She reached out, her fingers brushing the edge of her cell phone. Then, the wave hit her.

It didn't care about the solid oak door or the steel deadbolt. It radiated through the physical barrier—a heavy, suffocating blanket of calm that washed over her in an instant. The frantic, terrified hammering of her heart slowed to a sluggish, rhythmic thump. The desperate urge to run, to scream, to dial 911, simply evaporated, replaced by a golden, euphoric haze.

"Open the door," Adam said from the hallway. "It will be okay."

Elizabeth let her hand drop away from the phone. Paralyzed by the sheer, narcotic weight of his projection, she turned and walked back to the door like a woman in a trance.

She reached out, her fingers clumsy and relaxed, and unlocked the deadbolt. *There was no harm in this. Everything is okay.*

The brass handle depressed. The door swung slowly open.

Adam Basu stood on the threshold.

He wore a gray wool coat that looked too big for his slender frame. He wasn't holding a weapon. He stood with his hands folded politely in front of him.

He looked... serene.

"May I come in?" he asked.

She didn't move.

Adam stepped inside and pulled the door shut behind him. He locked the deadbolt, his movements precise and entirely unhurried. He didn't look around the apartment. He only looked at her.

"I... I helped you," she stammered, grasping desperately at the clinical straw. "I signed your release. I believed in you."

"You believed in the mask I wore for you. You looked at a

broken thing and called it whole because it made you feel powerful to do so. Like you were good at your job. You didn't heal me, Doctor. I healed myself. You only told yourself lies."

He took a step closer.

"I have seen your aura, Elizabeth. You are as dark as the rest of them. I'm going to let you feel some fear. You deserve it."

Icy terror broke through her paralysis. Her heart raced, slamming against her ribs so hard it hurt. Her legs gave out. She collapsed onto the hardwood floor, weeping, pulling her knees tightly to her chest.

"Please," she begged, looking up at him. "Please."

Adam paused.

The static in his head suddenly spiked—a sharp, dissonant scratch against the holy silence. For a fraction of a second, he saw her aura change. It wasn't the black, suffocating smog of the rot. It was a chaotic, multicolored. Desperate.

He blinked, forcing the vision away. *Vanity,* he told himself. *She wants to live for herself, not for anyone else.*

"The world will be safer without your lies," Adam said, his voice tighter than before.

He stepped into the kitchen and retrieved a blade from the knife block, then returned to her.

He crouched down. He reached a hand to her forehead.

"Be not afraid," he whispered.

He felt the remaining resistance drain out of her. Her rigid shoulders dropped. The frantic, terrified pulse visible in the veins of her neck slowed, forced into a sluggish rhythm. The scream building in her throat dissolved into a long, ragged sigh.

"There," Adam said gently.

She stared up at him, the terror entirely gone, replaced by a glassy, vacant look. She wasn't seeing a monster anymore; she was seeing the inevitable. He held her gaze, letting her see his absolute conviction, showing no malice in this act. Only necessity.

"Why?" she said.

"Because you are infected," Adam said, reaching into his heavy coat. "Your vanity is a rot, Elizabeth. It blinds you. I am here to free you."

A single tear rolled down her cheek.

It took only a few seconds for him to unroll the sheet of plastic across the beige living room rug. She rested upon it, as he asked.

"It will all be okay, soon," he said.

The blade caught the amber light of the kitchen—a flash of silver against the beige.

She didn't scream and didn't scramble away. She simply watched the blade come while she was pinned to the plastic by the suffocating quiet he had draped over her mind.

"Close your eyes," he said.

She obeyed.

Then, she died.

Afterward, when the blood had stopped flowing, Adam stood over the body for a long time.

She looked peaceful, now. Didn't she?

He tilted his head. The deep lines of stress around her eyes were gone, yes. The fear was gone. But something was missing. With Randall, with Eric, there had been a glow in his chest—a residual warmth of the transition. A message from the Most High that the sacrifice had been a holy act.

He bit his lip as he waited for it—the approval that filled him after a cleansing.

But it didn't come.

He wiped the blade clean on a linen napkin taken from the dining table.

He should feel lighter. That was how it worked. You cut away the rot, and the burden lifted. The noise stopped.

But as he looked down at Dr. Carter, the absolute silence in his head fractured.

A high-pitched whine, like the feedback of a microphone, started to drill into his inner ear. It sounded like a woman screaming from a great distance.

He touched his nose. His fingers came away wet and red.

Bleeding again.

Adam frowned. He looked at his hands. They were trembling violently.

"Why?" he said to the empty room. "I cleansed her. I finished your work in her!"

The whine grew louder.

Did you? a voice in the static seemed to ask.

He stumbled backward, gripping the edge of the leather sofa to steady himself.

It wasn't enough. It wasn't right.

He sank onto the beige cushions, the expensive leather creaking beneath his weight. He stared at Dr. Carter's face. The way her dark hair fanned out against the clear plastic... it triggered a memory he hadn't touched in years.

Suddenly, the beige walls of the condo dissolved.

He was a child. The air smelled of wet leaves and freshly turned earth. Rain fell, cold and relentless, plastering his dark hair to his skull.

He stood in a backyard, looking down into a deep hole.

She was there. His mother.

She rested in the box—simple birch, rough-hewn—her hands folded neatly over her chest just like Dr. Carter's were now. Her face was pale, luminous in the gloom of the wet earth. She didn't look afraid anymore. She didn't look sad.

She looked perfect.

"She is at peace, Adam," a voice rasped from above him. "We have returned her to the silence."

Adam looked up in the memory. His father stood at the edge of the grave, a muddy shovel heavy in his hands.

Adam had not possessed the vision to see it then, but he knew it now, the truth radiating through time.

The rot.

It had rolled off his father in suffocating, black waves. It stained the rain. It poisoned the very air.

His father hadn't buried her to give her peace. He had buried her to hide his own sin. He had covered her light with dirt because it revealed his own darkness.

The whine in Adam's ear shrieked—a deafening crescendo of revelation.

Adam looked down at his own hands in the dim light of the condo. Bloody, they were clutching the blade tightly, just like his father had once clutched that shovel.

A cold, terrifying thought pierced his delusion: *What if I am not the cure? What if I am just like my father? What if I'm just the gravedigger?*

No. He was the Ministrant. He was chosen.

But doubt was taking root.

A disease might have begun in that pulpit. And perhaps... the disease was in his blood.

He stood up. The trembling in his hands stopped, forced into stillness by sheer, terrifying will.

He put a finger to his lips. The blood tasted like iron, like the wet earth in that grave, so long ago.

He must go back. He must finish what started in the rain when he was a boy.

But first, he must rescue Thomas.

THIRTY-TWO

THE HOLDING CELL IN THE BASEMENT OF THE NESBETT Courthouse smelled of industrial disinfectant, a scent that clung to the cinderblock walls like a layer of grease. The cold, windowless box served to strip a man of his dignity as well as his freedom.

Thomas Dillon huddled in the corner of the communal tank, his knees pulled tight to his chest. Vibrating.

It wasn't just the cold. It was the absence. For days, he had been cut off from Adam. The peace Adam gave him had faded, drained by the fluorescent lights and the impersonal hands of the officers. Instead, the old noise returned to his mind, bringing the crushing weight of every mistake he had ever made.

"Dillon! Front and center!"

The voice boomed from the other side of the bars. A Judicial Services Officer—a thick-necked man with a buzz cut—stood holding a set of leg irons and belly chains.

Thomas squeezed his eyes shut. "No."

"We're not doing this again, Dillon. I told you when I picked you up from the jail, the judge is tired of waiting for you upstairs and has ordered you to show. Get your ass up."

"I can't," Thomas said. His teeth chattered, a staccato rhythm of panic. "I can't go out there. Not without him."

The cell door slid open with a heavy metallic clank. Two officers stepped in. They moved with the bored efficiency of men who handled the worst of humankind for a living.

"I have rights! I want to see my friend first!" Thomas pleaded.

One moved close. "Judge said, 'By any means necessary,' so you're going." He grabbed Thomas by the left arm, forcefully.

"Okay!" Thomas gasped and stopped resisting.

A moment later, the cold steel of the cuffs bit into his wrists as they were attached to the belly chains. The shackles snapped around his ankles, leaving a heavy chain dragging between his feet.

Without Adam, the world cut too sharp, too loud. He felt exposed, flayed open.

Thomas sobbed, snot running down his face. "Please, I've already confessed. I'll sign whatever you want. Just don't make me go out there alone."

They dragged him down the hallway, the chains rattling. Thomas hung his head, watching his orange slippers shuffle across the cold tiles. Alone. Adam had abandoned him. Lena, too. He was a junkie who killed for a lie, and now the world would eat him alive.

The elevator ride became a silent ascent into hell. When the elevator doors opened on the third floor, the noise hit him first.

Even through the closed oak doors of Courtroom 301, the hum of the crowd buzzed like a hive of angry hornets.

"Stand up straight," the officer said, gripping Thomas's biceps.

The doors swung open. It was bright. And loud. Thomas squinted, ducking his head, trying to shrink inside the oversized jumpsuit.

They led him to the defense table, where he joined his public defender. He'd met with her for five minutes a couple of days ago at the jail—a harried woman with coffee stains on her blouse.

A few minutes later, everyone rose as the judge entered the chamber and took her seat.

"Thomas Dillon," the judge said. "You are charged with three counts of murder in the first degree..."

Thomas didn't hear the rest. His heart thundered, a frantic

drumbeat that drowned out the legal jargon. He risked a glance over his shoulder.

Reporters with hungry eyes. Civilians with angry faces. Police officers, arms crossed, staring at him with pure hatred. A woman detective in the front row, a badge on her belt, looking smug.

They all wanted him dead. He knew it. The hostility radiated off them like heat from an oven.

Thomas started to shake again. He couldn't do this. He was going to vomit.

And then he saw *him*.

Sitting in the very back row, tucked into the shadow of a support pillar, was a young man in a dark wool coat. He looked like a college student who had wandered into the wrong lecture. His hands were folded calmly in his lap.

Adam.

Thomas's breath caught in his throat.

Adam wasn't looking at the judge. He wasn't looking at the cameras. His eyes were locked on Thomas.

He didn't smile. He didn't wave. He simply offered a single, imperceptible nod. A slow lowering of the chin as if to say, *I am here.*

Thomas's shoulders dropped. The shaking in his hands stopped. The roar of the blood in his ears vanished, replaced by a profound, velvety silence.

The fear evaporated. The entire courtroom seemed to quiet down.

He wasn't a prisoner anymore. He was a disciple once again. Suffering for the cause. And his master was watching.

"Mr. Dillon?" the judge asked, peering over her spectacles. "Do you understand the charges?"

Thomas turned back to the bench. He stood up straight, the chains clanking. He didn't look at his lawyer. He looked the judge in the eye.

"I understand," Thomas said. His voice was steady and clear.

The public defender blinked, clearly surprised by the sudden composure of her client. "Your Honor, we enter a plea of not guilty."

"Remanded without bail," the judge said, banging the gavel. "Next hearing is set for…"

Thomas didn't care about the dates. He didn't care about prison. He turned around, scanning the back of the room again.

The seat by the pillar was empty.

Adam was gone.

A smile touched Thomas's lips—not a nervous twitch, but a serene expression.

He has not abandoned me.

Outside, the Anchorage afternoon was gray and biting. The wind whipped down 4th Avenue, carrying the exhaust of idling cars.

Lena sat behind the wheel of a stolen Toyota Camry, her knuckles white as she gripped the steering wheel. The car was parked in a loading zone half a block down from the courthouse's east-side vehicle sally port—a large metal garage door. The engine hummed, the heater blasting, but she couldn't stop shivering.

This was insanity.

He's going to get us killed, she thought. *He's going to get himself killed.*

She watched the heavy steel roll-up door of the sally port. Where the vans came out. Vans with cops.

And Adam… Adam was just standing there.

It was the third day in a row that they'd come here, hoping for the arraignment to happen. It finally did. At no time did Adam complain about the cold. He never wondered out loud why Thomas hadn't been arraigned yet. He just waited patiently, as if he wasn't a man at all, but a part of nature itself. Strong. Inevitable.

He had exited the building fifteen minutes ago, walked to her door and told her it was happening. Today. He then walked to the sidewalk directly in front of the vehicle exit and stopped.

He now stood with his back to the street, facing the sally port. He looked small against the imposing architecture of the court-house. A young man in a coat.

Pedestrians walked past him, heads down against the wind. A few glanced at him, curious why he stood in the cold for so long, but they kept moving. Adam had that way about him—he could be the center of the universe or completely invisible, if that is what he needed.

Lena checked the rearview mirror. A police cruiser drove past, heading the other way. The officer didn't even turn his head.

How did he do that? How did he make himself part of the scenery?

The metal gate of the sally port rattled. It rose slowly, revealing the dark maw of the garage.

"Oh God," Lena breathed. She shifted the car into drive, her foot hovering on the brake.

A blue Ford transport van—unmarked, heavy-duty—nosed out of the darkness.

It rolled forward, gathering speed to merge into traffic.

And Adam didn't move.

Officer Barnes loved his job as a Court Services Officer, but loathed transporting prisoners. It was boring, the prison smelled like feet, and the midday traffic in downtown Anchorage was often a night-mare. He would much rather have been retrieving a fugitive on an out-of-state extradition, darting about the city serving writs, or even doing an eviction. That felt like real police work. But this?

"Let's get this guy back and grab some lunch," his partner, Officer Graves, said from the passenger seat. "I'm starving."

Barnes eased the van out of the garage, checking for pedestrians.

"Clear left," Graves said. "Clear ri—whoa."

Barnes slammed on the brakes. The heavy van lurched to a halt, the suspension groaning.

Standing directly in the center of the driveway, not ten feet from their bumper, was a guy.

"The hell is this idiot doing?" Barnes grumbled. He laid on the horn. *HONK.*

The man didn't flinch. He didn't jump. He didn't look at his phone. He just stood there, staring through the windshield with a terrifyingly blank expression.

"Move!" Graves yelled through the glass.

Barnes hit the siren—a quick *whoop-whoop* to startle the man.

Nothing. He remained planted, as still as a statue.

"Is he deaf?" Barnes asked, his irritation spiking into genuine anger. "I'm gonna go move him."

"Careful," Graves said, his hand resting on his radio. "Could be an ambush. Or a mental case."

Barnes unbuckled his seatbelt. "He's alone. I think we can handle him."

He reached for his mic to call dispatch when the man looked straight at Barnes.

And then it hit him.

It wasn't a sound. It wasn't a weapon. It was a wave.

It began at the base of Barnes's skull—a sudden, heavy warmth that washed down his spine and pooled in his stomach. It felt like that moment right before you fall asleep, that heavy, dragging gravity of exhaustion.

His anger... vanished.

It didn't just fade; it was deleted. The urgency of the transport, the hunger for lunch, the irritation at the pedestrian—it all seemed suddenly, profoundly unimportant.

His hand fell away from the door handle.

"Man," Graves murmured from the passenger seat. His voice was thick, slurred. "I feel..."

"Yeah," Barnes said. He blinked slowly. The world slowed down. Colors dulled. The sky looked soft. Comforting.

Why were they in a hurry? What was the point?

The man outside walked calmly to the driver's door.

Barnes watched him come close. Part of his brain—the trained part, the cop part—screamed a warning. *Secure the vehicle. Draw your weapon. Suspect approaching.*

But the scream sounded like it came from underwater. Distant. Irrelevant.

The man pointed at the door. He wanted Barnes to open it. What was the harm?

The door opened.

Barnes didn't reach for his gun. He didn't close the door. He just looked down at the young man.

Dark eyes. Deep, endless eyes.

"Shhh," the man said. He reached across Barnes toward the ignition.

Barnes smelled ozone and rain. The young man's arm brushed past his chest like a blessing.

His hand closed around the ignition key. He turned it off.

The engine died. The silence in the cab was absolute.

"It's all going to be okay," the young man whispered. He pulled the keys out.

Barnes let out a long, shuddering breath. "Okay," he said.

Then the man turned and walked toward the back of the van.

Barnes leaned his head back against the headrest. Heavy. Good. He closed his eyes.

In the back of the van, Thomas Dillon pressed against the wire mesh of the cage, watching.

He couldn't hear what was happening, but he felt the shift. The van had stopped. The engine died.

And the peace—the heavy, suffocating, blissful peace—rolled into the vehicle in waves.

The latch on the back door clicked.

Daylight flooded the compartment.

Adam stood there, framed by the open sally port behind him.

He held the keys in his hand. He didn't look hurried. He didn't look worried.

He unlocked the cage door. It swung open with a squeak.

"Come, Thomas," Adam said. His voice was low, but it carried the weight of a mountain. "The harvest waits."

Thomas moved forward slowly, the leg irons shortening his stride to a shuffle. He almost fell out of the back of the van, but Adam caught him.

Adam's hand was strong. He steadied Thomas, then half-lifted, half-guided Thomas back to his feet.

"We do not run," Adam said. "We walk."

Adam took Thomas's arm. He led him down the sidewalk.

A woman with a stroller walked toward them. She looked up, saw the man in the orange jumpsuit and shackles. Her eyes widened. She opened her mouth to scream or shout.

Adam turned his head to look at her.

The woman's expression went slack. She blinked, looked confused, and then turned her attention to her baby, pushing the stroller past them as if they were nothing more than a shadow on the wall.

A miracle. Thomas wept silently as he shuffled. They were invisible. They were ghosts walking through the world.

A gray sedan pulled up to the curb ten yards ahead. The passenger door flew open.

Lena sat behind the wheel, her face pale as a sheet.

Adam opened the back door. "In."

Thomas scrambled inside, dragging his chains. He laid down across the backseat, curling into a ball.

Adam slid into the front passenger seat, then closed the door.

"Drive," Adam said.

Lena didn't ask questions. She stomped on the gas. The car lurched away from the curb, merging into the flow of Anchorage traffic.

Inside the van, the spell broke like a window shattering.

Officer Barnes gasped, his eyes snapping open. The heavy, warm fog in his brain evaporated, replaced instantly by a spike of adrenaline so sharp it made him nauseous.

"What..." He looked down. The engine was off. The keys were gone.

He looked at Graves. His partner shook his head, blinking rapidly, looking around with wild, panicked eyes.

"Where did he go?" Graves shouted. "Where is that man?"

Barnes twisted in his seat to look through the mesh partition.

The back door was open, the prisoner was gone.

"Oh my God," Barnes breathed. The reality of what had just happened crashed down on him. They had been neutralized. Without a shot fired. Without a struggle.

They just sat there and let it happen... and felt good about it.

He grabbed the mic to the radio on his belt, his hand shaking so hard he almost dropped it.

"Matcom, 3-J-19!" he screamed, his voice cracking. "10-33! Emergency traffic! We have a prisoner escape! 4th Avenue outside Nesbett Courthouse! Suspects are... gone! They're just... gone!"

THIRTY-THREE

A FEW DAYS AGO, THE TASK FORCE'S WAR ROOM AT THE
Alaska Bureau of Investigation was a place of controlled chaos—
phones ringing, dry-erase markers squeaking against whiteboards,
the low hum of professional urgency.

Today, it was a tomb.

Lieutenant Kincaid stood before the main monitor wall, his
arms crossed so tightly that the fabric of his pin-striped dress shirt
strained at the seams. Sergeant Ballack stood beside him, looking
like a man who had just swallowed a mouthful of broken glass.

On the screen, high-definition footage from the courthouse
sally port played on an endless loop.

It was crisp. It was undeniable.

The gray, grainy ghost from the Talkeetna gas station
surveillance was gone. In his place was a young man in high resolution. He stood in the center of the driveway, hands at his sides, face
turned slightly toward the camera as the heavy transport van idled
helplessly before him.

Facial recognition software from the Feds had already run the
capture against the state DMV database. The match probability
hovered over ninety percent.

Basu, Adam. Age 22.

Kincaid stared at the image of the man who had just dismantled a prisoner transport team without drawing a weapon. They didn't need facial recognition software to see that Basu was their guy; placing the DMV photo side-by-side with the sally port still frame made it painfully obvious.

"He didn't even flinch," Kincaid said, his voice dangerous and low. "He stood in front of a four-ton vehicle and stopped them with a look."

"It matches the mechanics of the first two kills," Ballack said, though he sounded like he wished he was wrong. "No struggle. Complete compliance. Ward was right."

The door to the room banged open.

Detective Vanessa Miller strode in with an older investigator at her side. He was mostly bald and wore a worn leather jacket. Miller looked rattled. Her hair was windblown, and she gripped her tablet like it was a shield. She didn't wait for permission to speak.

"We found the sedan used in the courthouse escape—a Toyota Camry," she announced. "Abandoned in a parking lot off 3rd Avenue. Cell phone with a dead battery left in the glove compartment. But we lost them."

Kincaid turned slowly. "Lost them how? We have air assets up. We have the entire downtown grid locked down."

"They switched vehicles," Miller said. She threw her tablet onto the conference table, sliding it toward the bosses. "And Lieutenant, you will not believe how."

"Try me," Kincaid snapped.

The older investigator in the leather jacket piped up. "Miller interviewed a witness outside an eye care clinic—"

"Sir, this is Rod Hawthorne, a consultant from the FBI Behavioral Analysis Unit," Miller said. "Chief told me he's to work lockstep with us on this."

"Yeah, I got the message this morning," Kincaid said, giving a curt nod. "Nice to meet you, Rod. Continue."

Hawthorne cleared his throat. "The witness saw them ditch the sedan. Then, Basu approached a woman and her baby in the parking lot across the street. She was leaving a doctor's appointment. They took her Dodge Caravan."

"Carjacking," Ballack groaned. "Please tell me the kid is okay."

Miller looked at Ballack, her expression haunted. "They are fine. Dropped off a couple miles away. Here's the thing, Sarge. It wasn't a carjacking. Not in any way that makes sense."

She tapped the tablet's screen, pulling up her interview notes.

"The witness said Basu walked right up to her. No gun. No knife. He just... talked to her. For maybe five seconds. And then she smiled."

"She *smiled*?" Kincaid repeated in disbelief.

"She smiled and she opened the sliding door for Dillon," Miller said. "She helped a fugitive in leg irons and an orange jumpsuit climb into the backseat next to her infant son. Witness said she looked happy. Like she was picking up family from the airport."

The room went dead silent.

"The woman was chatting amiably with them as they drove off," Miller continued, her voice shaking slightly. "Just pulled right out into traffic like it was a Sunday outing. Her name was Sarah Jenkins—took a cab home after calling us."

Miller swallowed hard, her hand trembling as she swiped to the next screen on her tablet.

"And that's not all," she said, her voice dropping an octave. "I just got a message from dispatch. A housekeeper walked into a condo on Tudor Road a few minutes ago. She found the owner dead."

Kincaid's eyes narrowed. "Who?"

"A local psychiatrist," Miller said. "Patrol is on scene now. Throat slashed."

Ballack swore under his breath. "Another one?"

Kincaid shook his head. "Better head over there now, Miller."

Miller nodded, then left the room.

Kincaid ran a hand heavily over his face, dragging the skin down. "He overpowered a transport van without firing a shot, broke a serial killer out of custody, and then carjacked a mother and her infant? All right after murdering a shrink?"

Ballack looked at the screen again, staring at Adam Basu's calm, terrifyingly young face.

"Is he using some sort of chemical weapon?" Ballack asked. "Something that numbs people near him, calms them down, but doesn't affect him? Some new tech?"

Kincaid stared at the floor for a long moment. When he looked up, the arrogance that usually armored him was entirely gone, replaced by the grim calculation of a man realizing he was fighting a war he didn't understand.

"We've been chasing the wrong dog," Kincaid admitted.

"Ward knew," Ballack said. "He tried to tell us."

"He did." Kincaid gave a single, sharp nod. "Get him in here."

Ward walked into the briefing room ten minutes later.

He didn't gloat. He didn't shoot Miller an *I told you so* smirk, and he didn't wait for an apology from Kincaid. He just walked to the front of the room, plugged his laptop into the projector system, and waited for the massive screen to flicker to life.

The room was packed now—command staff from APD, the Troopers, and the U.S. Marshals had filed in. They were all looking at him.

Ward pulled up a file.

"Adam Basu," Ward said.

The name hung heavily in the air.

"We have the name," Kincaid said from the front row. "We got the hit off the sally port cam footage and the DMV. What we need to know is how you had it before we did."

Ward tapped a key. A spreadsheet filled the screen—thousands of rows of raw telecom data.

"This is the tower dump from the Talkeetna crime scene," Ward said. "I ran a script against the raw data to filter for subscriber devices present precisely during the window of Randall Tibeluk's murder. It spat out a lot of noise, but it gave me a few hits on young males who lingered at the scene, rather than just driving by on the highway. I tracked down one hit that mattered."

He highlighted a specific row.

907-555-0199 ... BASU, ADAM.

"He was there," Ward said. "While Tibeluk was bleeding out, Adam Basu's phone was pinging the tower less than a hundred yards away."

"Why didn't you bring this to us sooner?" Miller asked, though her voice lacked its usual sharp bite.

"Because you already had your guy, and you wouldn't listen to me. I needed something concrete to convince you, so I started digging. And I found it."

He clicked to the next slide. A newspaper clipping photo appeared, showing a younger Adam Basu standing proudly next to a high school science fair project.

"The phone just puts him near the scene," Ward continued. "It doesn't explain *why* he's doing this. For that, you have to look at where he came from."

"He's an addict," Kincaid said. "We pulled his record. He was caught with drugs on campus."

"He's a physicist," Ward said. "The drugs were Adderall, used to stay awake so he could study harder, not necessarily because he was looking for a high. It's not the same thing. Make no mistake, this kid is focused."

Ward let that sink in before continuing. "He had early enrollment at UAA. His faculty advisor was Professor Jan Mueller."

A visible ripple of recognition went through Ballack, who was standing a few feet away. Mueller was dead, but the university professor's deep connection to Richard Pagan's illicit research facility was a horrifying, open secret within the department's inner circle.

"Basu was recruited, exactly like Belle Anderson before him, by Mueller, and handed off directly to Richard Pagan," Ward said, his voice tightening. "He was fed into the same meat grinder I fell into. Basu didn't die, either. But his mind did break. And then, he found a way to put himself back together."

Ward clicked the presenter remote again. A new photo appeared.

It wasn't a crime scene. It was a screenshot of a church website. The image depicted a modest, vinyl-sided church building in Big Lake. Ward clicked to the next photo, showing a stark banner hanging directly behind a wooden pulpit.

PURIFICATION THROUGH SACRIFICE.

"I went to see his father yesterday," Ward said. "Malik Basu. He pastors this church."

Ballack sat up straighter. "You interviewed the father?"

"I did," Ward said. "And that's where the motive lives. Adam didn't hallucinate his theology in Pagan's lab. He learned it at his kitchen table. His father preaches a dark doctrine of literal cleansing —nothing like modern Judaism or Christianity. If anything, Malik Basu's ideology mirrors some of the forceful tenets of radical Islam. He believes sin is a physical rot that must be violently cut out. He uses the specific word 'Ministrant' to describe the hand of God that does the cutting."

Ward looked around the quiet room, making eye contact with Miller, then Kincaid. He noticed the new guy sitting next to Miller —the older man with steely eyes and the worn leather jacket. Hawthorne. The Fed.

"According to court records, the wife has been out of the picture for years. Ran out on the family when Adam was a kid; father got full custody. So there was nothing but his father's influence for his formative years."

The room was still quiet.

"Adam believes he is the hand of justice from his father's sermons," Ward continued. "He isn't killing for the thrill. He believes he is performing a medical procedure on a sick world."

"So he has some ability to brainwash people," Miller said, clearly struggling to process it.

"He didn't brainwash them," Ward said. "He removed their fear. He has the ability to take away the biological alarm bells that tell you to run or fight. Without fear, there is no resistance. Without resistance, there is only total compliance. It's a physiological adaptation he learned when he was a lab rat under Pagan's thumb and he's found some way to broadcast it."

They all knew Ward's terrifying history with Pagan. They knew he'd had a firsthand view of the same madness that warped Adam Basu. Ward sounded crazy right now, but he was the only one with all the pieces, and the silence in the room told him they were finally listening.

What else could they do?

Kincaid stood up slowly. He walked to the screen, staring hard at the photo of the church.

"So we have a name," Kincaid said. "We have a motive. And we have a profile."

"He's not hiding," Ward warned them. "He's refining. He started with a homeless man in a parking lot. Then a man in a secluded park. Now he's doing prison breaks at courthouses and converting citizens in broad daylight. He's escalating."

"Where is he going?" Ballack asked.

Ward looked at the map on the screen.

"I don't know if he tried to pass the torch to Thomas Dillon, or if Dillon took it upon himself," Ward said. "Either way, Dillon failed to duplicate the precise 'ritual,' which is what tipped us off that it was a different suspect."

His use of the word 'us' was charitable, but Ward hoped his effort to be a team player would repair the sudden rift he'd created with the bosses.

Ward clicked the remote one last time. The screen went black.

"But sooner or later, Basu is going to realize that these murders aren't satisfying him. He's living out a dysfunction that was taught by his father, but according to my interview with that man, he hasn't even heard from Adam in over a year. I believe him, but I have the gut feeling that Adam *will* go back," Ward said. "He's going to go for the source. He's going back to the man who first taught him about the rot."

"You think he's going to kill his own father?" Miller asked.

"He will at least contact him," Ward said. "Confront him. In person. If we want to catch Basu, we don't search for Thomas Dillon in an orange jumpsuit. Or a vehicle. Basu could have switched vehicles three times by now."

"Then what do we do?" Ballack asked.

"We go to the church," Ward said.

Kincaid stood up, his expression resolute.

"Ward, you're lead on the intelligence. Whatever you need, you get it."

"What I need is for us to get there before Adam does," Ward said. "And then we wait."

THIRTY-FOUR

ACCORDING TO THE CELL PROVIDER, BASU'S PHONE HAD gone silent. Technical Crimes confirmed it was the same device recovered from the abandoned Camry, making tracking of Basu no longer possible.

A cold, morning stakeout in Big Lake was their only remaining play.

Ten degrees below zero is the cold that turns the air into a physical weight. Under the vast, uncaring dome of the pre-dawn Alaskan morning, the woods surrounding the Church of the Sanctified Spirit stood like silent sentinels.

Ward leaned against the trunk of his assigned Ford Taurus, staring into the dark treeline. Behind him, the mobile command post—a black behemoth of an idling van—housed the brass. Inside, SWAT leaders, APD detectives, and a handful of troopers were busy monitoring the operation.

Ward wore no headset. He wasn't inside watching the glowing heat signatures of the tactical team lying prone in the snow.

He was feeling the pulse of the woods.

To Kincaid, to the SWAT commander, to the rest of the world, the perimeter seemed invisible. Ten highly trained, disciplined men held perfectly motionless. They were ghosts in white camouflage.

But to Ward, the setup felt... heavy.

It wasn't a specific sound or a visible flaw. It was the crushing, biological pressure of their presence. You couldn't pack that many armed men into a small patch of woods and expect the natural world to ignore it. Not with all their adrenaline and intent focused on a single point of impending violence. The ravens knew. The squirrels knew.

"Ward, get inside," Kincaid said, stepping out of the back of the command post with a steaming Styrofoam cup of coffee. "You're going to freeze to death out here."

Ward didn't turn. "It's too heavy, Lieutenant."

Kincaid frowned, looking out at the empty, ice-slicked road. "What are you talking about? We have total noise and light discipline. SWAT is invisible out there."

Invisible to eyes and ears, maybe, Ward thought. *But Basu is different.*

Ward desperately wanted to explain, but he bit his tongue. He knew exactly how it would sound. Kincaid hadn't been strapped to Pagan's metal table. He wasn't on the same wavelength. If Ward started talking about Belle Anderson's abilities, how they might be duplicated in some way in Basu, Kincaid would tell Ballack and Ward would go straight to a department shrink. They'd seen what Basu could do, but they didn't understand. Not really.

Ward rubbed his temples and carefully selected his words, offering a grounded, tactical translation instead.

"He's hyper-vigilant," Ward said, turning to face the APD Lieutenant. "He just pulled off a courthouse escape and multiple murders. He's going to be actively looking for a trap. An ambush this large... there are too many variables."

"We're doing it by the book," Kincaid said, his voice defensive. "Malik Basu is inside the church. When his son shows up to confront him, as you advised he will, we box him in. It's simple."

"Yeah, well, now I'm having a change of heart," Ward warned, keeping his voice level. "Basu operates differently. He's going to sense something is off before he even reaches the clearing, and he's going to bolt."

"He's a mental patient on a downward spiral, Jake," Kincaid said, shaking his head. "He won't know we're here until he feels the barrel of a rifle screwed into his ear."

Ward looked back at the trees.

"I hope you're right," Ward whispered.

A mile south, a silver Toyota Highlander moved slowly down the icy tarmac of Hollywood Road. They'd ditched the Dodge Caravan a few hours ago at the Walmart in East Anchorage and a little old man doing some late-night shopping had been all too willing to hand Adam his Toyota's keys.

Inside, the leather interior smelled strongly of vanilla air freshener. Lena sat behind the wheel. Her knuckles were white, her eyes darting constantly to the rearview mirror.

"Are we close?" she asked him.

Adam sat in the passenger seat, his head tipped back against the headrest.

"Yes," he said, smiling. He turned to look in the back seat.

Thomas Dillon sat still in the passenger seat behind Lena. He wasn't wearing his leg irons or belly chains anymore—a cuff key on the ring Adam had taken from the Court Services van had seen to that—but he still wore the bright orange jumpsuit, concealed beneath a heavy wool blanket they had taken from their apartment. Thomas now stared out the window at the passing trees, lips moving in a silent, frantic prayer.

Adam looked forward again. They were indeed approaching the turnoff for his father's church. The road curved ahead, disappearing into a dark tunnel of dense spruce.

He sat up, stiffly.

The air ahead wasn't empty. It was crowded. He looked through the windshield, squinting not at the physical road, but at something else.

He *saw* them.

They weren't men. To Adam, they appeared as jagged, violent spikes of red and gray light, rising from the snow like fiery thorns. They were everywhere—in the trees, in the ditch, and surrounding the small wooden building that sat in the clearing.

The aura of the ambush was so intense it almost blinded him. It was a forest of pure, concentrated hostility.

"What?" Lena gasped, seeing the sudden shift in his expression. "Did you see a cop?"

"More than one," Adam said.

He stared at the violent auras pulsating in the distance. They were waiting for him. The church wasn't his father's sanctuary anymore. It had been turned into a kill box.

"What do we do?" Thomas asked from the back seat, his voice trembling. "You said we had to confront the father. To cut out the root of the rot."

"We cannot cleanse what we cannot reach," Adam said.

He looked at the trap one last time. It was a crude thing. Loud. It lacked elegance.

"Just keep going straight," Adam ordered Lena. "Don't slow down. Don't look at them."

"Where are we going?" Lena asked, keeping her eyes locked straight ahead, terrified to even glance toward the church turnoff as they rolled past.

Adam didn't answer immediately. He turned his head, watching the angry red auras fade into the darkness behind them.

He felt suddenly unmoored. Floundering.

He had longed to confront his father. To diagnose the man who had first taught him about the rot. He needed that closure.

It didn't matter now. That way was shut.

He needed guidance. To understand the grand design.

"The library," Adam said suddenly.

Lena glanced at him. "The library? Adam, it's still too early. Everything is closed."

"Then we find a dark place to park, we sleep, and we go later."

"Why?" Lena asked. "What are we looking for?"

Adam looked down at his hands. They were steady now, but his spirit still ached from the hollow, echoing failure of Dr. Carter's death.

"I need to know where I came from," Adam said. "I wanted to confront my father, but he isn't the source. I need to find the one who made me."

Near the center of town, the Wasilla Public Library—a modern structure of glass and timber—sat quiet and dark. In its empty parking lot, the stolen Highlander idled, its heater fighting against the bitter morning chill while Lena and Thomas slept, slumped heavily against the windows.

But Adam couldn't sleep. He sat upright in the front passenger seat, thinking. Remembering.

He was revisiting the fragmented memories that still lingered in his mind about Richard Pagan's lab. He remembered the pain, the cold metal table, and ultimately, the agonizing gift that had propelled him forward. His holy mission hadn't come from his father's pulpit. It had come from Dr. Pagan.

Pagan was a prophet. A dark angel. Somehow, he was a Ministrant in his own right.

Adam needed to find him. Pagan would have answers. He could explain the noise returning to Adam's head, and the terrifying lack of fulfillment Adam felt after killing Dr. Carter.

But Adam didn't know where the lab was—it had been months since he'd been in that facility—and for all he knew, Pagan was long gone.

It was almost 8:00 a.m. when the heavy glass doors to the library finally unlocked.

Adam left Lena and Thomas in the running car.

"Keep the engine on," he told Lena, touching her shoulder lightly to wake her. "Do not look at anyone."

He walked into the vestibule. It smelled strongly of floor wax and old paper.

He found his way to the public bank of computers. His reflection in the dark glass of the monitor looked ghostly—hollow cheeks, pale skin.

He woke the computer and opened a browser window. His long fingers danced across the keyboard.

He typed: *Richard Pagan Alaska.*

The screen populated instantly.

SCIENTIST KILLED IN STANDOFF AT REMOTE LODGE

TROOPER KIDNAPPED, SURVIVES ORDEAL

LAB OF HORRORS DISCOVERED IN THE MAT-SU VALLEY

Adam clicked the first article. The dateline was six months ago.

He read voraciously, his eyes scanning the dense text. He read the sanitized media accounts about "unethical experiments" involving sensory deprivation and illicit drugs. He read about two bodies found buried on the property.

And then, he saw it.

"The standoff ended when Investigator Jake Ward, who had been held captive and tortured by Pagan, managed to free himself and fatally shoot the suspect."

Adam froze.

Pagan was dead.

It was unthinkable. He *needed* him. He had questions!

What would he do now?

Wait. There was another.

Jake Ward is his name.

Could he be… like me?

Adam clicked the blue hyperlink on the name. A news photo loaded on the screen.

It showed Ward sitting on the edge of an ambulance gurney, being examined by paramedics in the snow. His clothes were covered in blood. His face was a haunted mask—a thousand-yard stare locked on nothing. He looked entirely shattered.

Adam knew that look. He had seen it in the mirror. He leaned in, his breath fogging the monitor. Ward wasn't just a cop chasing a lead. He had been a subject. He had been strapped to the very same table, survived the same horrors, and carried the same despair.

Adam scrolled down. There were more recent, smaller articles.

INVESTIGATOR WARD COMMENDED FOR PAGAN CASE

INVESTIGATOR WARD RETURNS TO DUTY

Adam closed his eyes, and suddenly, the fractured pieces of the world clicked into perfect, divine place.

The heavily armed police waiting at the church—that was blunt force. That was the blind, ignorant government.

But Ward? Ward was different.

"He drank from the same cup," Adam whispered to the library. "He knows what I know."

A profound sense of clarity washed over him. He wasn't alone at all.

There was another Ministrant. One who had denied his calling. One who still slept, fighting the holy gift, trying to live in the noisy, rotting world of laws and badges.

Adam reached out and touched the screen, his fingertip tracing the sharp line of Ward's jaw in the photo.

"You are in pain, Jake," Adam said. "I can feel it. You are carrying the static, just like I was."

He knew exactly what to do.

His father was lost. Malik Basu was the past.

Jake Ward was the future.

If Adam could bring Ward back to the source—back to the lab where it all started—Ward would wake up. He would see the truth. They could finish the great work together.

But Ward wouldn't come willingly. He was too deep in the sleep. The fact that he was still acting as an agent of the government proved it. The man needed a push.

Adam stood up. He felt energized, divine purpose returning to his limbs with the violent force of a lightning strike.

He needed leverage. He needed to find out where Ward lived, or maybe where he worked.

He walked swiftly back out to the car.

Lena looked up anxiously as he pulled the car door open. "Did you find him? Did you find Pagan?"

"I found something much better," Adam said, sliding into the warm leather seat. "I found a brother."

He pointed toward the main road.

"Drive to Palmer," Adam commanded. "To the State Trooper post. I have an errand to run."

"Palmer?" Lena asked, her voice spiking with panic. "You want to drive straight to the cops?"

"Yes, I do," Adam said, a terrifying smile touching his lips. "We aren't hiding anymore."

THIRTY-FIVE

The building that housed the Alaska State Troopers detachment in Palmer was a study in sterile bureaucracy. A small entryway led to two public restrooms and a long, wooden bench that looked anything but comfortable.

Behind the bulletproof glass partition, Becky, the fifty-something front desk clerk, was trying to wake up while organizing a stack of files, frustrated at a million things that had happened in her chaotic life lately. Her daughter was in treatment. Her marriage of twenty years was on the rocks, and the rent was overdue.

She arrived to work today without crying, but she was confident she wouldn't make it past lunch.

The clock on the wall read 9:15 a.m.

Outside, the wind was howling, rattling the double doors. Becky shivered, pulling her cardigan tighter around her shoulders.

The outer door opened with a gust of blowing snow.

Becky looked up, expecting a delivery or a citizen requesting a copy of a police report.

A young man walked in.

He was slight, pale, dressed in a gray wool coat that looked insufficient to ward away the cold. He kicked the snow off his boots on the entryway mat and approached the glass.

He didn't look like the usual morning clientele—no urgency at all. He looked calm.

Becky keyed the intercom. "Can I help you?"

The young man smiled. It was a small, sad smile that seemed to reach right through the glass.

"I hope so," he said. His voice was soft, muffled slightly by the partition. "I'm looking for Investigator Ward. Jake Ward."

Becky frowned, glancing at the roster. "Investigator Ward doesn't work here. Well, not often. He's assigned to a unit in Anchorage. I can get a patrol officer to help you. What's this regarding?"

"Just a debt of gratitude. I'd like to speak with him."

He leaned closer to the glass. More people came into the lobby behind him, an old man and a couple, but she couldn't tear her eyes off the young man in front of her. His eyes were captivating.

"He helped me," he said. "But, I never got to thank him. I have something for him—a gift. I didn't want to leave it in the cold."

"You can leave it with me," Becky said. "I'll make sure he gets it when he checks in."

"I would," the young man said, "but it is fragile. And personal. I was hoping to just drop it on his porch. Let him find it when he gets home. A surprise."

Becky opened her mouth to recite the policy—*we cannot release home addresses of officers*—but the words died in her throat.

The young man placed his hand on the glass. Becky felt it instantly.

The cold draft in the lobby vanished. The fluorescent lights, usually so harsh and buzzing, seemed to soften into a warm, golden glow. A beautiful silence descended over her mind, quieting the boredom, the fatigue, the anxiety about her daughter. Her marriage.

It felt like sinking into a hot bath after a long walk in the snow. A peace she hadn't felt in years.

She looked at the young man's eyes—dark and endless. They weren't asking; they were inviting. The warmth in her mind was immediately associated with this young face staring at her. An angel of rest. The stress she carried with her every day was gone.

Why was I being so difficult to him? Becky thought, her mind sluggish and happy. *He just wants to say thank you. He's a good person. You can see it.*

But if she gave out the address, would she get in trouble with her supervisor? Probably. But that consequence was a distant notion, invoking no concern at all. All she cared about was the peace.

"He has an apartment here in town," Becky heard herself say. Her voice sounded distant, like it was coming from someone else.

"Is it far?" the young man asked.

"No," Becky said. She typed on her keyboard: *WARD, Jacob.* The address popped up on the screen. She was so glad she could help this nice young man.

"He's at the condos," she said, reading the screen. "On Elmwood Street. Unit 4B. The buildings with the blue siding."

"Unit 4B," the young man repeated. "Thank you. You are very kind."

"I try," Becky said, smiling.

She wrote it down on a yellow sticky note. She slid it through the metal pass-through tray beneath the glass.

The young man took the note. He folded it carefully and placed it in his pocket.

"Bless you," he said.

"You too," Becky said.

He turned and walked out.

Becky sat for a long time, staring at the empty lobby, a goofy smile plastered on her face. She felt wonderful. Light.

She should tell Investigator Ward the good news. She picked up the phone.

At the command post on Big Lake Road, the mood was funereal.

The sun wasn't up yet, but the darkness had shifted to a bruised purple. The ambush was a bust. The tactical teams were coming out of the woods, stiff with cold, their breath pluming in the air.

Investigator Ward sat in the back of the van.

"He knew," Ward said to the metal floor. "He must have seen us."

"We were hidden, Ward," Kincaid said, though he lacked his earlier fire. He was pouring coffee from a thermos, his hand shaking slightly from the caffeine and the cold. "Maybe he just didn't come. Maybe he fled north."

"He must have come," Ward said. "Probably one of those cars that passed by—he got close, sensed the trap, and turned around."

Ward stood up, pacing the small space. The anxiety was crawling under his skin like ants.

Adam Basu wasn't running. Ward knew that now. The profile he had given the brass—the zealot—was accurate, but it was incomplete.

If he couldn't get to his father, where would he go?

Ward had no idea.

His phone rang. It was the main line at Palmer Post.

"Ward."

"Investigator Ward," the voice said. It was Becky, one of the front desk clerks. "Hello."

"A man. He just missed you. He was so nice."

Ward froze. The hair on the back of his neck stood up.

"Who was nice, Becky?"

"The young man. He came in a few minutes ago. He wanted to speak with you."

Ward gripped the phone so hard the plastic creaked. "Becky. Listen to me. What did he look like?"

"Just... nice," she said. "Gray coat. Dark eyes. He had something for you."

"Did he leave it?"

"No," Becky said. "He wanted to surprise you. So I gave him your address."

The world stopped. The sound of the command post—the radio chatter, Kincaid's breathing, the wind outside—dropped away into a terrifying silence.

"You did what?" Ward asked.

"I gave him the address," Becky said, sounding confused now. "For your condo. On Elmwood. Was... was that okay?"

Ward didn't answer.

"Ward?" Kincaid asked, turning around. "What is it?"

Ward looked at him. His face was gray.

"He's not running north," Ward said, his voice strangling in his throat. "He's hunting."

"Who?"

"Me," Ward said. He grabbed his keys from the table.

Ward looked at his watch. The date. It was a state holiday—school was out.

"Ward, wait!" Kincaid said.

"There's no time!" Ward said, shoving past him. He burst out of the command post and sprinted to his car, the engine soon roaring to life.

As he peeled out onto the icy road, only one image filled his mind.

Emma.

She had a key. She went there to study, to get away from her mom, or just to watch TV.

If she was there this morning...

Ward slammed his foot to the floor, the speedometer climbing. Palmer Post was so much closer—Basu had a huge head start.

Please, he prayed to a God he hadn't spoken with in ages. *Not Emma.*

THIRTY-SIX

Thomas felt the Highlander slow, its tires
crunching onto the gravel shoulder of a desolate side street just off
the Glenn Highway.

He peered out the window. In the distance, the jagged silhouette
of Pioneer Peak struggled to pierce the hazy, gray light of the rising
sun. Through his exhausted, jittery gaze, the scattered neighbor-
hoods, strip malls, and copses of spruce all blurred together.

"Here," Adam said.

Lena braked hard, throwing Thomas forward against his seatbelt as she shifted the SUV into park.

"Why are we stopping?" Thomas asked from the back seat. He
pulled the scratchy blanket tighter around his shoulders, shivering
violently inside his thin orange jumpsuit.

"Because the road narrows here," Adam said. "And the path is
only wide enough for two."

Adam opened his door, and the biting wind instantly swirled
into the warm cabin, stealing Thomas's breath. He watched as
Adam stepped out onto the ice and drew himself up to his full
height. From where Thomas sat looking up, Adam appeared as an
immovable pillar of calm against the bleak morning sky.

Then Adam pulled the rear door open.

"Out."

Thomas blinked, tears of confusion pricking his eyes. "What? Is there a safe house? Are we meeting someone?"

"No," Adam said. "You are at the end of your service. Thank you."

Reluctantly, Thomas slid out into the freezing air, almost tripping over one of his prison-issue flip-flops. Without the protective shell of the vehicle, the cold bit straight into his bones. He hunched his shoulders, pulling his arms tight across his chest and curling inward to protect himself. Standing next to Adam's absolute stillness, Thomas felt tiny. He felt shattered. Pathetic. The wind whipped his thin, greasy hair across his face, but he didn't dare look away from his savior.

"I don't understand," Thomas stammered. "I'm ready. I can carry the burden for you."

"Right now, you *are* the burden," Adam said. To Thomas's horror, Adam didn't sound angry. He sounded perfectly calm, like a man setting down a heavy suitcase he no longer needed to carry. "You are loud, Thomas. You vibrate with fear. You need the peace just to breathe. A Ministrant does not need the medicine; he is the medicine."

"Please," Thomas whimpered. He reached out, his shaking hands grabbing fistfuls of Adam's coat. "Don't leave me. The noise... it can't come back. It will break me."

Adam peeled Thomas's trembling fingers off his coat, one by one.

"I have found a brother," Adam said. "One who walked through the fire and didn't burn. He is the partner I need. Not you."

Adam placed a flat hand against Thomas's chest. But he didn't project the holy peace. Thomas only felt the cold.

Adam pushed.

Thomas stumbled backward, falling hard onto the icy shoulder.

"The authorities will come," Adam commanded, looking down at him. "Tell them you were unworthy."

Adam got back into the car and pulled the door shut. He didn't look back.

"Adam!" Thomas screamed, the sound tearing out of his throat, raw and ugly.

The car pulled away, kicking up a harsh cloud of ice and gravel.

Thomas scrambled to his feet and ran a few steps after the tail-lights, slipping on the black ice, flailing under the blanket. He fell to his knees as the red lights faded into the gray morning mist.

The vast, frozen silence of the river valley descended on him.

But inside his head, the static screamed.

He curled into a ball on the side of the road and wailed.

THIRTY-SEVEN

THE CONDOMINIUM ON ELMWOOD STREET WAS QUIET.

Emma sat on Jake Ward's leather sofa, her legs tucked under her, a half-eaten Pop-Tart on the armrest. She was reading a paperback thriller—the kind with raised red lettering on the cover—but her eyes kept drifting to the clock on the wall.

10:00 a.m.

Jake wasn't home.

The only sound interrupting the quiet was the rhythmic bubbling of the aquarium filter in the corner of the living room. A couple of months ago, Jake had casually mentioned wanting a pet. A dog, maybe.

What an idiot, Emma had thought. *That guy is never home. How could he take care of a dog? The poor thing would be lonely as heck, and I'd be the one stuck walking it.*

So she had bought him a goldfish and a glass bowl, setting it squarely on his kitchen counter.

"A pet for you," she said when he finally came home.

He had laughed. A few days later, a high-end aquarium showed up in the living room.

She wondered where he was right now.

Not that she was worried about him. He was a trooper; long,

unpredictable shifts were part of the deal. But the local news had been relentless all morning, blaring updates about a serial killer and a brazen escape at the downtown courthouse in Anchorage.

The wall-to-wall coverage had spooked her enough that she didn't want to sit alone at her own house while her mom worked. Instead, she had let herself in using the spare key he kept hidden under the mat for "emergencies"—a term she loosely defined as when she needed Wi-Fi and snacks.

Besides, at least there was a fish to keep her company.

The apartment felt safe. It smelled like Old Spice, gun oil, and that specific, scentless clean of a person who didn't own enough clutter to gather dust.

The doorbell rang.

Emma jumped, exhaling a breath she hadn't realized she was holding.

He's home early. "Forgot your keys again, old man?" she said, unfolding her legs and standing up.

She walked toward the entryway in her oversized wool socks, sliding a bit on the laminate flooring. She didn't bother checking the peephole.

She unlocked the deadbolt and pulled the door open.

"You know, for a hotshot detective, you suck at—"

The words died in her throat.

It wasn't Jake.

Standing on the threshold was a man. He was tall but pale and slight, wrapped in a heavy gray wool coat that seemed to swallow him whole.

But it was his eyes that stopped her heart.

They were vast. Empty. And they were looking at her with an intimate familiarity that made her skin crawl.

"Hello," he said.

She tried to slam the door. It was pure, lizard-brain instinct.

A pale hand, impossibly fast, shot out and caught the edge of the door.

He didn't violently shove it open. He just held it in place. He wasn't even straining.

"Please," he said. "There is no need for noise."

"Get out!" Emma screamed, stumbling backward as the door was pushed open. She tripped over her own feet, her socks sliding on the laminate. "I'm calling the cops! Jake is a trooper!"

"I know," the young man said. He stepped inside and closed the door behind him. The deadbolt clicked shut. "That is why I am here."

He walked toward her.

Emma scrambled backward, knocking over a floor lamp. The bulb popped with a sharp crack. Panic seizing her throat, she grabbed the first weapon her hand found—a heavy hardback book sitting on the entryway table.

"Stay back!" she shrieked, raising the book like a club. Her hands were shaking violently.

The man stopped. He looked at the book, and then at her terrified face. He didn't look angry. He looked... sad.

"You are carrying so much weight," he said, then smiled. "Be not afraid."

The wave hit her.

It wasn't a physical force like wind or water. It was a sudden, crushing silence. A terrifying absence of feeling.

The heavy book suddenly felt ridiculous in her hand. Why was she holding it? It seemed silly. Dangerous, even. She should probably put it down before someone got hurt.

Her fingers went slack. The book slipped from her grip, falling to the floor.

Emma looked down at the mess. She knew she should be scared. She knew, logically, that a dangerous stranger was in the apartment and she was trapped. But the fear felt distant, like a police siren wailing miles away in another neighborhood.

Her knees felt loose. Warm.

"There," the soft voice said. He was closer now. "Better?"

Emma looked up. He was standing right in front of her. He smelled of ozone.

"Who are you?" she murmured, her tongue feeling thick and heavy in her mouth.

"I am the invitation," he said.

He offered her his hand.

"Come. My brother will be joining us."

Emma looked at his pale hand. It looked stable. Safe. She reached out, her own hand trembling—not with fear, but with gratitude.

As his long fingers closed around hers, the last spark of survival instinct in her mind flickered and went out.

On the couch, Emma's abandoned cell phone rang. The screen flashed brightly, displaying a photo of Jake Ward holding a fishbowl and smiling.

It went unanswered.

THIRTY-EIGHT

Lena sat in the driver's seat of the stolen Highlander, the engine idling, the heater blowing warm air against her frozen face.

She stared at the front door of the condominium. Unit 4B.

Adam had gone inside a few minutes ago.

He had told her to wait. He had said he was recruiting a brother.

She had watched him walk up the icy path, his coat flapping in the bitter wind. He hadn't looked like a savior in that moment. He had looked like a ghost.

She remembered the way his aura had felt after Dr. Carter. After he had abandoned Thomas on the side of the road. The holy, comforting peace was diminished, replaced by something jagged and desperate.

And now he was in there with a cop.

Lena gripped the steering wheel, anchoring herself to the present moment. The silence was suffocating. She expected to hear shouts. Gunshots, maybe. But there was nothing. Only the low hum of the Highlander's engine and the frantic, rabbit-quick beating of her own heart.

She couldn't stay here. If the police came, she was an accessory to murder. To multiple murders. She had driven the getaway car.

But she couldn't leave him. He was her anchor. Without his presence, the cravings would gnaw their way back to the surface. She would drown.

She looked at the clock on the dashboard.

10:03 a.m.

The minutes felt like an hour.

Suddenly, the front door of the condo building opened.

Lena leaned forward, her breath fogging the cold windshield.

It wasn't Adam.

It was a girl.

She was young, a teenager, wearing an oversized sweater and thick wool socks. No shoes. She walked out into the freezing snow as if she were strolling on a warm beach in July. Her eyes were wide, glassy, and perfectly blank.

Behind her, Adam emerged from the doorway. He had one hand resting on the back of the girl's neck.

Lena's stomach twisted.

Adam guided the girl down the icy path toward the Highlander. He opened the front passenger door, and the girl climbed in without a single word of protest. She didn't look at Lena. She didn't look at the interior of the car. She just stared straight ahead, a placid, empty doll.

Adam closed the door and walked around the front of the SUV to the driver's side. He pulled the door open. The biting Alaskan wind rushed into the warm cabin.

"Out," Adam said.

Lena stared up at him, her hands frozen on the steering wheel. "What? Adam, no. I'm driving. I'm coming with you."

"The path narrows here, Lena," Adam said, his dark eyes entirely devoid of warmth. "This final step is for my brother and me. We will return to where we were born. You cannot follow."

Panic clawed at her throat. The thought of being separated from him—from the narcotic peace he radiated—was physically agonizing. "You can't leave me here. The police..."

"They are blind to you," Adam assured her, reaching down to

pry her trembling fingers off the wheel. "Go north. Find a quiet place. Wait for me."

"Will you come back?" she begged, tears spilling hot down her freezing cheeks.

Adam smiled. It was the beatific, terrifying smile of a martyr. "I will find you when the work is done."

He stepped back, leaving the door open for her.

Lena's body moved on autopilot. The remaining residue of his peace forced her compliance. She slid out of the warm driver's seat and stepped onto the icy street. The wind immediately cut through her thin coat.

Adam slid into the car and pulled the door shut. He didn't look at her through the glass. He put the vehicle in gear and accelerated away.

She stood shivering in the snow, watching the red taillights fade into the gray Palmer morning.

Wait for me, he'd said.

But as the heavy, crushing noise of the world rushed back into her mind, drowning out the fading remnants of his holy calm, Lena knew the absolute truth.

She would never see him again.

THIRTY-NINE

Ward skidded around the corner onto Elmwood Street, the Ford Taurus fishtailing on the black ice. He didn't correct it; he just rode the slide, stomping on the gas as soon as the tires bit the asphalt.

Unit 4B was dark.

Ward slammed the vehicle into park before it had fully stopped, leaping out into the freezing air while the engine was still running. He drew his weapon—the Glock instantly becoming an extension of his hand—and sprinted up the icy walkway.

"Emma!" he yelled.

Silence.

The front door was closed.

Ward didn't bother digging for his keys. He didn't bother with a stealth approach. He hit the door just below the handle with the flat of his boot, putting all two hundred pounds of panic behind it.

CRACK.

The doorframe splintered. The door swung violently inward, banging against the drywall.

Ward swept the living room, his weapon up at guard in his right hand, his heavy flashlight in his left. He pressed the backs of his hands together, providing isometric tension for a stable, tactical grip.

He cleared the kitchen. He cleared the bedroom, the bathroom, and the closets.

The apartment was empty.

A floor lamp was knocked over. A book on the floor. Emma's boots.

The aquarium bubbled quietly in the corner.

On the sofa, her paperback thriller was face down, its spine cracked. Her cell phone sat next to it, the screen dark.

"Emma?" Ward said. The Glock lowered slightly.

She wasn't here.

He walked slowly back into the kitchen.

On the granite island, sitting squarely in the center of a place-mat, was a single sheet of paper. It had been torn from a notebook.

Ward holstered his weapon. His hands were shaking so badly he had to grip the cold edge of the counter to steady them.

He leaned over the note.

He recognized the handwriting:

> *Brother, you survived the fire, like me. Only those who have touched the infinite can understand the mission. Meet me where it began. Where he broke us. Come alone. If you bring the noise, the girl becomes the harvest.*

Ward stared at the words.

Where he broke us.

He closed his eyes. The familiar smell of his apartment vanished. In its place, he smelled the harsh, chemical antiseptic. The unnatural cleanliness. He heard the low, mechanical thrum of the genera-tor. He saw the stark concrete walls and the simple metal table. He remembered the voice of evil and felt the sharp stab of a needle sliding into his arm once again.

The lab.

Richard Pagan's house of horrors. The prison where Ward had been held for days, tortured until he finally clawed his way back to sanity and filled the madman's chest with lead.

Adam wasn't running away. He was going home.

Ward's phone buzzed violently in his pocket. It was a jarring, angry sound.

He pulled it out. Ballack.

"Ward!" the Sergeant's voice was tinny and frantic through the speaker. "What's the status? We have APD units two minutes out from your location."

Ward looked at the book on the floor. He looked at Emma's empty boots.

If you bring the noise, the girl becomes the harvest.

If the sirens came... if a tactical team swarmed the lab... Adam would sense the "noise." He would feel the aggression radiating from the perimeter—like he had at the church.

And Emma would die. She would just lie there on the cold concrete, smiling blissfully, while Adam cut her throat.

"Ward?" Ballack said over the radio chatter in the background. "Report!"

Ward swallowed the bile rising in his throat. He forced his voice to be flat. Dead.

"False alarm, Sergeant."

"What?"

"I said false alarm," Ward lied, his eyes fixed on the handwritten note. "I checked it out. It's all good. I just overreacted." He let out a manufactured sigh. "I'm exhausted. I'm going to crash here for a few hours. Call off the units."

There was a long, heavy pause on the line. "Um, you sure?"

"I'm positive, boss. And I'm spent. Need an hour or two at least, then I'll circle back with you guys on next steps."

"Okay. Get some sleep, Ward," Ballack said finally, his voice thick with suspicion. "You were up all night like the rest of us. We'll regroup at 1500 hours."

Click.

He walked to the hallway closet, pulled a high-output tactical light from his duty belt and slapped a fresh battery into it.

He checked the magazine in his Glock, then the spare in his mag pouch. Both were full, but it wasn't enough. Not for the lab. Not for a creature who had mastered fear.

He needed distance. His rifle.

He thought of the AR-15 locked in the rack of his unmarked Taurus parked outside, the polymer magazines each loaded with thirty rounds of 5.56mm duty ammo. He thought of the heavy external vest with the ceramic trauma plate sitting on the passenger seat.

Those were the proper tools for this nightmare. Today required overwhelming force.

"I'm coming... *brother*," Ward said.

He charged into the freezing Alaskan outdoors, leaving his front door broken and wide open behind him.

FORTY

The Major Crimes Unit office of the Alaska
Bureau of Investigation in Palmer was populated with metal file
cabinets and spartan furniture, making it functional, if unimagina-
tive. Today, however, the air in the room felt tense and heavy.

Investigator Bud Foley sat beside Becky, the front desk clerk.
She had her face buried in her hands, her shoulders heaving with
ragged sobs. Foster stood a few feet away, sipping from a foam coffee
cup, watching the meltdown.

"Start from the beginning," Foley said.

Becky looked up. Her face was a mask of red, blotchy terror,
dark rivulets of mascara tracking down her cheeks.

"I didn't know," she gasped, fighting for air. "Oh God, I didn't
know."

Foley placed a heavy, reassuring hand on her shoulder. "Tell me
exactly what happened, Becky. Deep breaths. Nice and slow."

"He was... overwhelming," Becky wailed, fresh tears spilling
over her lower lashes. "He said he wanted to speak to him. He asked
where Jake lived. I just wanted to help, Bud. I gave him the address."

"You did *what*?" Foley roared, his patience instantly evaporating.

"I gave him the address!" she shrieked, burying her face in her hands again.

Foley snatched his radio from his belt, his thumb jamming down on the transmit button to scream for a patrol unit to roll to Ward's apartment.

But before he could broadcast, the heavy front doors of the post blew open. A violent gust of wind and snow swirled across the linoleum floor, carrying the biting, subzero cold of the Mat-Su Valley morning.

Foley spun around, his hand dropping instinctively to his holster. Foster was already moving, his service weapon drawn and leveled at the entryway.

Foley expected Adam. He expected the Ministrant had come to finish the job, to cleanse the police station of its "rot."

Instead, a woman stumbled through the doors.

She looked like a shipwreck. Her hair was matted with ice, her face so pale and drawn she looked like a ghost haunting her own body. She wore a thin coat that was entirely inadequate for the weather, and her empty hands were already raised in the air, trembling violently.

She took a staggering step toward the bulletproof glass of the front counter, her hollow eyes darting between Foley and Foster.

"I'm looking for the State Troopers," she rasped. Her teeth chattered so hard the words were barely intelligible. "My name is Lena, and I need to report some murders."

Foley squinted against the harsh fluorescent light. He recognized her instantly from the BOLO photos Miller had circulated after the downtown courthouse escape. The getaway driver.

"Keep those hands where I can see them!" Foster said, a hand on his pistol grip. "Don't move!"

"Please don't hurt me," the woman said.

Foley and Foster pushed through the secure access door into the public lobby. The moment they cleared the threshold, the woman collapsed onto a wooden waiting bench as if her puppet strings had been cut. She slumped against the cinderblock wall, looking up at Foley with eyes that were clear, sharp, and utterly devastated.

"He's not here," Lena said, her voice hollow. "He's gone to find his brother."

"Stand up, slowly," Foley ordered. "Face the wall. I have to search you."

She complied numbly. Foley moved tactically behind her, securing both her wrists in handcuffs, then patted down her coat and pockets.

"No weapons," he said.

Foster keyed his shoulder mic. "Mat-Com, 2-1-55. We have a suspect detained at the front counter of the Palmer Post." He lowered the radio and glared at her. "Where is he?"

"He left us," Lena said, hot tears finally spilling over her cheeks.

Foley released his grip on her, and she sat on the bench once again.

"He found someone else," she said.

Foley turned to Foster, the blood draining from his face. "He's going after Ward."

"He's already been there," Lena said. She looked up, and the agony in her expression was raw.

Foley's stomach curled into a tight, icy knot. "Oh no... Emma."

"Who is Emma?" Foster asked.

"Jake's neighbor," Foley said, his voice tightening. "A kid. She feeds his fish. She's like his little sister."

"He took her," Lena said. "I watched him walk out of the building with her. He... he told me to walk away. That he would find me later. But he isn't coming back. I know that now."

"Where did he take her?" Foley stepped closer, crowding her space. "Listen to me. If you want to help yourself, you tell me where he took that girl."

Lena laughed—a dry, cracking sound devoid of any humor. "Help myself? You think I'm here to cut a deal?"

She pulled away from his grip and looked down, crying, tears hitting the old laminate tiles on the entryway floor.

"He talks about holiness," she said. "He talks about cleansing the rot. He made me feel... perfect. Like I was made of pure light. But it was a trick. It was just numbness. It wasn't holy."

She looked up, staring Foley dead in the eye.

"I want to be clean," she said, her voice finding a sudden, desperate strength. "And you don't get clean by skipping the pain. You get clean by walking through it. The blood isn't the price. Truth is the price."

"The location, Lena," Foley pressed, desperate. "Where did he go?"

"He mentioned their birthplace," she said. "Adam said he has to take his brother there."

Foley froze. He knew exactly where she meant. Knik River Road. Richard Pagan's lab.

He was already moving, grabbing his keys from his belt. "Foster, secure her in holding and call Ballack and Kincaid. Tell them it's the lab. Tell them to bring SWAT, but hold the perimeter. Absolutely no sirens."

Foley moved toward the exit, but paused at the double doors. He looked back at Lena, who was huddled on the wooden bench, weeping silently into her hands.

"Why?" Foley asked her. "Why did you come here instead of running?"

She slumped against the cinderblock, closing her eyes.

"Because that little girl is innocent," she said. "And saving her is the first true thing I've ever done in my life."

Foley turned and pushed through the doors, sprinting toward his vehicle. Ward was headed into this alone.

And this monster might finally be the end of him.

FORTY-ONE

The air in the command post trailer was stale, recycled through vents that probably needed cleaning. The early morning attempt to capture Basu in Big Lake had failed, Ward had bolted on a false alarm of some sort, and they were now trying to put the pieces back together.

Rod Hawthorne stood near the coffee station, watching Detective Miller furiously typing notes into her tablet, Kincaid looking over her shoulder and Ballack not far away.

Miller was good—tenacious, sharp—but she was playing checkers. The game Hawthorne played had no board, no rules, and the pieces were entirely disposable.

Miller's phone rang. Hawthorne moved closer.

"Go for Miller."

She listened for a moment, then looked up at Kincaid. "Foster has the getaway driver. At Palmer post."

Hawthorne's own phone buzzed against his hip.

He checked the screen. No phone number.

Sergeant Ballack turned toward him, his eyes tired. "Something?"

"Just my office," Hawthorne said smoothly. "Administrative nonsense. Give me a minute."

He stepped out of the trailer and walked until he found a quiet area near some trees.

He pressed the answer key and held the phone to his ear. He didn't speak.

"The situation has degraded," the voice on the other end said. It was metallic, flattened by encryption, but the authority behind it was unmistakable.

"I'm aware," Hawthorne said. "The psychiatrist. The courthouse."

"Asset AB has crossed the threshold. The psychological profile suggested a manageable messiah complex, but the public exposure has become... unacceptable."

Hawthorne watched a uniformed trooper walk past the far end of the trailer, oblivious to the shadow operative standing just yards away.

"Orders?"

"He's heading to the old lab. Get there now. End it."

The line went dead.

Hawthorne lowered the phone and slipped it into his pocket.

He looked at his reflection in side view mirror of a nearby patrol car. He looked old. But for the first time in weeks, a genuine smile touched his lips.

"It's about time," he said.

FORTY-TWO

The Old Glenn Highway was a blur of gray asphalt and packed snow, the scenery whipping past Ward's window at over eighty miles an hour.

His knuckles were bone-white on the steering wheel of the unmarked Taurus. The engine whined, but he didn't let up.

Every mile closer to the Knik River Bridge tightened the screw in his chest.

He had told himself he was going alone to protect Emma—to keep the tactical "noise" down so Adam wouldn't panic. But as the miles ticked by, the adrenaline curdled into something much colder: reality.

He was driving into a trap set by a man who could manipulate the human mind like a switchboard. A man who had dismantled an armed transport team without lifting a finger.

If Ward went in alone and failed, he had no Plan B. Emma would die.

And it would be his vanity that killed her.

He cursed violently, slamming his hand against the steering wheel. He wasn't a cowboy. He was a trooper.

He reached for his phone, punching Foley's speed dial before he could talk himself out of it.

It rang once.

"Jake." Foley's voice was tight.

"I'm on the Old Glenn," Ward said, his eyes locked on the horizon where the Chugach Mountains rose like jagged teeth. "He has Emma. He took her from my apartment."

"I know," Foley said. "We have Basu's driver. He's driving a silver Highlander."

Ward blinked. "What?"

"She walked into Palmer Post a few minutes ago. Gave herself up. Told us everything, Jake. She said he's taking his 'brother' back to the lab."

"Yes," Ward said, his jaw tight. "He is."

"Where are you?"

"Passing Sullivan Road," Ward said.

"I'm a few minutes behind you," Foley replied.

Ward exhaled a shaky breath, feeling a sickening mixture of relief and dread. "Who else is coming?"

"SWAT is spinning up, but they're a ways out. The roads are slick."

"Hold them back," Ward said.

"Jake—"

"I mean it, Bud. If he sees a convoy of Bearcats and light bars rolling up the driveway, he'll slit her throat. He's too sensitive. He'll feel you guys coming."

"It's a trap," Foley argued. "He's going to—"

"He's nuts, but he's looking for something," Ward said. "*Meaning*, maybe. Maybe I can talk him down."

"You can't talk down a madman."

"I can try," Ward said. "But I need you to hold the perimeter. I'm going in alone. Give me a couple minutes. If I can't fix it... then send in the cavalry."

A long pause hung on the line. Ward heard the road noise of Foley's vehicle, the engine roaring.

"A couple minutes," Foley agreed finally. "But Jake... there's something else."

"What?"

"Hawthorne."

The Fed. "What about him?"

"Ballack called. Hawthorne was in the command trailer when the call came in about arresting the driver. He didn't say a word. He just walked out. Miller tried to call him, but he's gone dark."

"He's going to the lab," Ward realized, a new layer of dread settling over him.

"That's my guess. That guy isn't who he says he is."

"You think he's one of the spooks who funded Pagan?" Foley asked.

"Yes," Ward said grimly. "Asset AB is a liability now. And maybe, so am I."

"Watch your back," Foley warned. "You're walking into a crossfire."

"Just get there, Bud. And bring the heavy iron."

Ward tossed the phone onto the passenger seat.

Ahead, the turnoff for Knik River Road approached. He took it fast, the tires of the Taurus sliding on the ice.

Time seemed to slow as he navigated Knik River Road. He was voluntarily heading back into the lion's den. The dread swelled, a weight pressing down on his chest.

But Emma needed him. He galvanized his resolve, forcing himself to accept what he was up against.

I'm afraid right now, he thought. *But I'm moving forward, anyway.*

Then, he saw it.

The access road leading into the woods. A single set of tire tracks had broken a shallow layer of snow—fresh marks.

Ward slowed.

He turned onto the road, the suspension lurching as the car fought through the frozen ruts below.

The trees closed in around him, tall and suffocating.

He knew this place.

Where he broke us.

Ward gripped harder. He wasn't that man anymore. He wasn't the victim strapped to the table. He was the one holding the wheel.

He looked over to the passenger seat and saw the tactical vest. His AR-15 was locked in the rack.

"I'm not going to lie down again," Ward said to himself. "I'm here to end it."

The car rolled slowly up the driveway, moving quietly toward the place where his nightmares were born.

FORTY-THREE

T HE ROAD ENDED IN A WIDE, SNOWY CLEARING WHERE
the trees had been pushed back years ago to make room for a
monster's ambition. Ahead, near the structure, the silver Highlander was parked.

Ward stopped the car just inside the treeline. He killed the
engine.

Silence rushed in to fill the void, heavy and suffocating.

He opened the door and stepped out. The air here tasted
different.

He donned his vest and grabbed his rifle, then quietly closed the
car door.

Moving forward, he stepped carefully into the existing tire
prints to mask the crunch of the snow. He glided toward the lab
door with the focus of a man who knew he was no longer the only
predator in the woods.

Ahead, the lab rose from the snow like a dark fortress. It stood
silent and imposing, a monolith of concrete and steel against the
sky. The windows were black eyes, staring blindly. The house where
Richard Pagan had played God.

Ward's breath hitched.

The last time he was here, the building was a prison. Now, it was a tomb.

He moved to the heavy steel door. Unlocked, it hung slightly ajar. He stepped inside.

The center of the main warehouse floor was a cavernous space, no longer filled with machinery. A single fluorescent light cast a harsh, white glare against the dust.

Ward moved closer, his rifle held low at the ready.

As his eyes adjusted to the light, he saw the tableau.

Adam had been busy.

He'd dragged several chairs into a rough semicircle, creating a makeshift theater with no witnesses to attend the show.

In the center, lying on a plastic sheet, was Emma.

Ward's heart hammered against his ribs.

Her hands were free. There were no ropes, no chains. She was just lying there in the dark, cold room, her hands folded on her chest. Her eyes were wide open, staring at the dark, corrugated steel of the ceiling with a look of terrifying vacuity.

Adam stood over her, knife poised near her neck, swaying back and forth, mumbling something. A shot from this distance would have to hit him in the head to be sure to stop him.

His movement made it too risky.

Ward stepped into the light.

"I'm here."

Adam turned, but the knife was still too close to Emma.

"Jake!" Adam cried out. "You came. I knew you would. The connection... it pulled you, didn't it?"

Ward didn't raise his rifle. He didn't shout commands. He just walked slowly, steadily across the concrete slab, stopping when Adam lowered the knife closer to Emma's throat.

Ward was about twenty feet away from his target, now. He'd practiced on the range from this distance. Seven yards. Fail-to-stop drill, two shots center-mass, then one to the head. His hands clenched the rifle with pent-up frustration.

The knife was so close. Still too risky.

"Let her go," Ward said.

Adam looked thinner than he did in the video at the court-house, but his eyes still burned with that feverish intensity.

"Welcome home, brother," Adam said. He gestured to the shadows around them. "Look. It's all still here. Not the machines. No, those are gone. But the energy. The silence. Can you feel it?"

"I feel it," Ward said, but he felt only a sick knot in his stomach.

Adam turned back to Emma. He touched her forehead tenderly.

"She is ready," Adam said. "She has accepted the peace. She is quiet inside."

"Emma?" Ward said.

Emma's eyes moved toward him. She smiled—a slow, sleepy expression that didn't reach her eyes.

"Hi, Jake," she murmured, her voice sounding like it came from the bottom of a well. "Adam says we're going to be clean. He says the noise will stop."

Ward swallowed the bile in his throat. The peace was a weapon, and Adam had smothered her with it.

"She doesn't need cleansing, Adam," Ward said, keeping his voice flat, reasonable. "She's innocent."

"No one is innocent!" Adam snapped. "That is the lie! We are born in the rot! We carry it in our blood! You know this, Jake. You saw the truth in this very room!"

Adam pointed a shaking finger at the floor beneath their feet.

"This is where he opened us," Adam said. "This is where he peeled back the layers and showed us the void."

"Yes, he hurt us," Ward said. "I, too, was afraid."

"At first," Adam said. "But then? When the fear broke? When the screaming stopped? What did you feel then?"

Ward remembered. He remembered when the terror disap-peared, replaced by peace. That infinite peace. Ward's experience hadn't broken him at all. If anything, it strengthened him. He'd seen paradise, and knew he'd never be alone again.

But that must not have happened to Adam. This poor kid had gone through hell and been forced to adapt.

"I don't know what I felt," Ward said.

Adam nodded vigorously. "It was silence! That is the gift, Jake. That is what we offer. We take the screaming away. We take the fear away."

Ward tensed, his finger pushing hard against the receiver of the AR-15.

He looked carefully at Adam's knife, a simple kitchen blade. The steel glinted in the harsh light.

"I brought her for us," Adam said, turning the knife in his hand. "A shared communion. I will open the gate, and you will witness the peace enter her. Then... we will go to the world. Two brothers on a mission of mercy. The left hand and the right hand."

"Adam, stop," Ward said.

Adam paused, looking back, confused. "Why? She is ready. Look at her. She isn't afraid."

"*I* am," Ward said.

Adam blinked. "What?"

"I'm afraid," Ward said. "For her."

Slowly, deliberately, he engaged the rifle's safety. He unclipped the sling.

He set the rifle down on the concrete floor.

He'd rather have his rifle right now, but he needed to make a gesture of de-escalation and that was all he could think of. He still carried his Glock in the holster on his hip. And with this dim light, the glowing, tritium sights on his pistol might be faster to acquire than the dull iron sights of the rifle. On the range, he'd practiced head shots with his pistol at three and five yards, but he was too far away for that right now.

He needed two more yards. At least.

Adam stared at him, the knife lowering slightly. "What are you doing?"

"I've put away the noise," Ward said. He took a step closer. "I'm not here to hurt you."

He held out his empty hands.

"I'm here as your brother. I'm here because I survived the fire, just like you."

Adam's expression wavered. The manic certainty slipped, replaced by a desperate, childlike hope.

"You... you accept it?"

"I remember it," Ward said. "I remember the table. I remember the straps on my wrists. I remember thinking that if I just died, it would be okay."

Ward took a step forward.

"Yes," Adam breathed. "Yes."

"But Adam," Ward said, taking another step. He was close now. Five yards. Close enough to see the dirt under Adam's fingernails. "Pagan lied to us."

Adam frowned, pulling the knife back away from Emma slightly. "No. He showed us the way."

"He lied, and then he broke us," Ward said. "He didn't make us holy. He made us bleed. And now... you're doing his work for him."

Ward looked at Emma.

"She isn't the sacrifice, Adam. She's just a girl. And you... you're just a young man who got hurt."

Adam flinched as if Ward had slapped him.

"I am the Ministrant!" Adam shouted, the knife close to her neck again. "I am the Divine Hand!"

"No," Ward said, his voice hardening as he took another step forward. Three yards away now. Close enough for a clean headshot —if the target wasn't moving.

Ward thought about the shot timer on the range. From the holster, he could get a shot on target in a little under two seconds. Head shots a little slower. But two seconds is an eternity when a madman has a knife at the throat of a little girl.

"You're Subject AB, Adam. They didn't even use your name. Not a human being, not a prophet. You're an experiment that they threw away because they broke you too badly to salvage."

"Liar!" Adam screamed.

"I read the reports, Adam. I watched the video of Pagan speaking with you. You weren't anointed for some holy mission. You were tortured because he was exploring how to make a human being touch the infinite. That was his real goal. But to pay the bills, to keep his shadow-funders happy, he had to crank out research that helped soldiers. He was trying to engineer fearlessness and control over pain."

Adam's eyes were wide.

"He used radiation and drugs to alter your brain. Somehow, Pagan gave you the ability to control your own fear, and the fear in others. It's like something out of a nightmare."

"No," Adam said. "That can't be. This is God at work in me."

"It all makes sense. You were taught a twisted theology by your father. Then you fell into a trap by yet another psycho. Pagan shattered your mind, gave you an ability no human being should have, and you took that as a gift. A mission. You fell back on the broken belief system of your childhood in order to give it all meaning."

Ward took a final step closer. His right elbow touching the grip of his sidearm, indexing it for what might happen next.

"True meaning doesn't come from power or death. It comes from service, Adam. We survived the fire so we could help people out of it, not throw them in. People matter. You matter." He gestured toward Emma. "She matters."

Adam's grip on the knife loosened. "If I don't have this... I don't know who I am."

What could Ward say to that? He wasn't a counselor, he was a cop. Maybe, right now, he just needed to be a human being.

"You are valuable, Adam. But because you're living, breathing, and on this earth. Not because of the horrible things that have been done to you, but despite them."

He looked Adam in the eye.

"Put the knife down. Let her go. Walk out of here with me. The nightmare is over."

FORTY-FOUR

"You aren't my brother," Adam said.

The words came out cold, stripped of the warmth he had projected only moments before. He looked at the man standing before him—the man who claimed to understand the fire.

Ward was lying, vibrating with the noise. Full of judgment, full of the laws of men. He didn't hear the music; he only heard the static.

"You are just another wall," Adam said. "And walls must be brought down."

He didn't raise a hand. He stopped holding back the reservoir of silence he had gathered, from the quiet of the woods, from the depths of his own soul. He pushed it all outward, focusing it into a dense, crushing wave directly at Ward.

Ward's eyes widened. His muscles tensed, fighting the intrusion, but he fought a tsunami with a sieve.

"Lie down," Adam commanded.

The impact hit Ward like a physical blow to the chest.

But he'd known this was coming. He didn't stagger back. He

leaned into it, planting his boots on the concrete, locking his knees against the invisible tide. It wasn't just a suggestion; it was a narcotic gravity, pushing at the marrow of his bones. His eyelids were dipped in lead. The anger he nurtured on the drive over, the sharp, tactical clarity he honed like a blade—it all blurred, softening into a warm, golden haze.

It was far stronger than he expected—he wouldn't last long.

He needed an anchor. Something sharp enough to pop the bubble.

Ward bit down on his lower lip. Hard.

He felt the skin break. The sharp, hot sting of the bite cut through the fog like a razor. The taste of blood flooded his mouth.

Pain is clarity, he told himself. *Pain is real.*

For a heartbeat, it worked. The golden haze fractured. The weight lifted just enough for him to breathe.

He forced his right arm up, his hand gripping his Glock pistol. He broke the gun free from the holster.

It moved in jagged, agonizing inches as if the gun weighed fifty pounds. His deltoids screamed as they fought his own mind, trying to bring the muzzle to bear on Adam's chest.

"I said... lie down," Adam said.

Adam's eyes narrowed.

Ward tasted the blood on his lip. Defiance.

Adam twitched a finger.

The pressure doubled and the pain in Ward's lip, his lifeline, suddenly washed away, smothered by the overwhelming, suffocating comfort of the peace.

Ward groaned, a guttural sound tearing from his throat. He imagined the path of his bullet. Adam falling. He just needed to reach the trigger to make it so.

Do it, he screamed at his finger. *Squeeze!*

But the signal wouldn't go through. His finger was numb, wrapped in cotton. The pain was gone. The fight, gone. He just couldn't see the point of it.

Desperate, Ward scrambled mentally, reaching into the back of his mind for the weapon he possessed the last time he was in this room. *The Options.*

In the lab, during the escape, time had fractured for him. He had been able to see the paths branching out—a split-second precognition that allowed him to choose the future where he survived. He clawed at his own psyche, battering against the door of his perception, begging to see the path where the gun fired, the path where he tackled Adam, the path where Emma lived.

But the toolbox was empty.

There were no visions. No branching paths. No "choose your own adventure." The trauma that unlocked that door had healed, sealing it shut. He was just a man, trapped in the linear march of seconds, standing opposite a god.

Damn you, Ward thought, his knees shaking violently as his legs weakened.

He looked at Adam. The kid frowned, tilting his head. He looked annoyed. Surprised that the wall hadn't crumbled yet. Adam lifted his arm and made a fist, then a sledgehammer of will slammed against his skull.

It wasn't fair. They'd both survived the fire. Both been broken by the same maker. But Adam came out of the kiln harder, sharper. Ward's will was a shield, but Adam's was a razor-sharp spear, and it drove deep into the soft meat of Ward's consciousness.

Ward's arm collapsed. The Glock clattered to the floor, the sound miles away.

The golden silence rose past his neck, filling his mouth, drowning his thoughts.

Please, he prayed, casting his mind back to the near-death experience that happened just a few feet away, right here in this lab. His mind grasped desperately for that being of infinite, terrifying love that had assured him he wasn't alone.

I am here, he screamed in the silence of his head. *I am fighting! Help me stand! If you are real, if you are the God of the broken, help!*

He waited for the thunder. He waited for the surge of strength, the flash of light, the divine intervention.

But there was no answer.

Only Adam. And a glorious peace.

It washed over his head, sealing him under. The prayer died on his lips, replaced by a sudden, sickening gratitude for the quiet.

The tension in Ward's jaw went slack. The defiance in his eyes melted into a glassy, euphoric stupor.

"Lie down," Adam commanded again.

Ward didn't fight this time. He couldn't. The fight was over, and oh, the peace was wonderful.

He moved forward a few steps, then crumpled, his knees hitting the concrete first, then his torso, moving with the heavy, fluid grace of a man sinking into a warm bath.

He stretched out next to the girl on the plastic. He closed his eyes.

Adam looked down at them. Side by side. The Trooper and the girl. Poetry.

"My father knew," Adam said, his voice echoing in the cavernous space. He wasn't speaking to them anymore; he was speaking to the shadows. "He told me the world burned, Jake. He said we were drowning in our own filth, and that only the fire could make it clean."

He circled the concrete slab, the knife loose in his hand.

"He will be so jealous," Adam said, a smile touching his lips. "When he sees what I have done. When he sees that I didn't just give empty sermons—I became the sermon. I am an instrument in God's hand."

He knelt in the dust, reached out and adjusted Ward's head, tilting it back to expose the throat. He did the same to Emma. They lied there, breathing in shallow, synchronized rhythm, lost in the beautiful nothingness he had gifted them.

Adam bowed his head.

"Lord, sanctify this harvest," he said. "Let the silence spread from this point. Let it cover the world."

He lifted the knife. He placed the cold steel against the pulse of Emma's neck.

Her skin was soft. Warm.

Adam paused.

He looked at her face. Really looked at her.

So young. Her face unlined, free of the ravages of time and sin that marked the adults he had cleansed. She looked like... a child.

A memory surfaced, unbidden. A Sunday morning in the stifling heat of the small church. His father, Malik, pounding the pulpit, sweat flying from his brow.

"The child is a vessel of grace!" Malik had thundered. "Until the age of accountability, the soul is white as snow! The sin of the father does not stain the child until the child chooses the darkness!"

Adam's hand trembled.

She is so young. She hasn't chosen, the voice in his head whispered. *So... she could be innocent.*

A whirlwind of recent memory struck him, a play-by-play of the last couple hours from the girl's perspective. Alone in an apartment, a strange man knocks at her door. She opens it, thinking it was someone she knew, someone she trusted. A stranger comes in. What terror that must have been!

Now, that same stranger had her laid flat on a cold concrete floor, a knife at her throat. This was different from his other kills. So obsessed had he been with luring his brother to the lab that he hadn't even looked at her aura.

He hadn't looked at her aura!

The noise of the police, looking for him. The urgency of his mission. Either he hadn't noticed her aura, or he hadn't been able to see it over the chaos.

The shock of the realization made him pull the knife back an inch.

He looked now.

White light. Shining, white, clean light. No darkness. None. No sin.

There was only light.

Using his left hand, he wiped his eyes and shook his head, hoping to clear his vision.

He looked again, and the aura remained clear.

He had kidnapped a sinless child.

And if she was innocent, then this wasn't a cleansing. He'd committed an offense against God.

Killing her would be... murder.

The thought struck him with the force of a physical blow. He froze, the knife hovering against her skin.

If I kill the innocent... then I am not the Ministrant.

He looked at the knife. It wasn't a holy relic. It was a cheap piece of cutlery stolen from a dead woman's kitchen.

He looked at the shadows of the lab. This wasn't a temple. It was a ruin. A place where a monster had hooked him up to machines and broken his mind until he couldn't tell the difference between holiness and madness.

Suddenly, the shadows of the warehouse warped. The smell of dust vanished, replaced by the sharp, chemical sting of antiseptic and burning ozone.

He wasn't standing over a girl anymore. He was strapped to the cold steel table.

"God, please," Adam heard his own voice begging, fractured with agony.

A face loomed over him, backlit by the blinding glare of an LED surgical light. Not an angel. Not his father. Dr. Pagan.

"We are inducing an acute amygdala response now, Adam," Pagan murmured, his eyes fixed on a humming monitor rather than the boy on the table. "The goal is to force neuroplastic adaptation under extreme duress. To let us document the exact threshold before psychological fracture."

A button was pressed. Fire flooded Adam's veins. He screamed until his vocal cords tore, his mind shattering into a million jagged pieces. He didn't find grace in the dark. He found a trapdoor. He fled into the absolute, dead silence of his own ruined brain just to survive the fire.

"Fascinating," Pagan's voice echoed through the static, sounding entirely devoid of empathy. "The subject is weaponizing his own dissociation. He's expanded the sensory collapse to those around him—I can feel it."

It was a memory he had buried because it didn't fit the story he wanted. Adam gasped, stumbling backward as the flashback released him, dropping him into the present.

Pagan lied, Ward had said. *Pagan lied.*

Doubt, cold and jagged, pierced the armor of his delusion.

I'm an experiment. A horrible accident! How many have I killed? Adam thought. The man at the gas station. The one in the park. Dr. Carter. How many more would there have been?

He told himself he was freeing them. But when he looked at the girl, the illusion had fallen apart.

He no longer saw souls ascending. He saw blood. Terror.

I am not the cure, Adam realized, the horror rising in his throat like bile. *I am the disease.*

He looked at his hands. They were filthy. Dripping with the blood of his victims.

Pagan didn't show me God, Adam thought, tears spilling hot and fast down his cheeks. *He just showed me how to turn off the lights.*

"I am the rot," he whispered. He felt his world collapsing. His mind breaking. His resolve, perched on the single hope that he was doing God's will, had left him entirely.

I'm a monster.

He lurched backward, away from his victims, scrambling crab-like across the concrete floor until his back hit a wall. He gasped for air, his chest heaving.

He withdrew the peace. He pulled the silence back into himself, sealing the breach.

He looked at the knife in his hand.

There was only one way to stop the noise. Only one way to finally, truly be clean.

He turned the blade inward, pressing the point against his own chest, right over his hammering heart.

———

Ward gasped, his eyes snapping open.

The world rushed back in a deafening crash of sensation—the cold of the concrete seeping into his back, the smell of dust, the sharp bite of adrenaline.

"Jake?"

Emma stirred beside him, clutching her throat, her eyes wide and terrified.

"I've got you," Ward rasped, scrambling to his knees. He grabbed her, pulling her into his chest, shielding her body with his own.

He looked around, searching for his pistol. It was only a few feet away.

"Stay down," he told her as he let her go and scrambled for the gun. He tapped the magazine firmly and racked the slide to ensure it was in battery, then held it out at guard, searching for the threat.

Adam was twenty feet away among the shadows. Ward squinted and saw him slumped against a wall, his face twisted in a rictus of absolute horror. He was weeping, silent, racking sobs that shook his thin frame. He held the knife with both hands, the tip pressed against his sternum.

He looked back at Ward. The madness in his eyes had broken.

"You were right," Adam choked out. "I am the sickness."

He tensed his arms, preparing to drive the blade home.

"No!" Ward shouted, taking a step toward Adam. "Adam, look at me! Look at me!"

Adam's eyes darted to Ward, wild and terrified. The prophet was gone; he was now in full, human panic. "It's the only way to be clean," he sobbed.

"You aren't the sickness," Ward said, fierce and fast. "You're just broken. And that's not your fault. You didn't ask for this. Pagan did this to you. His machines did this."

Ward took a step closer, ignoring the danger. Aware that at any second he could be back on the floor, preparing to die. But maybe he could save three lives here today.

"Don't let them win, Adam," Ward pleaded, taking another step. "If you do this, you're just hiding their secrets for them. You've lost enough already."

"I hurt people," Adam said, his voice trembling. "How did I go so wrong?"

"You did the best you could with what you were given, Adam. Like we all do. But the truth is, we only ever get to control one person. One. More than that, and we just cause pain."

"I didn't mean to be so lost. I have to fix it." His eyes were wide, desperate for redemption.

"We'll do it together," Ward said. "But not like this. There is a way back. I can show you. Just put the knife down and—"

CRACK.

The sound was sharp and dry...

Adam slumped against the wall, his eyes open but seeing nothing. A small, dark hole marred the center of his forehead.

"No!" Ward roared.

He spun toward the entrance, his weapon still at the guard.

In the shadows of the doorway, silhouetted by the growing daylight, stood a figure in a heavy coat. He lowered a suppressed rifle.

It wasn't Foley.

Special Agent Hawthorne stepped into the light, his face impassive, his eyes cold and dead as ice.

"Target neutralized," Hawthorne said calmly into his mic. "Secure the girl, Trooper."

FORTY-FIVE

The silence that followed Hawthorne's gunshot didn't last long.

Within minutes, Foley's cavalry arrived, flooding the scene with strobing lights and noise. But as the hour dragged on, the chaotic, desperate clamor of a rescue operation morphed into the precise, mechanical hum of a hostile takeover.

For every uniformed State Trooper Ward saw, there were two agents he didn't recognize wearing black tactical gear. The troopers were soon dismissed and the agents took over, moving with a synchronized, terrifying efficiency that unnerved him. They weren't securing a crime scene; they were scrubbing the site out of existence. Adam Basu, the kitchen knife, the stolen Highlander—it would all be gone soon.

Ward stood near the ambulance bumper right next to Emma. A trooper offered to fetch him a coat, but he refused, barely feeling the freezing air. His focus was entirely on the girl.

She was swathed in a heavy wool blanket, clutching a plastic bottle of water with both trembling hands. Her eyes were wide, staring blankly at the trampled snow near his boots. She looked fragile—like a porcelain doll that had been glued back together but might shatter again if the wind blew too hard.

"How is she?" Ward asked, looking up at the medic working over her.

Foley stood just a few feet away, watching them with a tight jaw.

"Shock," the medic replied quietly, clicking off his penlight. "Her vitals are stable, and there are no physical injuries. But she's just... quiet."

Ward crouched down, so he was eye-level with her and gently covered her freezing hands with his own.

"Emma," Ward said.

She blinked, her gaze rising slowly to meet his. Her eyes looked heavy.

"Jake," she whispered. It sounded more like a whimper.

"I've got you," he said. "You're safe."

"He told me..." Emma's voice trembled. "He said he was going to make me clean."

"He was sick, Em."

"Is he gone?"

"Yes. He's gone."

"Jake." The voice came from behind him.

Ward turned. It was Foley, nodding toward the lab's entrance, directing Ward's attention away from the girl.

Ward followed Foley's gaze. Two men in unmarked winter gear were walking out of the building. Between them, they carried a black body bag. They didn't struggle with the weight, and they moved quickly, entirely without ceremony or reverence.

There was no coroner. No scene tech snapping photos. No little yellow crime scene markers scattered about.

The men walked directly to a black Chevy Suburban idling near the tree line. The rear hatch popped open, and they tossed the heavy bag inside like it was a cheap piece of luggage—a broken prototype being returned to the factory.

Ward felt a flash of anger, hot and sharp. Adam Basu had become a monster, yes. But he had started as a victim. He had been a brilliant kid who loved science and just wanted to survive his father's suffocating expectations—until Richard Pagan turned him into a biological weapon to serve his dark masters.

And now, the very people who had funded his destruction were throwing him in the trash.

"He's gone," Ward repeated, turning his back on the Suburban and squeezing Emma's hand. "He can't hurt you again."

Emma leaned forward, resting her forehead heavily against Ward's shoulder. She finally started to cry—soft, hitching sobs that shook her small frame.

Ward wrapped his arms around her. He felt the massive, coiled spring of tension in his own chest begin to unwind.

He hadn't saved the others—not Randall Tibeluk or Eric Nolan or Elizabeth Carter. He hadn't saved Adam.

But he had saved *her*.

"I'm taking you home," Ward promised, his voice fierce. "I'm going to drive you myself. No more strangers."

"Okay," she breathed.

Behind him, the black Suburban peeled away, its heavy tires crunching on the frozen gravel. It disappeared down the dark access road, taking the Ministrant away forever.

Ward watched the red taillights fade into the distance.

This particular monster was gone. But the machine that built him was still running.

EPILOGUE

THE DRIVE AWAY FROM EMMA'S HOUSE WAS A BLUR OF pavement and regret. It ended with Ward parked on the frozen shoulder of the highway, his hands numb on the steering wheel.

He didn't know where to go, or what to do.

He'd expected Emma to bounce back—to crack a joke about police work or roll her eyes at her mother's frantic affection. That was the Emma he knew: the headstrong, fearless teenager who hung out in his apartment doing homework and feeding his fish.

But the girl he had just left standing in the doorway wasn't that person anymore. She had clung to her mother, looking small, trembling, her eyes wide and vacant as she replayed horrors in her mind that only she could see.

It would take a long time for the light to come back into those eyes, if it ever fully did.

Her mom hadn't asked many questions; she had just dropped to her knees and held onto her little girl.

The questions would come later. And he didn't have good answers.

A heavy wave of nausea rolled in his stomach. It wasn't just the adrenaline crash; it was the guilt. It sickened him to think that his relationship with her—his clumsy attempt at being a mentor, a big brother—had put a target on her back. He had brought evil directly to her doorstep.

He always thought of himself as a shield. A good force in a bad world. But tonight, watching the nameless spooks scrub the lab and the medics attend to a child he had failed to protect, he was reminded of a familiar, colder truth.

He was small. He was just a piece of driftwood subject to the violent ebbs and flows of a grand design far larger than he could comprehend.

I have to be better, he thought, gripping the steering wheel until his knuckles popped. *I have to be more careful.*

His phone buzzed in the cup holder. A text message from Ballack:

Go home. Get some rest. Write your report later.

Ward clenched his jaw. This would not be handled with a text message. He hit Ballack's contact and dialed.

Ballack answered on the first ring. "Are you okay, Jake?"

"How can they do that, boss?" Ward demanded. "Just sweep in and take over the scene? Hawthorne executed Basu right in front of me, and we're not handling this like an OIS?"

"Yes, an officer-involved shooting usually goes differently," Ballack said, his voice heavy with a tired sigh. "I got a call from the Colonel. The Commissioner was in his office. There was no discussion, Jake. The Governor decided. This is entirely in the hands of the Feds now."

"That's BS."

"I agree."

Ward stared out at the dark highway, then shook his head. "Goodbye, boss." He ended the call.

There was nothing he could do about Hawthorne, but he wouldn't go home, either. The apartment was too quiet.

He drove to work instead.

The building stood empty, the hallway lights dimmed to the

after-hours hum he knew so well. He walked to his desk, sat down, and opened up the records management system to the case file. It was gone.

He searched by persons: Dillon, Basu, Tibeluk.

Nothing. No file.

They'd learned from their mistake with Pagan's file and had already locked this one down.

He stopped looking and let his hands fall into his lap. As the cursor blinked in the search box, his mind finally absorbed the events of recent days.

Once again, he had walked into Richard Pagan's world, and once again, he had been helpless. Laid flat and at the mercy of a madman.

He hadn't survived because of his badge or his gun. He had survived because a broken kid found a flash of clarity before a bullet took him.

Ward rubbed his face. He felt old.

"You're working late."

He didn't jump. He simply exhaled and spun his chair around.

Rod Hawthorne stood in the doorway. He wore a heavy trench coat, his hands buried in the pockets. He looked relaxed, like a man stopping by for a casual chat, not an agent who had just executed a suspect.

"I have a supplement to write," Ward said.

"I wouldn't worry about the paperwork," Hawthorne said, stepping into the room. "The case file is closed to you. It will be… curated. Just like the last one. The official narrative is already being revised. Adam Basu as the mastermind. A couple of idiots followed him. Basu dead. The rest behind bars. Sad tragedy."

"You've found Dillon, then?" Ward asked.

"A couple of hours ago, half-frozen in a ditch off the Glenn Highway," Hawthorne said. "He's being secured at API, raving about being abandoned by a prophet. By the end of the week, he'll be declared incompetent to stand trial. Just a footnote, Jake."

Ward looked at him. The lines on his face, the deadness in his eyes. "You aren't FBI, are you?"

Hawthorne smiled faintly. "Does it matter?"

"It matters to me," Ward said. "Your people broke Adam."

Hawthorne pulled a chair from a nearby desk and sat down, spinning it backward to straddle it.

"I work for people who clean up their messes," Hawthorne said. "And Adam was a dangerous, unstable prototype. We watched, hoping you'd bring him in. We would have salvaged him if we could have, and in the end, probably waited too long to end it. Regrettable, but necessary."

"So it's my fault he's dead—because I didn't capture him?"

"I wouldn't put it that way. Let's just say he was too powerful a weapon for you to handle."

"He was a kid, Rod. If that's even your real name." Ward snapped. "A kid!"

"Maybe, but he was also a weapon," Hawthorne said. "And pointed in the wrong direction. We won't make that mistake again."

Hawthorne rubbed his jaw, a flash of genuine irritation cracking his calm facade. "My employers are tired of chasing ghosts through the ice. We prefer assets who understand how to be part of a team."

Hawthorne reached into his coat pocket. Ward tensed, his hand drifting instinctively toward his holster.

But he didn't pull a weapon. He pulled out a small, rectangular object.

He placed it on the edge of Ward's desk.

It was a card. Heavy stock. No logo. No agency seal. Just ten silver digits embossed in the center of a black background.

"I'm not playing your game," Ward said.

"Yes, you are, Jake. You have been part of my world since Pagan strapped you to his table."

Hawthorne leaned forward. The casual demeanor vanished, replaced by a sharp, predatory focus.

"My employers are fascinated by you. We know the precognition is gone. Faded, didn't it? A temporary side effect of the research. We've seen that before."

Ward didn't answer, keeping his face like stone.

"But the other stuff," Hawthorne said. "The regeneration. Increased pain tolerance. Those didn't fade, did they? You've healed far too quickly, and more than once, haven't you?"

Ward's heart hammered. "I don't know what you're talking about."

"Yes, you do," Hawthorne said, and smiled. "And we think that ability makes you a unique asset. Adam failed because his mind broke. But you... held. You adapted. Survived."

Hawthorne tapped the black card with his index finger.

"We want to bring you in, Jake. Not for experiments. You've had enough of those. For a debrief. To discuss a partnership. Imagine what you could do with the right resources. You want to protect the innocent? We can give you the tools to do that on a larger scale."

"I'm not your asset," Ward said, his voice low and dangerous. "I'm an Alaska State Trooper. Now get out of my office."

Hawthorne looked back at him. The man didn't look angry. He looked patient.

"You can refuse the offer," Hawthorne finally said. "But you can't escape this new biology of yours. You're carrying some of Pagan's legacy in your blood. And sooner or later, you're going to realize that a badge alone isn't enough to hold back the monsters we fight."

Hawthorne stood and walked to the door. He paused at the threshold, glancing back.

"One more thing. My employers have learned the cost of leaving their property unsecured. So choose wisely."

He walked out, his footsteps echoing down the empty hallway.

Ward sat in the silence.

He looked at the black card on his desk. The silver numbers caught the dim light of the monitor.

It was a key. A ticket to the inside. An invitation to become the very thing he hated.

He reached out and picked it up. It felt heavy. Expensive.

He didn't throw it in the trash.

Ward would not call. Not today. Maybe not ever. He had no intention of working for a shadow agency.

But he wouldn't burn that bridge, either.

He was just a trooper. He couldn't go on the offense against an organization like the one that sent Hawthorne. That battle would be lost before the first shot was fired.

But he didn't need to fight them. He might even need them, someday.

He took an oath to protect Alaska from all enemies, foreign and domestic. Sometimes those enemies were men like Adam. Sometimes they were worse. And if a day came when his badge wasn't enough to hold back the dark, he might need to make a deal with the devil to keep his state safe.

Until then, he would delay. As long as they thought he was a potential asset, they wouldn't treat him like a liability.

He opened his desk drawer and slid the card into the back corner, right next to the thumb drive Foley gave him.

The stolen files. And the card. Two choices.

He grabbed the thumb drive and inserted it into the USB port of his laptop. The directory popped up.

Ward clicked on the folder.

Let's see what else we have in here.

ABOUT THE AUTHOR

David A. Willson is a father, husband, pancreatic cancer survivor, and a retired Alaska State Trooper.

Much of his material is inspired by the 'Great Land' of Alaska, which he has called home for over 40 years. He is passionate about technology, faith, and fiction—not necessarily in that order. When not writing, he enjoys traveling, woodworking, brewing beer and wine, playing the acoustic guitar, and being a grandfather.

www.davidawillson.com